D0846945

Exit
Strategy

Joseph H Baskin

Copyright © 2018 Joseph H Baskin.

Cover Illustration: Tamara Viščović
Cover Design: Joseph H Baskin

All rights reserved. No part of this book may be reproduced, stored, or
transmitted by any means—whether auditory, graphic, mechanical, or
electronic—without written permission of both publisher and author, except
in the case of brief excerpts used in critical articles and reviews. Unauthorized
reproduction of any part of this work is illegal and is punishable by law.

For my mother

Through early morning fog I see,
Visions of the things to be,
The pains that are withheld for me,
I realize and I can see…

That suicide is painless,
It brings on many changes,
And I can take or leave it if I please.

The game of life is hard to play,
I'm gonna lose it anyway,
The losing hand I'll someday lay,
So this is all I have to say…

Suicide is Painless
Johnny Mandel

No pain.

She'd had enough of the constant worry, enough of the torment. She resolved to take matters into her own hands. The unknown didn't bother her, but the possibility of a painful exit did. It represented her last earthly concern. The chrome spigot ran with hot water, stirred up the soap and filled the air with a humid scent.

She took inventory like she'd done a thousand times before. Doors locked, note written, candles and steam creating the ambience she desired. The drugs kicked in; she floated on air. The Glenlivet's amber looked even nicer in this light.

When she first started these prescriptions they instantly took away the constant gerbil wheel in her mind, the racing thoughts that prevented a moment of peace. But their effect waned as time went on. Like an addict, she needed increasing doses just to get back to that blessed release from thought. Taking several week's worth in one shot along with a healthy dose of scotch returned her to that initial buzz.

Leaning over her Creed scented candle, she closed her eyes and inhaled deeply the strong scent of citrus and rose. It calmed her. She placed a hand on her chest and focused on the rhythm of her heart beating, the rise and fall of her chest with inspiration, exhalation. Finally, she achieved the centering her yoga teacher had exhorted all these years.

Eyes back open she reached over to the sink's edge and took hold of the knife. Its blade reflected the flickering flames as she turned it over in her hand. To do it out of the tub and jump in or cut while in the water? In the tub - the water would distort her actions, making it seem distant, less real.

The bastard hadn't shown, failed to live up to his end of the bargain. Why did this surprise her? Story of her life: everyone had always let her down, why should he be any different? Tears rolled down her cheeks. Not over what lay imminent, but that her faith in him wasn't rewarded; her love wasn't truly reciprocated. What a shame.

She dropped her robe to the bathroom floor. Tested the water with a toe. As she stood on one foot she grew unsteady, almost fell and had to grab the sides of the tub. The irony caused her to laugh out loud. Don't want to slip and break my neck; that's not part of the plan. She continued to giggle as she slid easily into the inviting water, sighing deeply, expelling her worries.

Her mind registered some booms outside the bathroom door. Maybe the fireworks on the esplanade. Or perhaps the boom from the Boston Pops setting off the cannon in concert to Tchaikovsky's 1812 overture. Not that it mattered. There would be no more July 4th's for her.

No wasted time. Now, while the pills and heat synergistically protected her in a cocoon. The first plunge in her medial thigh created no pain. She smiled, grateful that the plan would work and there'd be no suffering. The blood ran in pulsing rivers through the misty water forcing her to lift the other leg to locate the identical opposite spot. No pain with this cut, either. It was as if she were slicing through a foreign object. The crimson wasn't as intense with the second thigh, but she noted with satisfaction that both wounds continued to bleed.

The task complete, the job well done, she experienced the relief that had eluded her for too long. Her eyes fluttered close. The last thought that passed through her mind was gratitude that she succeeded with this, her final plan. A content smile came over her face as her head slowly submerged below the water line.

Archibald Wendt sat on a barstool, head slumped on his arms. He was deep into a bottle of blended whiskey. The choice of liquor a punishment for his behavior, though his intoxicated mind struggled to call up this particular sin. It gnawed at him in an offhand way.

In the background the Red Sox played on the boxed television that hung in chains from the bar's ceiling. His mind registered some booms. Big Papi had hit another long ball and the stadium was celebrating with congratulatory fireworks. The bar erupted raucously, patrons high fiving each other. With supreme effort he lifted his head off of his arms and made to signal the bartender for another round. As he did, he lost his balance, slipped off the stool and fell to the floor with a thud.

The bartender took his eyes from the television for a minute and investigated the commotion. Finding Archie on the ground didn't faze him; he'd let the psychiatrist lie there for a time knowing the man would soon wake up and stumble out of the bar on his own. As he'd done countless times before.

P er usual he awoke early, at five, like when he ran on the banks of the Charles. His current route wended its way next to the flood wall, the smell of the paper mill hovering like an invisible cloud over the town. When he first came to Harding, Ohio he thought he would never get used to the pungent reek; in Autumn, all smells are particularly intensified. He offered silent thanks for olfactory fatigue.

His many times bleached socks acted as reflectors in the predawn light. The five-mile run took him through most of the town and gave him enough time to shed some emotional baggage and sweat out the excesses of the night before. His breathing produced a calming rhythm. The initial burn of the cold morning air faded and the ever present morning headache receded.

Without the running he knew he would foray deeper into insanity. As it was, he had to run on the left side of the road. He could cross a street only if there were no cars in sight. If there was a car on the horizon he forced himself to hold his crossing until the last possible moment tempting the driver to run him over - a human squirrel. He timed his runs to the second; they had to end on an even number of minutes.

Wendt grew up in a small New England city, so this town of twenty thousand held a nostalgic sentiment for him. After the hustle and bustle of Boston, he welcomed the change of pace. A warm feeling of anonymity accompanied him when he arrived. While it lasted, he savored the release from notoriety. In a town this small it couldn't last forever.

Immersing himself in work, he neglected a social life and his demeanor propagated the isolation. So used to the gruff comportment of New Englanders, he almost told the first person who wished him a good morning to go fuck themselves before realizing that they weren't trying to pry into his business. Just being friendly. He chuckled aloud at that memory.

Turning from Riverside onto Bridge he made his way back home. His lodging was a Bed and Breakfast. An old house with several bedrooms and crooked stairs, the kind a AAA travel guide might describe as charming. The proprietress, Lillie, a woman in her fifties, had bought the house with her husband intending it to be a pseudo-retirement. The husband had other plans that included his twenty something secretary and South Florida. When the soon-to-be-ex tried to snake the house from under Lillie she fought in court and got him to concede the property as part of the divorce settlement.

Wendt intended it to be a temporary solution until he found his own place. That was nine months ago. Comfort and company kept him there. Lillie kept a warm house and attracted some interesting lodgers. One, Trent, alternated between intense work in the ER and safari trips to Africa. The nights that he returned from the hunt the three of them would stay up, drink wine, and listen to Trent's stories. Like sharing a house with Ernest Hemingway. Wendt had little incentive to find other accommodations. Lillie offered him a good monthly price.

Wendt came from Boston with enough savings to get by while he built his practice. He took over a retiring psychiatrist's office and slowly built up through word of mouth. It wasn't long before his practice was full of the usual mixture of depressives, neurotics, substance abusers, and the occasional manic and psychotic to keep things interesting.

He jogged up the stairs of the B&B. The front was a two door frosted glass job. He ran up and down the stairs a few times, his goal to extract as much from the workout that he could. Satisfied, he unlocked the door and went inside the still quiet house. He walked up the creaking stairs, stopped at the landing and listened. Archie heard movement in Lillie's room. That meant that breakfast would soon be in the offing. He went into his little room, outfitted with a queen size bed and a roll-top desk. In the latter he kept provisions for an emergency: gin, vodka, rum, and tequila. If all hell broke out in society, Archie was at least going to able to make a decent Long Island Iced Tea. He had some V8 there, too, because one needed vegetables. He opened it and gave it a hesitant sniff. A fifty fifty proposition, he shrugged and poured - if it's turned, the alcohol in the vodka should kill off anything harmful. After downing the Bloody Mary he showered and dressed.

Coming down the carpeted stairs he smelled the reassuring combination of coffee and toast. That aroma alone made the monthly rent worthwhile. Lillie sat in her robe chatting with a couple in the dining room. Probably visiting Amish country.

"Good morning, Arch. These are the Bennetts. Here for some antiquing." That would have been his second guess. "This is Dr. Wendt, a local psychiatrist."

The man smiled and held up his hands in surrender. "Oh! Guess we won't be speaking anymore; wouldn't want to be analyzed."

Lillie cringed. She knew that particular reaction to Wendt's profession rubbed him the wrong way. He likened it to the assumption that a hooker would give you a freebie roll in the hay just by dint of her being a prostitute.

Archie handled it with a smile. "Tell you what, unless you put two hundred dollars on the table, I'll assume you don't want my professional services and I'll just share breakfast with you."

Smiles and laughs all around.

"What will it be this morning, Arch?"

"Just coffee and a slice of toast, Lil. I'm in a bit of a rush." He really wasn't. She knew it. If it were just the two of them he would take his time. But he didn't have the energy to make small talk and couldn't tolerate the discomfort of eating in silence. Or having to explain to the Bennett's that he preferred they just shut the fuck up while he talked to Lillie.

Wendt walked to his office the same time every day; it was less than a mile from the B&B, a nice benefit to living in a small town. He loathed the lengthy car commutes in Boston. Out in the elements under the power of his own feet proved liberating. The cold never bothered him; just a matter of good layering and wearing a warm hat. He recognized some of the folks with similar routines making their way to work in the morning. He offered little half nods in response to friendly greetings while mourning his lack of spontaneity; if he were the target of a whacking, he'd be as predictable as a Swiss train.

His office was situated on the second story of a downtown building above a barbershop, part of a series of attached two story brick structures. The spinning barber's pole sealed the deal for him - the mesmerizing red and white a holdover from when barbers doubled as surgeons. Patients entered through a set of steep stairs to an anteroom sporting a couple of chairs, a table and some magazines: *Playboy* for the sex addicts, *MAD* magazine for the psychotics, and *Sports Illustrated* for all the rest. In actuality, no magazines. No one took their eyes off their own smartphones long enough to read. His entrance was in the back allowing him to come and go without encountering patients in the waiting room. He answered his own phones and did his own scheduling so no need for a secretary . During a normal day Wendt saw between ten to fifteen patients depending on the type of visit, whether for pills, therapy, or both.

The office accommodated a desk, two armchairs and a sofa. The lighting was muted and on the walls he hung some Monet prints figuring the pastoral scenes would be soothing. He thought Jackson Pollock and M.C. Esher might be off-putting to the more fragile minded. Archie put his briefcase down (containing food items) and looked at the schedule. A formality. He always memorized the next day's schedule before leaving the previous night. This allowed him to run the list of patients and determine what type of day it would be. Some included names that made him cringe, others brought smiles as he looked forward to finding out how they'd been and what progress they'd made. First name on this morning's list: Lorna Smith. An interesting woman.

She left her father's home at nineteen to make a new one with her husband. They were married for over forty years until he got cancer. She nursed him through the worst of it and had to watch as he deteriorated before her eyes. After his death her grief was intense. She didn't see Archie about that, though. Widowed in her early sixties, she was still an attractive woman and when she started a new relationship she experienced a tidal wave of guilt with each sexual encounter. Lorna couldn't shake the feeling that she was repeatedly cheating on her dead husband.

She came in every Monday morning to give a rundown of her weekend events. Wendt opened the door to the waiting room to find her sitting demurely, head hung low.

"Good morning, Mrs. Smith."

"Good morning, Doctor."

Lorna walked in and took the seat on the chair opposite his. He always offered the couch, not to lie down, just to be more comfortable. She preferred to start in the seat until she felt ready and then would move to the couch.

"How are you doing today?"

"Just lousy," she said while looking at the ground. This was how every session started.

"Tell me about lousy."

She shifted uncomfortably in the chair, never looking up. "I just feel lost, like I want to die. I don't see a reason to keep on living."

"That's horrible."

"Well, Doctor, you know, I'm not a good person. I saw that man again. He came over on Friday night. And I told him that we couldn't engage in any physical contact. Well, one thing led to another and I let him touch me in places he shouldn't have, so I don't deserve to live."

Wendt stayed silent. She slowly made her way over to the sofa.

"I just feel so lousy. I have sinned against my husband and my Lord."

"Your husband is no longer alive, Mrs. Smith."

"I know, but I'm sure he's ashamed of me."

"Because you went on with your life?"

"Because I've engaged in sexual relations while married."

"Till death do you part, Mrs. Smith, till death."

She didn't have a retort for that.

"What do you think your husband would say about this?"

She looked up, more energy in her voice and said. "He would say, 'Darlin', get on with your life. No point in being miserable.'"

This was how each session went. Grief coupled with a healthy dose of amnesia for any gains made during therapy. The endless loop of Mrs. Smith's more carnal desires getting the better of her and the backlash of intense guilt. Monday morning absolution with Dr. Wendt, then back at it again. Not for the first time it dawned on Archie just how similar the psychiatrist's role was to that of the priest.

The last patient completed, notes written, he swiveled in his chair contemplating the next move. So often his mood was predicated on how he felt he did for each patient. Right now he felt some mild satisfaction, but still struggled with the feeling he should have done more. Wendt opened a bottom drawer and took out the bottle of Glenfiddich, poured himself an end of the day drink. The first swallow helped melt away those reflective thoughts and his mind moved to musings at the strangeness of not having someone to go home to.

Paul McCartney's "My Brave Face" played in his head. Someone to whom he was accountable, he left that with his practice in Boston. Collateral damage from the incident. That was how he had walled it off in his own mind. The Incident. Not to be explored, but placed in deep storage like the Ark at the end of Raiders.

Having no need to rush home left him with a lot of time to think. And drink for that matter. Time required effort to keep certain suppressed issues at bay. The alcohol only went so far. He decided to go to Howard's and get drunk with someone rather than do it pathetically alone. That should prove he wasn't a full blown alcoholic. Only mostly blown.

When Archie left (fled?) Boston, he consulted an older mentor of his who suggested Harding, Ohio as a place to lay low and collect himself. He recommended Archie look up Howard Rogoff, a psychiatrist with whom he'd trained years ago. The timing couldn't be more serendipitous; Howard wanted to retire and sell his practice just as Archie hit town. Their collaboration made the process near seamless for the patients.

Archie locked his office and walked down the stairs, out onto the street and drew deep breaths. The row of buildings reminded him of Paris. He enjoyed that and the light traffic. After so many years commuting with

Massholes, he was grateful to see cars move freely. Lost in his thoughts he failed to notice the figure that shadowed him.

"Dr. Wendt, right?"

He stopped and turned.

"You are Archibald Wendt?" The man looked to be in his sixties, well over 6', well-dressed and in good shape. He had a shock of thick white hair on his head; it might have been red as a younger man, because he had a light complexion and piercing green eyes. He had the tall man's habit of putting his hand on smaller men's shoulders as he was doing now to Archie. It made the psychiatrist uneasy and he pulled away slowly.

"In the flesh. And you are..?"

"Virgil Morgenstern. You think I could walk with you back to Lillie's?"

Morgenstern. The name was all over town. Real estate holdings, and such.

"You related to the realtor Morgenstern?"

"The very same. But I'm not really a realtor, I just own a lot of property."

I'll say. The guy seemed to own half the town. It disturbed Archie a little to have been snuck up on by Morgenstern. However, the fact that he knew where Archie lived and worked didn't make him Poirot; he'd already seen that everybody knew everything here.

"I don't mind the company. But I'm not going to Lil's. I'm going over to Dr. Rogoff's. You know him?"

"What kind of question is that? I doubt there's a soul in this town I don't know." Morgenstern said.

They began walking. "So what can I do for you Mr. Morgenstern?"

"Virgil, please. I don't want anything from you. Just wanted to make your acquaintance. You've been here, what, nine months?"

"That's a very accurate guess. How long have you been here?"

"All my adult life. Grew up in a town smaller than this. Came here when I finished high school. Didn't plan on staying, but things happened that led me to plant my roots here. You're from Boston, right?"

"Originally from Gloucester, but I came here from Boston. I guess word gets around." Archie said.

"It's a small town, to be sure. But I have to admit that I've looked into you."

"Have you now. And what have you found?"

"Well, educated at Bard College, then Tufts for medical school. Residency at Harvard. You worked with some heavy hitters there then ventured out on your own. What I'm curious about is why a guy like you comes to a place like this?"

Both men stopped and looked at each other.

"What's a nice guy like me doing in a place like this? That's a hell of a line."

Morgenstern held up his hands and smiled. "Hey, sorry about that, I can come on strong. I wasn't meaning to put you on the defensive. Just curious about you, that's all."

Wendt began walking again and the older man kept pace. "In my business, Mr. Morgenstern, people rarely are without numerous motives. So tell me, what can I do for you?"

"I'm glad to see you're a man who doesn't bullshit around. My interest in you is wanting to know what kind of man you are. Can you be trusted? Are you sharp, able to cut through the crap? I'm always on the lookout for such men." Morgenstern stopped. "I'm going to leave you alone now, but I will be following up with you, Doc. Thanks for your time."

He walked away and Wendt continued on to Howard's house.

"You'll never guess who stalked me just now."

Wendt walked in the front door; the older psychiatrist stepped aside to let him in. Rogoff wore his usual blue robe with Homer Simpson slippers. It was the only TV show he watched religiously. He said when they go off the air he would cancel his cable.

"Was it a woman, shortish, with long graying hair, few teeth, really bad breath, and a tendency to defecate on rugs?"

Wendt stopped in the foyer. "That's a hell of a specific guess. But, no. Who is it you're referring to?"

"Oh, nobody. Certainly not a former patient who still lives in the area. Who stalked you?"

They walked down the hallway into his den. There was already a bottle of scotch sitting out. Glenlivet. God bless Howard.

His was a modest colonial. He lost his wife to breast cancer a couple of years before. When asked about her Howard would say that he'd been with her as long as the Good Lord allowed. He was wistful, but not dramatic. His home bore the signs of being well appointed and cared for by the late Mrs. Rogoff. There was a spacious living room/dining room, kitchen and den on the first floor. Howard and Archie spent their time in the den. There were two plush chairs that framed an elaborate fireplace that Howard promised to fire up on special occasions. Clearly Wendt didn't rate special; it'd never been lit when Archie was there. Their discussions typically took place over a chess board in a game that rarely finished. If Archie was losing, as was usual, he would simply stall with conversation.

Howard followed Archie into the den. "You're keeping me in suspense on purpose? That's good. Build the tension." He sat and poured the two men a healthy shot. Archie lifted his glass towards the light admiring the color. He tilted it towards Rogoff then took a sip.

"Virgil Morgenstern."

"Interesting. What did he want?" Howard asked.

"Want? He just wanted to make my acquaintance, said he."

"You believe that then I want to talk to you about a bridge I have for sale."

"Well, he also hinted that he was looking for someone to give it back to him straight. What do you know about him?"

"He's the guy every town has." Howard said after a swallow. "The one who owns practically everything and everyone. The proverbial big fish in the little pond. He's got the requisite narcissism for how important he actually is to this burg."

"Is he a decent guy?"

Howard thought that over. "I have no reason to say he isn't. I'm not aware of any scuttlebutt to the contrary."

They were quiet for a minute. Rogoff spoke softly.

"How are the dreams?"

Archie smiled. "They aren't like they were when I was a teenager. I'm holding out for a return of the good old fuck dreams."

"You want to talk about them?"

"What's there to talk about? Run of the mill shit. They'd probably bore you to an earlier grave. But thanks. Instead I thought I'd kick your ass in chess."

"Then you better wait until I'm drunk so you'll have a fighting chance."

"I can't wait that long, I'm due at the Club later."

"Due. You're funny. Let's play a quick one."

CHAPTER

6

By now Wendt's thoughts came swiftly, one on top of the other, pushing the next one of a cliff like so many lemmings. He'd lost count how many drinks were in his system, but the buzz was intense and steady, just the way he liked it when he needed to disgorge a painful story.

"Garrett Portman came from a prominent family. Lots of money; some inherited, some earned. His father, Hunter, was a partner in a Wall Street firm whose name was recognizable the world over. Are you listening to me?"

The bartender stopped wiping the counter with his rag. The copper edge sported swirls of grease that reflected all the colors of the rainbow. Archie ran his finger over it creating new designs.

"I've got other clients, you know," the bartender said.

"Who, Drunky Jones over there? He's in the bag. Look at him, he can't even keep his head up. I've got things to get off my chest so you need to focus your attention on me."

"At least *Fred* is a regular who gets nicer as he gets drunk. You're a mean ass drunk and your stories are sad as hell."

"Be that as it may," Wendt continued, "it is your duty as the barman to listen to my shitty musings." He put on his best Sinatra: "It's quarter to three, there's no one in the place, 'cept you and me…make it one for my baby, and another one for the road."

The barman sighed, dropped his rag, and placed his elbows on the bar, face in his hands.

The President's Club was a hole in the wall downtown. The name, a nod to Warren G. Harding, the 29th president and a man whose name became synonymous with corruption, lent a grandiosity not matched by the decor. Like a Chicago railroad apartment it couldn't be more than fifteen feet wide. It stretched a ways lengthwise, one side dominated by a wooden bar, mirrored back. Stools, a few small tables, and at the end of the room a little used pool table rounded out the accoutrement.

Wendt swirled his glass to see the scotch sparkle. "Where was I? Oh yeah, telling you about Garrett's papa. Though he spent little time at home he took great interest in his only son. Hunter had much to be proud of; Garrett was an excellent high school student who parlayed his achievements at Dalton into a Harvard admission. When he got there, though, he became overwhelmed with the competitiveness and grew depressed. That was how he came to be in the care of yours truly. I began seeing him weekly. Some medication, but mostly therapy."

"Should you be telling me such details. I mean, isn't it private information?" Mike offered a final plea to shut the doctor up. His given name was well known to Wendt, though he insisted on calling him Barkeep.

"What are you a medical information cop? Don't interrupt me. So Garrett and I explored his issues of low self-esteem. Living up to Daddy's expectations proved overwhelming. He lamented the clichéd nature of his malady while at the same time acknowledging a desire to piss off his old man. Somewhere in there he discovered jazz and a passion for music was ignited. The Berklee College of Music just across the river seemed too good to be true. Well, even a nitwit like you can figure out the rest."

"Why do you ask me to give of my time to listen to your tales of woe and then insult me? What kind of shit is that? Besides, I have no desire to figure out the rest. If you're telling the story it has to have a sad and horrible ending." Mike said.

"I don't insult. I state only what is perfectly obvious to any observer. You wipe the counter with a greasy rag, effectively spreading dirt rather than cleaning it. Clearly you're not a Mensa candidate. Be that as it may, I will spell out the rest of the story. Garrett wanted to leave Harvard and attend Berklee to develop his interest. The predictable row with his father ensued. Son declared his intention to leave Harvard forthwith, Father forbad such a move, and round and round it went. Garrett grew increasingly despondent with each confrontation with his dad. Our sessions became marked by his swelling hopelessness. Then, quite suddenly a distinct change; Garrett appeared more upbeat. He couldn't say why he was feeling better about his circumstances, but he had come to terms with his father's dictates and was going to make the most of his education."

"Hey alright. It doesn't turn out bad." Mike began walking away. Wendt stood on his stool's crossbar and held onto the crook of Mike's elbow.

"Hold your horses, Barkeep. Garrett missed his next appointment and a call from me went unanswered. Concerned, I reached out to his father who informed me: 'Garrett took his life this morning.' Roommate noticed that Garrett hadn't slept in his bed, and puzzled, went to the bathroom and discovered Garrett hanging in one of the stalls."

Mike shook his arm free and tossed the rag at Wendt's chest. "I knew it. Fuck you, man. You always tell the shittiest stories. Why did you set me up like that, telling me that he was looking better?"

"Can I help it? It's part of the process, my good man. See, when someone makes a definitive decision to off themselves they often experience some peace of mind that can be misconstrued as an improvement in their mood. It wasn't intended to make the ending harsher for you. Or me for that matter."

Mike softened. "You're an asshole, yeah, but you've paid some dues." He reached into the well and brought up the house vodka. Have one on the house."

"Well vodka, you cheap bastard?"

"Even when I'm nice and offer you a gift you have to bite my hand off. Be polite or I won't pour."

"You're right. I apologize profusely and am grateful for your generosity."

"That's more like it." He shook out the remainder of the scotch and poured the vodka.

Wendt drank the proffered freebie in one shot. "Cheap bastard." He said in a low voice.

"Prick." Mike grinned despite himself.

Archie waited patiently. He couldn't remember how long he'd been waiting, but the room was comfortable so he didn't mind. The patient finally came in and sat down sideways, his long legs draped over the arm of the lounge chair. Hard to make out his features, but Wendt knew who he was. In good shape, he honed his ropey musculature on a boat in the

Charles. Like his father before him, a rower. He wore his usual hat, the one with Harvard Crew stitched across the front. He had removed the middle 'rva' so that it read Hard Crew. Big smile on his face, like when he discovered Kind of Blue.

"How's it going, Doc?"

"I'm okay. Worried about you; you haven't been coming to your appointments. I'm wondering how've you been?" Wendt said.

"Hangin' in there. Ahhhhh! Too soon, Doc?"

"That's not funny. You caused heartache to a lot of people."

"You gonna give me a guilt trip? I'm free of that tyrant's grips. You should be happy for me; I finally did something for myself."

"Is that how you see it? Did something for yourself? You robbed the world of a talented young man. Who knows what great things you might have accomplished."

"Or how many people I would have disappointed." Garrett retorted. "Look, we'll never know will we. But there's no reason to dwell on the past. Although, you have your share of skeletons in your closet, doncha?" He laughed again.

"I don't remember you being cruel, Garrett."

"This is your gig, Doc, any cruelty comes from you."

"Maybe, but you could take it easy on me. I cared a great deal for you and mourned your death."

The young man straightened up in the chair, leaned forward elbows on knees. His face came into focus and held a look of genuine concern. "I know you did. That's why I want to help you."

"That's a switch, huh? You helping me."

"We all can use help. You folks are the last to ask for help."

"You folks?"

"Doctors, psychiatrists. The old, 'doctor, heal thyself' and all that shit."

"It's 'physician,' and it was an admonition to clean your own house before you criticized another's." Wendt said.

Garrett waved that off. "Regardless, Dr. Wendt, the point I'm trying to make is you're still beating yourself up over the one that got away. You know, she never held you responsible; why do you refuse to move on?"

"I wish it were that easy."

Garrett put a reassuring hand on the psychiatrist's knee, offered a comforting smile. In his face Wendt could see someone else swirling around, but it didn't come into focus.

Wendt awoke with a start in a chair in front of the television. He was in the den of the B&B and didn't remember how he got there. The dream quickly faded, but the residue it imparted on him was a powerful mix of emotions that cut through the inebriation and left him feeling empty and wasted. He turned the TV off, staggered upstairs into his bedroom, and collapsed on the bed fully clothed for not the hundredth time.

CHAPTER

7

The next day's schedule was light. Some cancellations, one no-show. When he was on salary for a hospital he loved the no-shows because it gave him time to catch up. In a private practice no shows were a colossal waste of time and money. He tried to bill for them, but rarely was he able to recoup the lost time and income. Sighing, he collected his things and locked up.

An unseasonably warm day, he thought he might go for a long walk. The run from that morning hadn't cleared out the previous night's dreams. Wendt exited onto the street rubbing his jaw, a habit (a tic?) he developed when under stress unaware that he continually did it. He closed his eyes and tilted his head towards the sun. It felt good on his face. The smell of spring was strong in the air - a cruel trick of nature as they were a good six months from the real thing.

"Good to see you again, Dr. Wendt."

His reverie disturbed, Archie looked in the direction of the voice. It took a minute to pull focus.

"Mr. Morgenstern. I can't imagine this is a coincidence."

"I was waiting for you."

"You know, pretty soon I'll have to charge you for these impromptu sessions."

Morgenstern smiled. "I don't need therapy or pills. I'm doing great."

"That's wonderful for you. If that's the case, I'll be on my way."

"I *do* have something to discuss with you." Morgenstern said, unperturbed by Wendt's dismissal.

"Okay, what can I do for you today?"

"You can tell me a little bit about yourself. You Jewish?"

"That's a hell of an icebreaker. You always start with that?"

"Just wondering. I mean, you're a psychiatrist from the east coast. It's a reasonable assumption."

Wendt stayed silent impassively looking at the taller man. Virgil grew tense then said, "I'm half Jewish. I mean, my father was Jewish, but apparently didn't have much faith. I don't have much use for religion. Seems to me it's just another racket looking to take your money."

Archie appraised Morgenstern as he spoke. He could see what made the man successful. Virgil had a disarming demeanor. His smile was open and exuded sincerity; he carried himself well, embodying both confidence and an ease with himself that affected Archie despite his annoyance at the intrusion.

Both men began walking. This out-of-context meeting proved difficult for Archie, the psychiatrist. So used to not revealing information about himself to patients he was at a loss for how to approach this conversation. It felt like the older man was probing, putting feelers out for how treatment would be; back door therapy, if you will. That put Archie on edge because it intruded on non-work time, when his professional demeanor could be set aside. Almost reading his mind Morgenstern added, "What *would* you be willing to share with me?"

Archie thought for a minute. "I'm a big Celtics fan."

"Okay, that's a start. I respect their history, Cousy, Russell, Havlicek, Bird. But it pissed me off how they bought the last championship by bringing Garnett and Allen aboard."

"A banner is a banner."

"Fair enough. Did you go to many games?"

"It was my one indulgence." Archie said. "I had season tickets and tried to be at every game. I was a kid when Bird was doing his thing. I promised myself that when I was old enough and could afford it I would be a season ticket holder."

Virgil smiled. "That wasn't so hard, was it?"

"No, it wasn't. But I get the distinct feeling there's more you want from me than reminiscing about my Garden days."

"You're right, there is something. I would like you to come to dinner this Friday night."

"Dinner?"

"Yeah. The last meal of the day. I want to break bread with you and have you meet my family. How about it?"

Wendt looked into Morgenstern's eyes and knew instantly that this man's endurance for pestering would far outstrip Archie's ability to parry the thrusts. "Sure. What time?"

"Come to the house at eight. Do you know where I live?"

"I have a feeling I'll find it."

They shook hands and parted. Morgenstern called after him.

"You know, you never answered my question about whether or not you're Jewish."

Archie stopped and turned. "True. It must be an unusual experience for you not to get your way."

Morgenstern smiled. "You got balls, Doc, I'll give you that. I like that in a man."

"Glad to oblige."

"I'll work on you more at dinner." He pointed at Archie. "So, great, I'll see you then."

P aul Stringer was a good surgeon. To say gifted would be overstating it, but he used his skills effectively and generously to alleviate the spinal problems of numerous grateful patients. However, shortly after finishing his neurosurgery residency he was diagnosed with a rare movement disorder; it manifested as a tremor and jeopardized his prospects for operating. Stringer's world came crashing down until his neurologist assured him that it could be controlled with medications and he could still perform surgery. That proved the case for many happy years until the medications could no longer hold back the tremors. Two decades into his flourishing professional career, when his mastery of skills allowed him to be a near virtuoso in the operating theatre, the medications ceased being effective. The end came suddenly, without warning or ceremony.

Dr. Stringer stood in the operating room engaged in a routine case. Dissecting through the tough muscles of the back his hands stopped following the routine commands his brain gave as they had on so many previous cases. They refused to stay still. He looked up to find his longtime assistant staring at him with a visage equal parts pity and panic. Stringer sucked it up and gave it another go. No dice. The more effort he exerted the more tremulous his hands became. Beads of sweat formed just below his surgical cap, perspiration he hadn't experienced since his early days of being a resident when the attending stood over him cursing his technique.

With a tidal wave of nausea he realized this was the day he long feared. The day that haunted his dreams and wakened him from sleep sweating, his heart threatening to pound out of his chest. He nearly collapsed right there in the OR. He croaked out to his assistant that he'd eaten some bad seafood and asked him to fetch Dr. O'Leary to finish the case.

Now he stood at the doorframe of his final humiliation, crossing a threshold that would cement his loss of face and put the final nail in the coffin of his aspirations.

Wendt opened the door and invited the surgeon in. Stringer had the look of a man who would have preferred a simultaneous colonoscopy and root canal rather than seeing a psychiatrist. Not unusual; surgeons generally harbored a crooked eye towards psychiatry. Wendt sat in his chair and offered the couch with his hand. Stringer plopped down on it; Archie focused his attention away from Stringer's gyrating hands and waited for the surgeon to begin.

"I'm only here to placate my wife. I have no desire to be on medication or engage in psychotherapy."

"Okay."

"This is going to be a collosal waste of time."

"Gotcha."

Stringer shifted uncomfortably in his chair; Archie rescued him. "Well, as part of the placating, tell me what's been going on that led you to have to do the placating."

The surgeon sighed. "Alright. I don't know how much you already know, but I had to stop operating three months ago."

"I know you're a neurosurgeon who specializes in the spine because that's what your wife told me over the phone. She worries that you're despondent since the tremors hampered your ability to operate."

"That about sums it up," he said, smacking his thighs and then folding his hands under his legs in an obvious attempt to hide the shaking. "Aside from the 'hamper' part. The goddamned tremors have taken away my ability to operate altogether."

"You've gotten a second opinion?"

Stringer grew more irritated. "Second and third and fourth."

"Nobody could offer you help?"

"Holy shit. Are you trying to make me relive the crushing disappointment? That modern medicine in all its technological glory has failed me and the best advice I could get was enjoy what I've got because it's only downhill from here. That I am going to slowly and painfully lose my dexterity. Is that your deal?"

Wendt held up his hands, spoke softly. "Sorry, sorry. You're right. That doesn't help."

They sat, the only sound coming from Stringer's heavy breathing as he calmed down. When he felt enough time passed, Wendt tried again.

"Do you agree with your wife's assessment about your depression."

"Depression? Shit, I'm more than depressed if there is such a thing. I'm crushed. I can no longer see a reason to keep living." Stringer slumped into the cushion so thoroughly it looked like the only thing preventing him from melting into the floor. Invisible weights pulled at the features of his face. His eyes were dull; no fight in them.

Wendt shifted gears. "Your wife mentioned kids. How old are they?"

"We got two. My daughter is a senior at Cornell. My son, a freshman at Ohio State."

"I'm sure they worry about you."

Stringer said nothing.

"Do you wonder how they will handle it if you kill yourself?"

This caused him to shift in his chair uneasily. "I don't see how that's going to help me. I mean, I see what you're doing, but that doesn't make a difference."

"Why doesn't it make a difference?"

No answer.

Wendt spoke softly. "Paul, have you thought about how you'd kill yourself?"

"I don't really want to answer that question. It could put me in danger of being thrown in the pretzel factory."

"No hospital. Just trying to gauge where your head is."

"Look. I can't do what I love anymore. Do you know what that's like? Huh? Have *you* had to give up what you love to do?" He leaned forward in his chair, looked down at his tremulous hands. His voice dropped a few registers. "In my dreams at night I still operate, using my hands as I once did. Then I wake up each morning and that's when the nightmare begins. Can you imagine? I struggle to find things to keep me busy. I was so used to working sixteen, eighteen hour days. Now I have nothing but time on my hands. And to make it shittier, there isn't a lot my hands will let me do with that time."

"What about non-operative medicine?"

Big sigh from Stringer. "Doesn't do it for me, though I wish it did."

They sat in silence, though now the surgeon appeared less uncomfortable.

"Will you let me work with you to find a way through that doesn't end with your kids grieving the loss of their father?"

Stringer offered a wan smile. "At the very least it will keep my wife off my back."

+ ✦ ✦ ✦ ✦ +

Rogoff came to the door in his bathrobe and slippers. He already had a drink in his hand. He tilted it towards Archie and said, "You got some catching up to do, young man."

They went into the den where Rogoff poured a glass of Glendronach.

"The good stuff. What's the occasion?"

They sat down, Rogoff dropping heavily into his high back chair. "Anniversary of the wife's departure from this life." He lifted his glass high. "To a woman who must have gone straight to heaven after a lifetime of dealing with a mamzer like me."

Archie lifted his glass. "To your wife."

"So Archie, what brings you here this evening? You look like a man with much on his mind."

"After I enjoy your company I will be heading to the Morgenstern's for a late dinner with hizzoner. I wanted to game plan a little before I jumped into the deep end."

"You think he wants something from you. And you'd be right."

Archie nodded, "It doesn't feel like a run of the mill back door therapy."

"I'm sure I don't know what he wants, but he's a guy used to getting his way. A narcissist who's been successful. With each milestone reached the sense of entitlement and infallibility becomes more entrenched. Not easy to contend with."

"And you say no skeletons in his closet. How is that possible?"

Rogoff shrugged. "None that I'm aware of. He wasn't born of money; he married the tycoon's daughter. To get to his position I'm sure he pissed off a lot of people so there have to be a lot of folks who have an ax to grind with him. Then again, maybe he wants from you what he says he wants,

26

you know, a new person, untainted by prejudice, who can give him honest feedback. The opposite of a 'yes' man, if you will."

"I suppose that would be the best-case scenario."

"You're a curious sort. That's why you went into Psychiatry. Go and explore."

Archie stood. "You going to be okay?"

The older man waved Archie off. "You go. I have my scotch. Promise me you'll fill me in the details."

"Will do." He saw himself out.

It was an impressive, Tudor style home sitting atop a hill. He caught his breath at the top, looking at a nice view of the river. A liveried woman answered the door, her back to a foyer boasting an expanse of hard wood floors covered with Persian rugs. The mammoth grandfather clock to her right chimed eight times.

"You are Dr. Wendt." It wasn't a question.

"Yes, I am."

"I'm Linda. Mr. Morgenstern asked me to escort you to the sitting room. He'll be with you shortly."

She led him down a wood lined hallway past a formal living room that stretched to his left, then a wide and winding set of plush stairs, into another living room, this less formal, with a pool table and bar at one end. Seated on deep leather couches were two men, looked to be in their thirties. A woman with dirty blond hair lounged in an Eames Chair. Archie noted the same type of piercing green eyes clearly inherited from her father. Naturally pretty without make-up, she sported worry lines discordant with her youthful appearance.

"Mr. Morgenstern will be out shortly. Can I offer you a drink?" Linda said.

"Scotch on the rocks, please."

One of the men on the couch piped up. "Dad only has bourbon."

Wendt smiled. "That will be fine. Also with ice." Linda nodded and went to the bar. The psychiatrist stood for a minute, not uncomfortable, then walked to the couch and extended his hand to the man who had spoken.

"I'm Archie Wendt."

The man attempted to stand, but owing to the depth of the couch fell back with a grunt. He got up again looking sheepish and shook hands.

"I'm Luke Morgenstern. This is Jed Miller, a friend of mine and that there is my sister, Rose."

"That there? Is that how you talk after father spent so much money to afford you the ability to drop out of Yale?" Turning to Archie, Rose said, "It's nice to meet you."

"Go to hell." Luke said and dropped back into the deep couch.

Wendt looked Luke over. He was a good looking guy wearing trendy clothes. The petulance on his face appeared worn in. The other fellow, Jed, appeared…well, *hungrier*, was the only word suitable. Like a man who wanted what he saw, but was unsure how to get it short of taking it by force.

"Have a seat Dr. Wendt. My brother lacks basic manners and his pet Jed is little more than a common street hood. Hey, I'm sure you've been told this many times: your name is a sentence. Archie Wendt. Kind of like mine, though only in a school setting where they say your last name first. Morgenstern, Rose. Sounds kind of religious, doesn't it?"

Linda brought the bourbon on a serving tray. Wendt took it and thanked her as she disappeared into another room. Already a little buzzed from the earlier scotch and not wanting to fall flat on his face, Archie sipped cautiously. He took in the rest of the room. On one wall hung an immense flat screen TV that hovered over wood cabinetry of a light tan. The adjacent wall was all sliding glass doors looking out on a back yard that stretched to forever. Lined with lights and hedges it looked like a Polo commercial. In the background Luke bickered with Rose as only siblings can.

"People are the same. Every generation says that the one that follows is more bratty and entitled. We're no worse than the one that came before us."

Rose looked amused. "You don't have any context for what you're saying. All your friends are lazy and entitled. Not one of them knows how to do any real work, so your frame of reference is shit."

"Just because you went to that dyke school, Smith," Luke spat.

"I went to Vassar you shithead, not Smith and it's co-ed now."

"As I was saying, just because you went to that liberal dyke school doesn't make you an authority on anything but hairy legs and Birkenstocks."

Rose stood out of the lounge chair. "That's very enlightened of you, Luke. You're a real man of the world, you know that?"

Luke turned to Wendt who made every effort to appear immersed in thought by the pool table. He had no desire to wade into this internecine nonsense. "Doc, hey doc, you must have an opinion on this, right?"

Wendt stopped in mid sip then thought better and made it a gulp. "Anyone can have an opinion. The question is whether it means something to you."

That seemed to perplex Luke. It didn't escape Rose. "Try speaking more concretely to my brother. Whatever sharp edges my brother's intellect had have been buffed dull with copious amounts of weed."

"Doc, are people more spoiled now than they were or are people just people?" Luke asked.

"The Bible tells us that there's nothing new under the sun. But I would say that with each generation of plenty, there is an increase of the expectation that all needs will be met." Archie turned to Rose. "How's that?"

"I thought it was classic shrinkinese. You successfully straddled both sides."

"Rose ain't right, that's all I know." Luke said then returned to his brooding.

"Look who made it to my humble abode." Virgil Morgenstern's voice boomed out as he came in through the sliding doors from the outside. Wendt wondered where he'd been, but then took another sip and the bourbon jettisoned his curiosity.

"I see you've met my progeny. My pride and or joy." He put his arm around Rose who lifted her face and gave him a kiss on the cheek.

"Hi, Daddy. Does this mean we can finally eat? Because I'm famished."

"Yes, why don't we eat. We'll start without your mother who is off at some charity event or another. Let's go to the table. Except you, Miller, you're not invited."

Luke stamped his foot. "Are you serious? Come on, why pick on Jed?"

"Because I'm not supporting him any longer. We've been through this. Sorry, Jed, you have to leave."

Jed put his glass down with a small bang and stalked out of the room. Luke fumed, but said no more. The family turned away; only Wendt kept his eyes on Jed and saw the pall cover his face as he walked out. It was an unmistakable mix of rage and resolve.

"Linda! Linda!" Virgil bellowed. She appeared at the doorway. If there'd been a blast of smoke and smell of crimson surrounding her entrance it would not have shocked Wendt.

"Yes, Mr. Morgenstern."

"Is dinner ready?"

"It is. Are we waiting on Mrs. Morgenstern?"

"No."

This sense of formality in small town Ohio struck Wendt as out of place. He'd seen his fair share of wealth among the Brahmin in Boston. There they touted all the trappings of class: breeding, education, wealth. He knew that Morgenstern came from humble beginnings, so Archie chalked all this up to showing off for him.

They made their way back towards the winding stairway and the formal living room on the right. Off to the left was a dining room only slightly smaller than Archie's apartment in Boston. It had the requisite chandelier and table that seemed to stretch for miles. Great smells emanated from the kitchen. Morgenstern sat at the head and offered his right hand to Wendt. He didn't seem to care where his children sat.

"You should feel special Dr. Wendt. We never do this," Rose said as she sat down opposite the psychiatrist. Luke sat to his right.

"What do you usually do?"

"Linda offers to fix us a family dinner, but Mother is out doing something, and Daddy is working, I scrounge for myself, and Arby's next to you…well, you get the picture."

This Rose was a hot sketch. Clearly she had inherited her father's wit and presence. Wendt put his napkin on his lap and sat quietly. Morgenstern did the same, but was quiet for one millisecond.

"Linda! Where's the food and where's my drink?"

On cue Linda came in with a tray. It had four soup bowls and a martini glass. The drink came first to the table. She knew her priorities. The soup looked to be a cream of something or other. Wendt waited for everyone to be served before digging in to his. Virgil did not. He ate with gusto right away.

"Linda makes the best goddamned soup. Normally I can't stand the idea of courses. Like food foreplay. I like to get right to the main course, if you know what I mean." He offered a salacious grin to Wendt. "But Linda outdoes herself every time."

After Wednt tasted his he nodded and said. "Quite good."

"Daddy, I'm wondering what you think of the argument Luke and I had just before you came in the room."

Luke got up and stalked to the kitchen.

Unflustered Rose continued. "You see, I was saying that with each generation the youth in this country grow more emboldened and entitled. Conversely, or more likely as a corollary, they are less inclined to put in the hard work that's needed to pay dues."

"I'm curious," Wendt interjected, "what is it you do for a living?"

"I am vice president of Morgenstern Holdings and manage all of the residential properties." Rose said.

"And one day she will manage the entirety of Morgenstern Holdings." Virgil's eyes oozed pride. His face soured when Luke returned to the table with a highball of something clear.

"So, Daddy, what say you." Rose stared at Luke as she spoke.

"C'mon, you're still on that subject? Get a life." Luke said in between swigs from his glass.

"What did the good doctor have to say on the subject?" Virgil asked.

"He waffled like all good shrinks do." Rose offered a playful smile to Wendt.

Virgil expounded. "Well, I would have to say that it becomes harder for each subsequent generation, especially when the parents have had success."

Rose turned to her father. "Elaborate."

Wendt could see that Virgil would do just about anything for his little girl. "I came up the hard way. Had to earn everything. My mother taught me values, but she couldn't teach me how to scrap and persevere; that I learned on my own. My children didn't have to do struggle, a fact for which I am thankful, but I deprived you of the opportunity to scrape and scrimp for yourselves. Sometimes I don't know if I helped or crippled you. It seems I have done a bit of both." He gave a sly nod towards his son.

"Don't make it personal," Luke said. "We were talking about society in general."

"As pertains to society," Virgil picked up his martini glass and swirled the olive around in the liquid, "the parents of the baby boom generation, many of them children of privation from the Great Depression, now with abundance naturally spoiled their kids. With extra time on their hands these boomers used it to smoke dope and protest every goddamned thing under the sun. They never held a rally against laziness, that's for sure. But, however entitled they were, they remained tethered to their parents and thus, by extension, maintained a grasp on the concept of hard work.

"The boomers then had children. Themselves given to a lax approach to rules and discipline, especially as it pertained to drug use, it would be only natural that their progeny would push the envelope. So while the hippies were smoking a weak dope, their children now partook in significantly stronger weed and dabbled in powerful narcotic pain relievers, ecstasy, and heroin. The baby boomers' kids, not being tethered to the generation that had to sacrifice, have proved more disconnected from the mother ship. You can't even shame them. They have little sense of propriety and even less a sense of self awareness. How's that for an answer."

"Dr. Wendt said something vaguely like that." Rose said. "Give us a definitive answer, Dr. Wendt." Virgil and Rose looked at him expectantly; Luke appeared not to give two shits. Linda came in and collected the bowls. As she receded, Wendt spoke.

"I'm in your home so please call me Archie. Your answer, Virgil, has some merits. However, it is a gross generalization. I could find you numerous examples of laziness even in the face of privation. The hobos preceded the hippies and they were content to ride the trains. They didn't consider themselves homeless, they just embraced an untethered life if you'll allow me to borrow a word from your monologue. And among today's youth you have twenty something millionaires who revolutionized commerce with the internet. Not to mention Mark Zuckerberg who changed the entire landscape of socializing."

Virgil waved it off. "Outliers and exceptions. They don't prove the rule."

"I do agree that substance abuse is more rampant and destructive. But I think of it as a good example of entropy." He explained further. "Things always move towards greater disorder, not vice versa. So if you start with a generation that is more lax than its predecessor, say on sex and drugs, it only stands to reason that their own offspring will demonstrate an even more lenient view of those subjects."

"We had sex in my generation just like those hippies, we just were more discreet about it. Those baby boomers think they invented everything."

"Daddy, you were born in '41. You're the same age as that generation."

"No, I most certainly am not. I had respect for my elders. I knew the value of hard work and dedication to my craft. And I didn't feel compelled to piss in everyone's pool just because the "Red Man" got no justice."

Rose turned to Wendt. "Daddy loves to demonstrate how unpolitically correct he is. Please don't take offense."

"I don't take offense. It would be hard to do what I do and take offense at people's idiosyncrasies and foibles. I wouldn't be a very good psychiatrist."

"Good point, Doc." Virgil raised his glass in salute and took a sip. Rose put a hand on his arm. "Maybe you shouldn't drink any more. You appear unsteady."

He winked at Wendt, talked to Rose. "I'm fine, honey. Thanks for the concern. Luke, you haven't clarified your position. Please enlighten us."

Luke, abandoning his sulky demeanor, perked up to answer.

"I think you're all wrong. All part of that same cantankerous 'your generation is worse than mine' bullshit. Like those dudes on the Muppets who sit in the balcony and have nothing but criticism and bile for everything anyone else does."

"Like the word bile and nice imagery with The Muppets reference."

"Quiet Rose, let him expound. Nice to hear him take any position."

Luke ignored the back-handed compliment from his father. "I don't think my generation is any more entitled or self-absorbed than any other. Besides, I don't think that selfishness is wrong or a problem. If everybody acted in their own self-interest, honestly and without bullshit, this would be a better world."

"Not that Ayn Rand shit again, Luke. Didn't you outgrow that?"

"Chide all you want, Rose. She was a genius and people like you are only interested in squashing genius to make everyone equal. But we weren't all born equal. We were born, some of us, with talents that need to be expressed."

"What talent are you expressing currently, o' brother of mine. Smoking weed, playing video games?"

Linda came in with a wheeled cart and served dinner. Wendt

desperately wanted another drink, but held off. Luke didn't have the same compunction; he accepted a fresh glass from Linda while everyone enjoyed a conversational respite while she served. Wendt took the opportunity to look around the room as a way of avoiding returning to the heated topic. It was purely classical in decor. Persian rug underfoot, long, wooden dining table. Chandelier that wasn't too gaudy. On the wall opposite him were what he assumed were Chagall originals. The whole effect was impressive. On the wall behind Morgenstern there was a wooden buffet. Above it was a reprint of DaVinci's Last Supper. That made Wendt laugh.

"What's funny?" Morgenstern inquired.

"The Last Supper."

"Yeah. Ain't that a hoot? I thought it went well with the room."

The meal was excellent. Pork medallions in a mushroom sauce. On the side was a dumpling type of dish that puzzled, but delighted Wendt. He looked up at Virgil, some of it on his fork.

"Spätzel. Linda's mother was Swiss." Virgil said.

They ate in silence. Wendt was glad they didn't renew the argument with Luke. He could feel Rose's real anger beneath the playful sarcasm. He didn't like the negative energy that came with the jibes. When Virgil finished he put his silverware and napkin on his plate and called out loudly.

"Linda, I'm going to take my dessert and brandy in the library with the doctor. Send it in five minutes."

He didn't wait for a reply, just stood. Wendt looked wistfully at what remained on his plate, but understood that his gustatory needs had to come second to those of the host. Rose and Luke made no protest; it seemed they were used to this type of arrangement. They stood and scattered, Rose with a sarcastic yet playful curtsy to Archie.

Wendt wiped his mouth and stood. Lil cooked, but not like this. Many nights he got a sandwich from a late night deli. This repast was as good as he'd eaten in a long time.

10

He followed Virgil out of the dining room and into the formal living room. You could host a president, czar, and emir in there and not feel ashamed. Midway through the room Virgil lost his balance; Archie reached out and steadied him.

"I guess I had more to drink than I realized."

Curious statement because Archie hadn't seen him drink that much and had noticed no obvious signs of intoxication.

At the end of the living room stood an archway with an impressive oak door crossed by iron bands. Very medieval looking. Virgil pulled out a large skeleton key. He smiled behind his shoulder to Archie as he opened the door.

"I enjoy both security and theatrics as you can see."

"Security from whom? You must have a hell of an alarm on the house."

"Son had a bit of a drug problem. Got into a stealing phase. It was a long time ago, but old habits die hard."

"Whose habits have died hardest?"

Virgil wagged his finger at Archie. "Good question."

He turned back to the lock, opened the door and switched on an impressive chandelier that hung from the middle of a vaulted ceiling. They stepped into a beautiful room. An oak and leather overdose with maroon accents. Any bigger and you could toss in some old white haired men sitting in high back chairs smoking cigars and reading the Wall Street Journal.

"I find this room very soothing." Archie said.

"Thanks. Me, too."

"I've dreamt of an office like this. These types of leather high back chairs."

"My wife decorated the house, but I kept her out of here and picked the style. What you see here are my ideas without the interference of a feminine touch."

"What's your wife like, if you don't mind the prying."

"Not at all," Virgil said, "in fact, I'd be interested in your opinion after you meet her. Very sharp woman. Grew up wealthy and she carries it in her bearing. I charmed her into marrying me. She bored of me quickly, but we've managed to stay together. Not an easy feat these days, what with all the divorces."

They were interrupted when Linda came in with the wheeled cart. On it was coffee in a French Press and a decadent looking chocolate cake.

"Thank you, Linda. Dr. Wendt, as you can see I have a weakness for the finer things. Brandy, cigars, chocolate, booze, women, gambling... I got a lot of weaknesses." He chuckled good naturedly.

Archie stood and walked over to the bookshelves and looked at the titles. He pulled on some of the books.

"They're all real. No props there."

"You're a smart man, Mr. Morgenstern. I did wonder."

"I've read most of them, but some I still haven't gotten to. Reading is a passion of mine."

"I notice you have a lot of Russian literature."

"Can't get enough of it. Amazing culture filled with talented people amid societal pathology. First the czars, then the Communists, now it's all oligarchs and criminals. But the writers in that country were astounding: Dostoevsky, Tolstoy, Pushkin, Turgenev, Chekhov, and the list goes on and on."

"Nabokov." Archie added.

Virgil smiled. "Yes, Nabokov with his love of pre-pubertal girls. I imagine that would be interesting to a psychiatrist."

"He lived for a short while in Cambridge, Massachusetts. I used to walk by his old house."

"Interesting. Doctor, sit, please, and have some cake and coffee with me. Then, if you're willing, a nice cigar."

They sat and ate cake. Archie drank the coffee, noticing that Virgil didn't touch his. Archie nodded when Virgil offered him a cigar. They lit up and puffed contentedly. Virgil turned on an air purifier.

"I'm sure you believe that I had ulterior motives for having you come here."

"It crossed my mind." Archie blew smoke to the ceiling.

"Perhaps it's unfair to call them ulterior; they certainly aren't nefarious and I'll share them with you." He leaned forward in his chair, holding his cigar between his index and middle fingers. "This is a pretty small town as you've seen. Once you get to be a big enough fish it's difficult not to be told what others think you want to hear. I've grown tired of people rubber stamping any opinion or idea I throw out there. I heard there was a new doctor in town and my curiosity had me seek you out. Now that we've met and spent some time together it confirms my hopes - you could be the type who shoots straight from the hip and I'm in need of someone like that." He sat back and resumed puffing on his cigar.

Archie leaned forward in his chair and unconsciously mimicked the position Virgil just abandoned. "Two things, Virgil. One, I'm flattered that you would consider me such a man, but you don't know me at all. Not in any real way that justifies your faith. Secondly, what exactly could I do for you aside from offering psychiatric services that you've already indicated are unnecessary?"

Virgil leaned in again; he seemed to be enjoying this. "It's precisely that kind of push back that I want. You don't have to only provide psychiatric services. I mean, your position allows for counseling, as well, doesn't it?"

"Counseling?"

"Yes. I need counsel, not for my own mental issues, but for my businesses, my holdings…" He waved his hand around looking for a word. "My life, Dr. Wendt. My life. I have come to a point where I need some advice and I believe you're the kind of man to give it."

"What kind of advice are you seeking?" Archie asked.

"I want your opinion of my kids. I am making estate plans and having difficulty." Virgil stood suddenly and paced the room. "My thoughts on them are stale and unimaginative and because of that I'm not able to see what I can't see, if you know what I mean. It's important I know what they're made of, what they're capable of."

"Mr. Morgenstern, Virgil, again, I'm flattered that you would think so highly of me in so quick a time. But, I'm not a mind reader nor do I have a crystal ball. Your impression of them after so many years is infinitely better than anything I could come up with in such a short order."

"I appreciate your humility. I really do. But you underestimate yourself and the perspective you can bring. I'm a father. It's in my nature to want to see the best, and sometimes worst, in my kids. I need a professional to size up their character."

"Rose is angry and Luke is lazy."

"Thanks, Sigmund, for picking at the low hanging fruit."

"Aren't you trying to get me to help you? Should you be insulting me?"

Virgil laughed. "You're right. But I want a more in depth understanding."

"Seems to me that Rose, however, pissed off she is, is not the problem you're focused on, but Luke."

Virgil nodded. "He is the more troublesome one. But sometimes the quieter ones worry me more, in business and in family. Though Rose appears loud, she keeps her inner feelings well guarded. So, will you do it?"

"How did you imagine I would carry this out? Neither seems likely to want to meet with me under the pretense of sizing them up for their inheritance." Archie said.

"No, I agree. You'll come here and meet them informally, taking in observations. If you come to feel that's insufficient we'll come up with a solution then. Sound reasonable?"

"I'll give it my best. Did you have some remuneration plan in mind?"

"Money? That's the easy part. Anytime in life you can solve a problem with money, and like me, you've got it? Hell, I'll take that any day."

Archie enjoyed the moment - cigar, caffeine, and repartee. "You're an interesting man in your own right."

"Coming from an educated man like yourself I'll take that as a compliment," Morgenstern said. "Anyway, I want you to come back for dinner on Sunday night. My kids'll be there as well as my wife, I promise. You can tell me what you think of her, too. There will be one other couple: an old friend and his wife. He's also my personal attorney." Virgil stood. "So it's settled." He offered his hand to Archie then called out to Linda who appeared at the door. "Will you please see Dr. Wendt to the door and make sure he leaves without stealing anything."

"Thank you for a lovely evening, Mr. Morgenstern. And thank you, Linda, for a truly magnificent meal." She blushed, but said nothing as she led him to the front door. The night air cooled his face pleasingly. He lingered by his car for a few moments finishing his cigar then contemplated driving back to the bed and breakfast, but decided on a detour to Rogoff's house instead. Had to keep his promise.

"So he asked you to come back in a couple of days?"

"Yes. So I could size up his son and daughter."

They were seated in the den. Archie had a drink in hand; Rogoff did not.

"You know, inviting you like that reminds me of the story read on the Jewish holiday of Purim. You familiar?"

"No."

"It's a ripping yarn. Happened more than two thousand years ago. Esther is a Jew and she's been made queen, but she doesn't share with the king, Ahasuerus, that she's Jewish. The villain, Haman, you might have heard of; he pays a premium to the king to have all the Jews killed.

"Esther, the secret Jewess queen, fearing for her life hosts a party for Haman and Ahasuerus, who is ready to give up half his kingdom for her youthful honeypot. She plays it real cool. When the king asks what he can do for her, she tells him come back for another party with Haman. When they return for the second party she flips the script on Haman and exposes him in front of the king who, in his rage, has Haman hanged from the very yardarm Haman had prepared for his enemy, Esther's uncle. Good story, like I said."

"You think Morgenstern has something sinister set up for me? Why? It doesn't make sense; I harbor no ill will towards him."

"I don't think he harbors any ill will towards you, it's just the way you described it made me associate to that story."

Archie shrugged and said: "He has a very nice house, I'll tell you that."

"I would imagine," Howard said, "rumors are he's worth over a hundred million."

"The place looks every bit of it. What do you know about the son?"

"I know the scuttlebutt I've heard over the years. Got into some drug trouble a few years back, but no major felonies. Father sent him to an expensive rehab place in California. He came back and has been living at home since. I don't think he has much to do with the business."

"He doesn't. The daughter does." Archie said.

"Yes, Rose. Bright girl. I think Virgil's most concerned about her finding a suitable spouse. Not easy given her moneyed status. I imagine she must be in her early thirties by now."

"It was an interesting evening to be sure. I felt like I had been transported to another age. The pomp, circumstance, the meal - the guy puts on a good show."

"Sounds like he piqued your curiosity. I'll be interested in hearing how things go from here. It should make for a good story."

Howard had no idea just how right he would be.

When Archie finally made it back to his room at the B&B, dog tired, he trudged up the stairs holding on to the railing knowing it was going to be a rough night of sleep. Falling into bad habits like before, drinking to avoid dealing with issues. He wondered why he should be stressed; they weren't his issues. He absently rubbed his jaw, now showing traces of red from irritation. As he opened the door to his room he heard movement behind him. Lillie stood in her doorway in a negligee, back to the mantle, one leg bent and the arms held over her head in a classic pose.

"How about a little nightcap, sailor."

She might have been in her late fifties, but she still had the goods. They had broken the seal on copulation a few months back. There was an unspoken understanding that they weren't dating, necessarily, but he worried about the potential for things to go bad. His instincts had been to avoid this kind of entanglement; he needed a place to stay and not the potential complication. But one night when he had too much to drink he was vulnerable and maudlin. The rest played out in a predictable way.

"You look ravishing, Lil. I would love nothing more than to rip off that negligee and..." His words tailed off as his legs gave out. She sighed, walked over to him and put her head in an armpit, lifting him as best she could. His legs worked like that of a newborn foal so she mostly dragged him to the bed, plopping him down with perhaps more force than his weight would predict. His last conscious thought was about the convenience of passing out - he avoided a poor performance and the inevitable damage to Lil's vulnerable psyche.

The proprietress turned off the light and walked out of the room muttering angrily. That night Wendt slept like the dead, sans dreams; the hangover was significant, but he would take a dreamless night every day of the week even if it meant a more wicked headache the next day.

CHAPTER
12

The President's Club on a weekend enjoyed slightly more business than during the week. Regulars, plus a few weekend tourists who came for Amish country and indulged in alcohol as a reaction to the teetotaler tradition of their daytime hosts. They tested Mike's ability to concoct newfangled drinks. More frustratingly to Wendt, they kept Mike away from serving his role as a sympathetic ear.

"Mike, get your ass over here 'cause I'm not done with the story."

The bartender slowly made his way down the bar to the belligerent psychiatrist.

"You see, I knew she was going to be a pain in the ass," Wendt launched into a loud monologue. "Could tell from the referral. It was from a family friend and I wanted to do him a favor. Always a mistake, I can tell you. But I'd gotten to a point where I felt capable of helping anyone and I relished the challenge." He swirled the liquid in his nearly empty glass.

"You going to want a refill on that?" Mike asked, grimy towel in hand.

"Mike, I keep tellin' you not to interrupt me when I get going 'cause it derails my train of thought. I mean, you should know that by now, right? How hard a concept is that, for chrissakes? And I always want a refill, you should know that as well, you cretin." He made sure to pronounce it pretentiously with the "eh" first syllable rather than long "e".

Mike poured from a height with his finger on the gin bottle's spout top, an old trick bartenders use to make it seem like they're giving more than they are. Wendt was too drunk to notice.

"As I was saying, I knew she would be a pain in the ass. Had already attempted suicide several times. And these weren't the 'look at me' type of attempts, no, these were the "nobody is home and I'm going to see how many sedatives I can fire down with a bottle of wine until I die or pass out

44

trying kind." He tipped back the rest of his drink. The movement caused him to sway on the barstool. Mike leaned across the bar and steadied him.

"Okay. Easy there now, Dr. Wendt. Time for you to call it a night."

"No. No, please, I need to get this out. I know I'm a pain in the ass, but you gotta do this for me." he pleaded. The change in tone took Mike by surprise. He'd tended bar long enough to develop a thick skin for the crap you took from drunks. You couldn't take them seriously because they didn't remember half the shit they said, anyway, so why take any of it personally? Also, and more importantly, regulars kept bars like his in business. He tried not to think too much about it because when he did he invariably felt guilty. Wendt was different, though. Mike knew that Wendt'd taken over Howard's practice and the retired shrink spoke well of the new doctor's dedication. In a way Mike felt like he contributed to the wellness of all those patients by listening to Wendt vent. It was detoxifying for the psychiatrist and kept him on a more even keel. Detoxifying the shrink by making him intoxicated.

"What the hell are you smiling about, you old fuck?"

That brought Mike back quickly. "You knew she was going to be trouble…" He prompted Wendt and offered a refill of mostly Collins with very little Tom.

"Right. She comes in and gives me her pertinents. Was young when her parents divorced, became her mother's confidante at too early an age. She —"

"You didn't mention her name."

Wendt slammed a hand on the bar. "Goddammit, Barkeep, I asked you not to interrupt." He then lapsed into silence and took a deep breath. "Sorry, Mike, you're right, I didn't give you the name. I know how important a name can be in a story 'cause it lets you develop a mental image. Her name was Janine Frank.

"So, young Janine's mom did her level best to ingrain disappointment in her young daughter; that is disappointment in everyone and everything and you'll always be let down eventually so trust nobody. Negativity and hopelessness as regular a part of her childhood as burnt meals.

"But our Janine had resilience. I mean, she studied hard and got into Radcliffe, escaped her mother's clutches and worked her ass off to find her way in the world. A bachelor's degree in fine arts, then a masters of the same at Harvard. From there she landed a plum job at the Boston Institute of Contemporary Art. But it never proved enough, you know? She always thought of herself as a piece of shit no matter what type of success she achieved.

"We worked hard to piece together her self-esteem, to give her some satisfaction from her hard work and success. Slowly things started to improve for Janine."

Wendt couldn't bring himself to take more ownership for her improvements, to tell Mike that at the time he sincerely thought he'd changed her trajectory. She handled things better and exhibited a healthier outlook, even experiencing joyous moments. Archie'd let himself believe that she was going to make it - no more suicide attempts. Then she fell in love with a man.

He drank down the last few swallows of his highball, looked at the glass, then at Mike to let him know *he* knew it was watered down. Then he continued. "I had her squared away, Mike, I had her deriving pleasure from life. I was home free. If I could I would have stopped time and therapy then I would have." He looked through Mike, through the dusty bottles lining the wall, into the mirror behind the bar, and beyond. Transported back to that moment in time.

Mike leaned forward on his elbows. "Give it to me, Arch. Tell me what happened."

"She got involved with the wrong man. Janine threw herself in this guy, you know, just lost herself in his world, riding his ups and downs without regard for her own safety. I saw it coming like the light on a freight train and did my level best to anticipate and ease the impact.

"She didn't show for an appointment. Police found her submerged in the bathtub, her thighs cut open. Toxicology report showed she'd taken pills, as well, to ensure success. The triple attempt."

Mike shook his head. "I'm sorry, man. You did the best you could, I'm sure. Can't win 'em all, huh?"

Archie put his head on the bar and spoke to the floor. "Can't remember the last time I won even one, Mike. It's been a long time."

Garrett barged in the office.

"Hiya, Doc. What's shakin'?" He pulled a chair out and arranged it in front of Archie. then a second and a third.

"Why so many chairs?" Archie asked.

"We got company, man. I, for one, am excited. While I do so enjoy the one on one with you, I've been longing for some group therapy."

"I don't do groups. They always get taken over by a narcissistic loudmouth and the needier people shy away. No groups for me."

"You don't have much of a choice, do you? They should be here any minute. How you been doing in the interim, huh? Hitting the sauce hard, I see. You know what that does to your dreams. Ah, here they are." He stood.

The door opened and in walked Janine, wearing a sun dress and looking pretty and care free. Just seeing her face brought a flood of emotions to Archie - he'd forgotten how she exuded vulnerability. It perpetually came as shock to him that she could be so unaware of the effect she had on men. Especially him. Low self-esteem kept Janine oblivious to her own beauty. Nothing he ever said disabused her of that dissonance.

Janine sat and offered a smile. "How are you, Dr. Wendt? I want you to know I'm not angry with you. I know how hard you worked to make me feel better about myself. It was somewhat disappointing that you didn't keep your end of the bargain, but I don't hold that against you."

He didn't answer. Before she had a chance to speak again the door opened. All three turned to watch Father Damian Karras, the priest/psychiatrist from *The Exorcist*, enter.

"What the hell?" Archie said to Garrett.

Garrett shrugged. "I told you before this is your gig."

Karras sat down. "Hi, Archie, I can answer your question. You always felt a kinship with me having briefly flirted with the clergy before ultimately choosing psychiatry. I embodied both those worlds to you, the religious and psychiatric. When you saw *The Exorcist* you identified with the duality of my role as both a man of science and the cloth."

"It was a very brief flirtation with the clergy, I can assure you." Archie said. "But, it was more than those things; I remember feeling the intensity of your isolation. The shitty little room you lived in and how you mourned the loss of your mother, tormenting yourself that you'd let her down. It must mean that I crave that kind of guilt as an excuse to be reclusive and unobligated to other humans." Archie turned to Garrett, the makeshift MC. "Is Damian here as a patient or group leader?"

"There are no rules here. We're all here for some enlightenment and who better to help us than a man who has spent a lifetime straddling the physical and spiritual worlds. Personally, I think it's a great choice on your part." Garrett smiled and clapped his hands together as if readying for a scrum.

Damian slapped his hands on his thighs. "Let's begin."

Everybody sat silently. Archie cracked and spoke first.

"I don't think any of this is necessary. I mean, you guys did what you did for yourselves. Only Damian's suicide served someone else; it was a heroic gesture, saving Regan." He tipped his head to the priest then looked at Garrett and Janine. "You two should start if there are things that need to be said."

Janine said, "It's probably foolish to say that it wasn't personal. But you must know that it wasn't directed at you. In the end, I felt sorry you got hurt."

"I'm not sorry." Garrett jumped in. "It had nothing to with the good doctor. I mean, do cardiologists look for forgiveness from their heart attack patients when they don't respond to the CPR being performed on them? You worked on us like somebody in the intensive care unit after a bad accident. If the body is beyond repair no amount of ministrations will make a difference. If the body is broken, baby, it is broken. It was our souls that were beyond help, our psyches."

"I consider those the same things," Damian added.

"Let's not get technical, Padre." Garret said. "Don't get your ecumenical undergarments in a bunch. You understood my meaning. The very essence of our being cried out for an escape from the daily agony of living with the psychic pain. Archie gallantly tried, Lord knows he did." Garrett said.

"Does he?" Archie asked looking around the room.

"We don't have those kinds of answers for you. It doesn't work that way." Damian said.

"I thought you'd give me that kind of shitty response."

Janine leaned in and put her hand on his knee. "You're a good man, Archie. You need to ease up on yourself. I don't hold you responsible; I'm only left with the good memories. You remember how we spoke of our good friends Glen and Val?"

Archie sagged in his chair. "Glen and Val. Two buddies I haven't thought of for a while. Sure, I remember them well. That was the deal you and I made, but then you took it literally whereas I just wanted to keep you tethered to earth."

She looked into his eyes as if she wanted to enter his soul. "Those were my demons, not yours. You couldn't take them away, no matter how hard you tried."

Archie's eyes welled up. He hadn't cried since losing Bud, his Dalmation, as a little boy. "God knows I didn't want you to die."

He awakened with a start to doors slamming in the house. Even his addled head grasped that Lil was still pissed off about the other night. He sat up at the edge of the bed and the dream ebbed slowly from his consciousness. Archie poured the needed eye opener with one shaky hand as he wiped the tears with the other.

Wendt did little on Saturday. He endeavored to jog, but his energy flagged so he mostly walked. The fresh air helped. So, too, staying away from the visual daggers Lillie sent him. He could feel them through the walls. Sleeping with her turned out to be a bad idea. Who would have thought? They warned about shitting where you eat, not where you sleep. They should have been more specific.

He circled around to Rogoff's house only to find the classic Mercedes not in its usual parking spot. A rare sight, but telling; no car equaled no Howard.

Archie returned to an empty B&B. Thank God for small favors. He showered quickly and left with the plan to spend the rest of the weekend in his office if need be. He bought a sandwich and a drink and went up the stairs. Paperwork and the bottle of scotch in his drawer would keep him busy and away from any confrontations at home.

Sunday night arrived. Brimming with anticipation, curious about Mrs. Virgil Morgenstern, and frankly eager to see Rose again, Archie dressed with more care than usual. His stomach growled with anticipation of Linda's cooking.

She greeted him at the door. "Good evening, Dr. Wendt. Let me take your jacket. Is that a package for the Morgensterns?"

"Yes, but I'd like to present it to them if you don't mind." They walked down the hall to the second living room. "I'm looking forward to another of your meals. The last one stands fixed in my memory."

She smiled in response and quietly led the way. Virgil was already seated with a drink in his hand. He had on black wingtips, gray slacks, a black turtleneck, and a black blazer. It looked good with his white hair. Soft jazz played in the background. Morgenstern got out of his chair and stood next to a woman in her sixties. Very stylish looking. Gray hair in a bun so tight it forbad any strays. Navy pants and a silky cream top, expensive looking. And everywhere, the sparkle of jewelry.

"Great to see you, Dr. Wendt." Virgil smiled, put an arm around his wife's shoulders. "Katherine, I'd like to present to you Dr. Archibald Wendt, new to our fair town of Harding. Dr. Wendt, the love of my life, Katherine."

She didn't smile, but offered her hand palm down. Archie offered his palm up and gave her manicured hand a gentle shake. Her grip was firm, the skin smooth as butter. Like Virgil described: she bore all the hallmarks of good breeding and wealth.

Rose stood. "Hello again, Dr. Wendt. How the hell are you?"

Archie smiled broadly at the sound of her voice. "Archie, please. And I'm good, how about you?"

"Is that package for us?" Virgil inquired. Rose sat down with a look from her mother that didn't escape Archie's notice.

"Yes, it is." He turned to Mrs. Morgenstern. "My apologies in advance, ma'am, I bought a gift that I fear only your husband will like. Though I could be wrong." He handed a bag over to Virgil who pulled out a bottle of Jim Beam Devil's Cut.

"The proprietor of the liquor store said that it is a highly rated bourbon."

Virgil smiled. "I've seen it advertised, but haven't yet tried it. Creature of habit, you know. Let's open it and find out."

He waved away Linda's attempt to take the bottle and walked across the room to get fresh glasses. Wendt sat down opposite Rose, ensconced again in the Eames chair.

"It's nice to see you again, Rose. How was your weekend?"

"Rose, please don't sit with your legs across the chair. You know I don't like that."

"Mother, I hope you'll be sharing in the bounty that Archie brought."

"Don't be sassy, Rose; put your feet on the floor. That should do the trick."

Moving with the speed of a teenager, Rose straightened herself and turned her attention to Archie. "Bringing my father bourbon is a shrewd move. You're looking to become his personal shrink, aren't you, you crafty devil."

"Really, Rose, why do you insist on being as shocking as possible. It's terribly boring, you know. You aren't a teenager any longer."

Rose didn't take her mother's bait, but looked at Archie. "I, for one am excited for a taste. Devil's Cut. What a great name."

Virgil brought a tray with glasses and ice. He poured four and held out the tray for his wife, daughter, and Archie. Only Katherine demurred.

Still standing, Morgenstern raised his glass. Rose and Archie raised theirs.

"To children carrying on the good work. To Rose."

"To Rose," Archie repeated. They drank.

"Hey, that's pretty good." Virgil said.

"They're all the same to me," Rose chimed in.

For Archie, used to his single malts, it went down like rusty screws. He held his tongue and smiled. They sipped silently as Linda walked in trailing a couple. "Mr. and Mrs. Daugherty are here."

Morgenstern smiled and walked across the room to greet the newcomers. Placing his arms around the shoulders of both he faced Archie.

"Dr. Wendt, this here is David Daugherty, my long time attorney, and his wife, Laura."

Archie shook hands with both. Laura stood half a head taller than her husband, her dyed hair coiffed to additional heights. David wore an ill-fitting suit, had a red, pinched face and a bad comb-over.

Morgenstern rubbed his hands together. "What say we eat?" He led the way to the dining room. The attorney hung back to walk with Archie; he looped an arm around Archie's biceps as they went into the dining room.

"Virgil told me about you. He talked you up, in fact."

"Really." Archie wasn't comfortable with Daugherty's arm looped inside his own. It felt overly intimate and too much like they were in the 1920's. Daugherty put his face close to Archie's, his breath smelling of a head start to the night's drinking.

"Yeah. It's a small town, I don't have to tell you. Everyone knows everyone. So for Virgil to feel he has found someone he can talk to, someone he can confide in, well, that's something special for him."

"He doesn't feel you're enough?"

David threw his head back and laughed. "Oh, you're good. I can see why he likes you. There's no lie in you."

"Wait till I get more booze in my system," Archie replied sotto voce.

Katherine Morgenstern appeared confident as the hostess, gesturing the others into the dining room.

"There are no assigned seats. Please be comfortable."

Virgil pointed at Archie and David. "You guys over here, on each side of me."

They sat. Linda and an additional helper laid out salad plates.

"So, Dr. Wendt, I understand that my husband is getting free therapy from you."

Before Archie could answer, Katherine continued. "I'm curious about your training. Do you just prescribe or do you do therapy, as well."

"I do both."

"What school of therapy do you subscribe to?"

"It would best be described as analytical psychotherapy. The tradition that Freud started."

Luke snorted. Archie hadn't noticed him slink in.

"Dear, I do wish you would learn to speak." Katherine said. Archie made a note not to be offended by her; she doled out her sneer equally, sparing no one.

"Doctor, you can see that my darling wife and son are not as open minded to psychiatry as I am."

"Open minded, dear? You don't have the courage to see the man properly. You do it on the sly."

"You see, Doctor, what an enlightened man has to go through in his own home."

"Why are you speaking as if I am not in the room, Virgil, speak right to me." Katherine said without missing a beat.

"So you subscribe to Freud's theories?" Luke asked. "I thought his ideas were debunked, like, I don't know, a hundred years ago?"

"Luke, shut your mouth, okay? You don't know shit about anything. If it's not written on the back of a cereal box or the label of a beer bottle, you're not familiar with it."

"Fuck you and the horse you rode in on, Rose."

"My children, Dr. Wendt. Out in the open for your viewing pleasure."

"Virgil, don't be ashamed of our kids. If you had wanted a hand in their upbringing, you would have been around more often."

"The old standby, Katherine. So glad you dusted it off and brought it out."

"I'm curious, Dr. Wendt, did you know that Freud was a coke head?" Luke said.

"Don't answer that, Archie. My brother's knowledge is like a shallow lake. He only knows enough to spout off, but below a thin veneer, his ability to discuss any topic intelligently is severely hampered."

Luke shot back. "Archie? What the fuck is that? You're so sophisticated that only a first name basis will do?"

Archie took a slug of the bourbon. The pain of it going down took his mind off the forced family therapy underway. The lawyer and his wife looked like they had stumbled upon an indecent scene.

Linda returned pushing that cart of hers while the second server took off the salad plates. Everyone took the help's presence to cool down and admire the fare: veal scaloppini, roasted potatoes, and a vegetable concoction that looked like linguini.

Archie scanned the faces at the table. Virgil looked uncomfortable, like he had something on his mind. Katherine sat as if there were a steel rod jammed up her posterior. Rose slouched while Luke looked pissed and bored at once. The lawyer and his wife had on 'public faces', the smile pasted on like make-up when they left their house.

"This is Virgil's favorite meal, Dr. Wendt." Katherine said.

"It looks delicious." He said to the matron and then turned to Luke and made sure his tone was light-hearted. "You're right that Freud had a bout of cocaine addiction. In fact, he thought it such a miracle drug he got one of his best friends hooked. That friend eventually died due to various addictions."

"You see, Rose, you know it all bitch."

Virgil put his fork down hard. "How about you act nicely while we're at the table. You're messing up a fine meal."

David, ever the lawyer, cleared his throat to speak and put on a face that suggested what he had to say represented the highest authority. Archie didn't like him already. "You have to understand, Dr. Wendt, to the layperson, the things that go on in a psychiatrist's office are a mystery unless one has been through treatment. It can be very intimidating to think that there is someone who can see through you and speak of your darkest natures."

Archie spoke to the table at large. "These days I spend little time analyzing people, as it were. Most of my efforts are basic treatments for depression and anxiety." He lied easily. The analyzing wasn't something he could turn off. Archie often lamented that this tendency stayed lit like a hundred year bulb, shining on others. Over the years he learned to share little of what he gleaned unless paid the price of admission. Even if someone inquired playfully he knew the kind of pain in the ass a shrink could be at a cocktail party, analyzing people like a carnival guess your weight guy.

Rose smiled at Archie. "Those of us who have an education understand that the psychiatrist's role is to help people like any other doctor tries to do. I hope you're not offended by my brother. He gets his opinions from talk radio."

"Thank you for the vote of confidence, Rose, but I don't take offense at anyone's misgivings with psychiatry. I even understand it having been a patient myself."

Quiet descended as everyone attended to their plates. When Virgil was done he sat back with a smile on his face. He looked across the table at Rose.

"Rosie, what do you think of Archie here? You think he's a good man?"

She looked at Wendt and cocked her head. "I do."

Virgil nodded and turned to Archie. "I agree. I'm a good judge of character, but my daughter is heads and shoulders above me. She sizes people up like nobody I know." He smacked the table. "That clinches it. I made the right decision with you, Doc. You are my man. Thanks, Rose." He got up and walked around to his daughter, gave her a long kiss on the head. "She's a good one, this girl of mine."

Morgenstern walked out of the room. As the echoes of his footfalls receded, Katherine cleared her throat and put her napkin down. "I don't know what kind of doctor you are, but I don't like your presence here in my family. It seems a conflict of interest. Either you're a doctor in your office with scheduled times, or you're a guest setting aside your clinical persona."

"I agree Mother. I don't like him, either."

"Keep your mouth closed and your ears open, Luke," she snapped.

"Mrs. Morgenstern, I came here tonight not in a professional capacity, but at the invite of your husband. I'm just here to enjoy the company and this excellent food."

The lawyer spoke up, again with a preceding ahem. "Dr. Wendt, you'll have to pardon our curiosity, which must seem hostile to you. Virgil is a powerful man with a great many responsibilities. Anything or anyone new in his world is viewed with skepticism."

Archie took another sip of bourbon, put his glass down, and held his hands up. "I take no offense. Believe me, I wouldn't be much of a psychiatrist if I took people's barbs personally. You love your husband, father, client. Nothing wrong with that. Of course, I *was* invited into your home. That should entitle me at the very least to the courtesy you might afford any guest."

"You're right. Perhaps I've been less than hospitable. Then again, most guests do not seem to have my husband's ear so quickly. I'm sure you can understand my concern."

Rose stood. "You know, I think we've been over this territory already. Nothing more to be gained." Looking at Archie she said, "How would you like a tour of the house?"

"That would be very nice." He stood, made a little bow to the hostess. "This was a lovely meal. Truly. Please give my compliments to Linda."

As Rose and Archie walked out they could hear Katherine mumble, "Give it to her your goddamned self."

Archie spoke softly. "Wow, it usually takes me a lot longer to piss people off."

"Don't mind her. She should have divorced Daddy years ago, she just didn't have the stones to do it."

"That's an interesting opinion."

"Interesting how? What do you mean?" She said as she gestured liked she was giving a tour of the White House. "This is the foyer. This is the second foyer."

"Just that you seem to be the apple of your father's eye. Interesting that you side with your mother."

"I don't side with her. Look, I love my father more than anyone. Look up to him. But he's been a lousy husband, always concerned with events outside the house, ignoring the needs here. I mean, you see my brother.

Even in the brief time you've been around he has amply demonstrated what a screwball he is. He needed a firmer hand coming up and Daddy wasn't around to do the job. Come this way I'll show you the servant's quarters."

"Screwball. That's a term you don't hear often enough. Are there really servant quarters?"

Rose smiled and touched his arm affectionately. "Neh. I just like to call it that. It's living quarters that Linda uses if she's here late. Sometimes Mom likes her to stay if Daddy is out of town. Which can be often."

"You live here?"

"No. Luke crashes here a lot and if he and I had to live again under the same roof, we'd tear this place apart. I have my own condo outside of town."

They walked to the other side of the kitchen entrance down a long hallway that ended in what looked like a little apartment. It had a sitting room, bedroom, and a full bath replete with a black toilet.

"I hate the black toilet when I crap. The camouflaging makes me feel like I didn't accomplish anything."

"Why Dr. Wendt, you're a comedian. And scatological humor is the height of comedy, let me tell you."

"Scatatogical. Screwball. You're just a walking thesaurus." Archie said.

"Did Daddy show you his dungeon?"

"If you mean the study that sits behind the medieval oak door, then yes."

"That's the one. He must have gone there to hide. Let's go spoil his reverie."

They walked back passed the second living room and into the first and took a right. Crossing over the length of the room they came to the oak door. Rose knocked lightly.

"Daddy, let me in."

No answer. She knocked more loudly. It was such a heavy door that even rapping her knuckles on it didn't produce much noise. She grew more insistent.

"Fuck it," she said. "I know where there's a spare key. He's probably got his headphones on. Whenever he gets pissed off he puts on Larry Carlton to calm himself down. Stay here, I'll be right back."

Archie sat down on a sofa and waited. It really was a tastefully done room, he thought, as he looked around. Katherine had a good eye. Or hired someone who did.

"I'm back." Rose put the skeleton key in and opened the door. "Daddy, what are you do-——."

She stopped in the doorway, the blood fleeing her face. Archie jumped off the sofa and pushed passed Rose to get inside. At first he didn't see anything unusual and was momentarily confused as to why she looked upset. The next moment lasted an eternity as his eyes fixed on a sight his brain struggled to comprehend.

Virgil Morgenstern's lifeless body hung from a well-made noose affixed to the study's chandelier.

CHAPTER

14

Archie's paralysis broke and he ran over, grabbed the legs and heaved upwards.

"Rose, go call 911. Now, run, call 911."

She remained standing. "Rose! Call 911." She finally snapped out of it and acknowledged the order.

With Rose gone he dispensed with lifting the body and looked up to see how he could get Virgil down. He righted a chair from underneath the body, clearly the one Virgil had used for his own purposes. It took some maneuvering and grunting, but he was able to loosen the knot and slip it over Virgil's head. His body fell to the ground with an unceremonious thud.

Archie jumped down, placed his fingers in the groove between the neck muscles and the knobby trachea. Nothing. Not that he expected any different. He looked down at the face. It was ruddy, but tranquil. It seemed prudent to do CPR until paramedics arrived so he started pumping the chest rhythmically. It had been years since he had done this, but the memory of it came back easily. Nights on the hospital floor when he was an intern in medicine, presiding over the death throes of many patients. Always the dead of night, two, three in the morning when they elected to run for the border - how one of his senior resident's referred to the dying patient.

As he performed the chest compressions, his mind mulled over the night's events. He recalled an episode in the psych hospital when he ran to a patient's room to find a nurse frantically trying to cut through a bed sheet tied around a patient's neck. The patient had tossed it over the door, closed it, and fell forward. That had been enough to do the trick.

He wondered then as now. Why anyone would do this to themselves? Once done, impossible to undo. That concept proved hard for Archie to get his mind around. The finality of it. The absolute fucking finality. The whole world coming to an end. And for the people they left behind, a lifetime of torment. Questioning every interaction. What did I do? What didn't I do? What could I have done? Archie shook his head as anger welled up and intensified with each chest compression.

He heard rapidly approaching footsteps. A paramedic ran in and got on the floor with Archie.

"I'm Dr. Wendt. We found him about fifteen minutes ago. I've been doing chest compressions during that time. No pulse. It was only, like ten minutes, that he was alone. Let's say it took him two minutes to get into the noose." *How long had Virgil been planning this?* "That means he was hanging for perhaps eight minutes."

"Thank you, we'll take it from here." The medic took a stethoscope from around his neck and placed it on the chest. Wendt stood up and wiped his brow as the second medic came in wheeling a stretcher. The guy on the floor shook his head to his partner. They got Virgil onto the stretcher and moved him out of the library. Archie followed behind and found Rose in the dining room hugging her mother, talking to an officer in a tan uniform. Archie suddenly felt like he was imposing, that it was obscene for him to be there. But he had to make sure Rose was okay.

"Dr. Wendt was here the whole time. He found Daddy with me. I'm sure he's in a better state to answer your questions."

"Okay, Rose, you're right. Take your mother and go with the medics to the hospital. I'll get what I need from Dr. Wendt." The officer walked over to Archie. A big man, maybe six two and broad in the shoulders, like a lifter; he filled out the uniform.

"Dr. Wendt? I'm Sheriff Hidalgo. Difficult time, I know, but if you could fill in some details for me, it would be helpful."

"Is there a criminal charge for a suicide?" Archie asked, unable to keep shakiness out of his voice. The sheriff was nonplussed.

"No. And I obviously don't suspect foul play, but I was very fond of Virgil. I was on duty when I heard the nine eleven call go out to the medics. The address obviously got my attention."

Archie softened. "We can walk the scene if it helps."

"Please." They walked into the library. Aside from the noose, there was no evidence of anything out of place. Both men stood silently for a moment.

Then: "How long did you know Virgil?"

"I just met him. He approached me on the street and befriended me." Archie answered.

"So you didn't see him professionally?"

Archie cocked his head and looked at the Sheriff. "If I were seeing him professionally, dead or not, I wouldn't be able to divulge that information. But it so happens I wasn't. I knew him socially, such as it was. This was my second dinner in less than a week and on both occasions Virgil acted pleasantly, the perfect host. He didn't strike me as depressed at all. Then tonight he excused himself from the table after dinner." Archie stopped and looked off into the distance. "Actually, come to think of it, he didn't excuse himself. He just stood, kissed his daughter and walked away from the table." The full weight of the night's events rained down on Archie as he thought of that last kiss. It was going to haunt Rose for the rest of her life.

Hidalgo got onto the chair and pulled on the noose then untied it from the chandelier. He got down and shook his head. "That's one strong chandelier."

"I had the same thought when I first saw it."

The sheriff stepped back to the floor and shook his head. "What the hell? It just doesn't make sense, I mean the guy was on top of the world. Always the life of the party."

"Was he in any financial trouble?" Archie asked.

"Not that I've heard."

"Scandal coming down the pike?"

"I'm not that hooked in to the gossip."

"I thought this was a small town? Maybe Daugherty knows. He was here for dinner, too." Archie said.

"I didn't see him when I came in." The sheriff responded. "Can you tell me more about the dinner party?"

"You know what, this is all quite overwhelming for me. Do you mind if we do this later? I just met all these people; I feel like an intruder on their moment. If it's okay with you, I really just want to go home."

"I understand and appreciate the stress you must be under. Maybe you want to go to the hospital as well? Get treated for shock?"

Archie searched the face for ulterior motive, but found nothing but concern. "Thank you, sheriff. It's not my first rodeo, though. I think I'll just go home."

"I understand. Thanks for the info. I'm going to linger here for a little while, help the family if they need it."

They walked out of the library.

"Just what are you doing in my crime scene?"

A man walked towards them in the dark living room. He seemed to be a different brand of law officer - dark blue uniform, leather coat, gun on his right hip and a silver nameplate illegible in the poor light.

Hidalgo spoke from behind Archie. "Dr. Wendt, this is Horace Lynne, Chief of Police of Harding. Chief, Dr. Wendt."

"That's right, sheriff, and last time I checked, I have jurisdiction over this type of situation." He pronounced it sichayshun. Lynne had the rugged look of a man in his fifties who spent a lifetime with a Marlboro planted between his lips.

"I'm not here in an official capacity. Just as a friend to the family."

"And who is this you're talking to?"

Lynne addressed the question to Hidalgo, but looked at Archie.

"I'm Dr. Wendt, Chief Lynne. Family friend, too."

"You the one that cut down the deceased?"

"Yes."

Lynne took out a pad and a pencil. He looked up at Hidalgo, a taller man by a half a foot. A silent message passed between the two; the sheriff tipped his hat to Archie and walked away.

"Mr. Wendt, I'm going to need you to give me a blow-by-blow description of everything you have seen and done since you arrived here this evening."

Archie noted the stripping of his degree and the officiousness of the request. His energy waning he sat. "Okay if we sit as I tell you?"

The Chief shook his head. "No. It isn't. Rise and begin."

Archie had no fight in him and did as he was told, gave as accurate a description as his memory allowed. He got through the recitation by fixating his mind on all the shots he would do after he left this house. Lynne took his phone number and address and advised him to return his call should he need clarification on something.

"Am I missing something, Chief? Did a crime occur tonight?"

"We'll see. If there was, you can bet your smart ass I'll find out."

Archie headed to the front door, paused and looked back. Linda sat on the bottom of the staircase, her face in her hands, her body shaking gently.

Archie debriefed Howard of the night's events. It would be anathema to pound scotch, so Archie opted for rum even if it meant an ice pick through the top of his head come morning.

"No warning signs?"

"None. I mean, looking back on it I can see that his language had the vague feel of goodbye, but I mistook it as his style. As did everybody, I believe."

Howard raised his glass. "Now you got your answer as to why he wanted you around."

"What do you mean?"

"He probably thought of you like a game warden in the safari. For his family. You know, an expert who can guide them through the jungle of post suicide feelings."

"You have a way with words, Howard, but I don't see any good explanation for this clusterfuck. Morgenstern ambushed me; put me in a shitty predicament. Far as I'm concerned just another selfish prick deciding what's best for him and not being around to see the aftershocks." He ran his hand across his jaw. "Just like the fucking rich to dump this on me and think I'll be there to pick up the pieces."

"You have a lot of anger, young man."

"You're goddamned right I do. What kind of shit is that? You invite me to your fucking house and then hang yourself before dessert? I didn't even get a piece of fucking cake." He laughed maniacally.

Howard sat back and waited until Archie regained control over himself.

"I guess I'm still in shock," Archie finally said.

"No shit, Arch. We're accustomed to hearing about these things in the office, not being a part of the drama."

"You ever witness something like this?"

Howard shook his head. "Hey, why don't you lay off the rum, get a good night's rest. Take the next few days off."

"That probably would be best." But Archie knew that he wasn't going to lay off the rum and a good night's rest would once again prove elusive.

John Hidalgo tipped his cap to Lynne in the Morgenstern living room and took his leave. He did it out of habit. In the face of ignorance it's best to smile and engage in passive aggression, Virgil liked to say. He also said he didn't need a two thousand year old Chinese philosopher to tell him let your enemies underestimate you.

"If they're ignorant, John, don't educate them. Use their blockheadedness to your advantage."

And there didn't exist a more ignorant soul than Horace Lynne. Virgil pounded that into the young man's head when he pushed him to run for county sheriff.

After his time in the Marines, John toured the country doing odd jobs, taking joy in being aimless. The service had shown him the broadness of experience to be had; he couldn't just return to small town Ohio. He needed more.

But like many before him who foreswore returning to their roots, a death brought him back. In this case his father. Not his biological one, but the man he knew to be Dad. His own flesh and blood was a KIA in Vietnam. All John knew of him was the little his mother told him. She didn't even have a photo. He suspected his mother harbored shame over their brief coupling before he got shipped overseas.

After his father's funeral John knew he wouldn't leave his newly widowed mother alone. His options for employment limited, his mother reached out to Virgil Morgenstern, a high school classmate.

John arrived at Virgil's house hat in hand, but Marine proud. Virgil opened the door and looked John squarely in the eyes. Unusual for both men given their statures. They shared an instant connection. From then on Virgil took a great interest in John's career, first as a sheriff's deputy, then eventually bankrolling him to position of elected sheriff. Through it all, a steady stream of advice for the younger man.

"Don't ever trust Lynne. He has his own agenda that won't often jibe with your own." Virgil dispensed his words of wisdom with an arm around Hidalgo's shoulder. Virgil guided him through the election and beyond, available to bounce ideas and vent frustrations. The politics between sheriff and police chief always a source of tension while Lynne ran the latter.

A less secure man would have seen Lynne's dismissal as a slight. They were both law enforcement agents in this small town and professional courtesy should be a given. John walked to his Jeep comfortable in the knowledge that the chief of police was a small man who bristled at any challenge to his authority. His hand on the car's doorjamb John looked over the roof at the house where he spent many hours soaking up every moment with Virgil, the man who served as mentor, father figure, sage advice giver.

John drove aimlessly through town lost in his thoughts. He forced himself to focus on his next moves. Because this much he knew; this process stood at the beginning. New insights tumbled into place as he integrated recent conversations with Virgil into this night's shocking event.

One particular memory - sitting, as usual, in Virgil's study.

"I want you to get me background information on someone."

"Who?" John asked.

"A new doctor in town. Archibald Wendt. Heard of him?"

"Yes. Shrink from Boston. Took that space above the barbershop, used to belong to the accountant who got in trouble with the IRS."

"Find me anything you can."

Virgil often asked John to do discrete inquiries into people's backgrounds, usually for business purposes, sometimes personal. He never questioned the older man's motives, however, this request felt different. He pointed that out at the time.

"Well, John, you know I'm always looking for talent in unusual places." He flashed the smile he used so effectively to sway others to his position.

Now that very same psychiatrist cuts down a suicided Virgil. John pulled his cruiser into the parking spot in front of his station house and understood, as certain as if Virgil had told him outright, that this had all been arranged. He placed a hand on his left chest and felt the bulge of an envelope Virgil recently entrusted to him. A chill ran down his spine as he realized it was time to complete whatever machinations Virgil set in motion with his sudden and violent departure.

CHAPTER

16

rchie returned home after dark, drunk, but not blindingly so.
Lil's light showed under her closed door. He tiptoed passed it
with his shoes in his hand. Like a teenager again, coming home
after curfew.

He slept fitfully with nightmares of a different sort. He's in college and
finals have arrived. The last exam is today and it's for a class he could have
sworn he had withdrawn from. Archie raced down the hallway to the class
to tell the instructor that it was a mistake. When the door opened it was
Lil wearing a teddy, garters, and carrying a riding crop. Wendt woke up
relieved and vowed not to explore his unconscious's new sexual proclivity.
He had enough on his plate already.

A couple of days passed and the town buzzed with news of the suicide.
By the third day the retelling had about six hundred people storming in
on the hanging body, though some of the rumor came close to the truth;
someone on the inside had loose lips.

Archie took Howard's advice on taking some time off. He phoned his
patients and cancelled the whole week. Mentioned a nephew's wedding in
Florida. Quite unnecessary given that everyone knew it was Wendt who
cut Morgenstern down.

He went to his office daily to get some quiet, away from the furtive
glances of the townsfolk. His answering machine light blinked. He ignored
it as long as his obsessive mind allowed, then pressed the button.

"Ahem, uh, Dr. Wendt, this is David Daugherty, Mr. Morgenstern's
personal attorney. We met on the night…ahem, earlier this week before
the unfortunate happening. Anyway, uh…I was hoping you would come
to the funeral and, uh…be a support for the family. Given your unique
position as both, uh… a professional and a witness to Virgil's, uh…last

days…Well, it's tomorrow and I think it would mean a lot to the family if you came. You don't have to RSVP or anything, just —"

Daugherty exceeded the machine's time limit. That usually only happened to Wendt's most neurotic patients.

Virgil requested a graveside service on a picturesque hill just outside of town. The height offered a view of the twisting river and the flood wall. A beautiful Saturday morning, crisp, in the 50's. Clear blue sky without a cloud to be seen. Wendt, in his one black suit, walked up the hill. It was the only formal wear he brought with him from Boston. He figured it would cover all bases: weddings, funerals, and everything in between.

His simple wooden coffin sat next to an already prepared hole. A tent covered several rows of chairs already filled. Standing room only. Archie spotted Rose and her mother in the front. Behind them he recognized Linda, David Daugherty and his wife. He scanned the remaining rows and found Luke skulking in the back, biting his nails. Jed stood to his right, dressed like he planned on going to see a grunge band in someone's basement. Archie hung out on the side, enjoying the warmth of the sun.

They kept the service brief. From a lectern erected at the front of the chairs several people spoke including Harding's Mayor who waxed about Morgenstern, the giant of industry who put the town on his back and took it for a ride. He must have meant it; Virgil couldn't give him any more donations. A pastor talked briefly about how much Morgenstern meant to various charities around town. Finally, Rose stood up. She looked remarkably composed, considering all she'd endured. She gripped the edges of the lectern tightly.

"I appreciate all you being here. I just want to say a few words." She paused, put a fist to her mouth. "Daddy would have asked it be kept brief, wanting all of us to get back to work. (A muted chuckle from all.) I would be remiss if I didn't speak about the private man that few knew." She caught her breath and turned away for a few seconds. Beginning to sob, she continued. "This is such a beautiful spot. Daddy loved the view from this hill. He was a man who never forgot the little things. He became a rich man, but he earned his money through hard work and no matter how much money he made, he never sought much for himself. Always wanted the best for those he loved. God, I will miss him more than anything. He was my rock, my mentor. I will miss him so much…"

Archie looked around, waiting for someone from the family to rise, comfort her, envelope her. Nothing. Rose backed away from the podium, turned towards the coffin. The pastor gave a nod to some men in overalls. The men lowered the coffin; Rose quietly sobbed.

Archie looked over at Katherine. Hair perfectly in place. A stoic look on her face as the backhoe whirred into life after they lowered her husband's casket. Everyone sat mesmerized by the machine - or paralyzed by the moment. The only sounds came from the joint man and machine work of entombing Virgil for eternity. Archie walked over to Rose and gently put his arm around her. She didn't notice him walk up and startled slightly, but looked grateful for the support.

The group amassed under the tent took this as a sign things were over and trekked back down the hill. Only family and the attorney remained. Rose didn't move, so Wendt followed suit. He watched Luke and Jed make their way to the front row.

"Well, he's in the ground. I guess we move on now."

"What kind of statement is that, huh, Luke?" Rose looked closely at his face. "Your eyes are bloodshot. I'm sure you haven't been crying, so you came to your father's funeral stoned? Is that your show of respect?"

"Give me a break, will ya? I wouldn't have been able to make it otherwise."

"You chickenshit."

"That's enough, Rose." Katherine stood.

Jed nudged Luke, cupped his hand over Luke's ear and whispered something. Luke pushed the hand away as if shooing a fly and got closer to his mother. He said in a low voice, "Mom, I was wondering when I could get an advance on the inheritance."

Rose threw off Archie's arm. "You filthy piece of shit. That's all Dad ever was to you, an ATM."

"Are you kidding? He never gave me anything, preferring the perfect Rose over me. But now I'm going to get the back pay I am owed."

It didn't seem possible, but Rose turned a further shade of crimson. Before she could start yelling her mother intervened. "Could we please just have the funeral without any sibling rivalry. Rose, go cool off. Luke, the reading of the will is on Monday. Until then, stop hounding me."

Archie watched these proceedings with a dispassionate eye. He didn't have enough emotion invested in Morgenstern to mourn him, though he remained shaken by the suicide. The whole thing felt surreal. To be mired in this family dynamic, seeing it so close was a new experience. Patients reported these types of interactions frequently when seated in the comfort and safety of his office. Out here he felt like a journalist cataloguing war, just as subject to the possibility of injury as the combatants.

Lost in his own thoughts he failed to register that he stood alone. The only men left wore work uniforms and rounded off the mound with hand held spades. They ignored him while he paid his final respects. He thought of the lifetime efforts of Virgil Morgenstern. It must have broken his heart to see a wife so cynical and a son so worthless. It made sense that he put all his love and attention into Rose.

At the time those graveside thoughts seemed so profound to Archie. As if he'd really understood the situation and sized it up appropriately. He would later reflect on those initial musings and marvel at the superficiality of his grasp of events. In this instance, as in most cases, first blush analyses proved erroneous in explaining the deeper truths later to be revealed.

CHAPTER

17

After the funeral Archie bypassed home and went straight to the bar. He sat down on a stool and smacked a fifty down.

"This is one of those times, Mike, where a single glass just won't do. What will a Grant get me?"

Mike put the soiled towel over his shoulder and stood with both hands on the bar eyeing the fifty dollar bill. "Doc, for a fifty I'll give you a bottle of most anything we got."

"Give me something worth thirty and keep the change."

"We'll make it thirty-five seeing as how you were the one that found Virgil and all."

"Seems that should be worth more than just five dollars."

"Indeed it should." Mike pulled a bottle of Johnny Walker Black, showed the unbroken seal to Wendt who nodded his head. Mike opened it, placed it and two highball glasses next to Archie who poured out two shots. Archie tilted the glass towards the bar's mirror in salute and prepared to take a healthy swig.

"Hold on, Doc." Mike raised his glass and said in a loud voice, "To Virgil Morgenstern, a hell of a guy."

Others in the bar stopped what they were doing and raised a glass in unison.

"You knew him?" Archie laughed. "Dumb question, right? Small town and all."

"Right, Doc. Small town."

Archie drank and a spring that'd been welling up since the funeral came to the surface. He wiped his mouth, scrubbed his jaw, and launched into a tirade. "Who, Mike, tell me, who invites a man to his house only to hang himself after dinner? Is that not the most fucked up thing you can think of? I was with his beloved daughter who he must have known would be the one to come looking for him. It wouldn't be his frigid wife or retarded son. No, it would be the one person on earth who would be most grievously injured by the discovery." He took another swig, the glass already half empty. "I'm no longer cut out for this type of shock." Archie said just above a whisper.

"Hang in there, Doc."

Archie looked up, a puzzled look on his face. Mike got the reference and blushed. "You know what I mean, don't *hang* anywhere, just keep on keeping on."

Eager to change the subject Mike picked up dirty glasses and dunked them for a brief cleansing before putting them on a rack. "Everyone in town is familiar with the ice queen, Katherine Morgenstern. You know, there was scuttlebutt about her knocking boots with some other fellow."

"Anybody I would know?"

"Word was it was the personal attorney of Morgenstern."

"No shit." Archie shook his head. "I met that guy. Odd bird."

"You never know about rumors of that sort in a small town. Could be someone started that just to make the wife look bad. Or the lawyer. Never was a lawyer I knew of didn't have his share of enemies, you know."

"That's very perceptive of you, Mike.

"Even a blind squirrel finds a nut every once in a while, right Doc." He winked at Archie.

"I just don't like being involved in this. It was because of this kind of toxic shit that I left Boston."

The bars phone rang; Mike walked to the end of the bar and answered and looked over at Archie.

"It's for you." He walked the receiver over. "Why don't you get your own goddamned cellphone, huh? Join the 21st century."

"Where would the fun of that be? Anyway, I relish making you work for me."

Archie took the receiver. "Yeah?"

"Dr. Wendt?"

"That's right."

"Uh, Dr. Wendt, this is, uh, David Daugherty, Mr. Morgenstern's personal attorney. We met at his house."

Wendt rolled his eyes. "I remember who you are."

"Great, anyway, I appreciate that you were at the funeral today.

Appreciated even more, uh… your handling of, uh…Rose's situation. On that front, I am requesting you be there on Monday morning for the reading of the will. In the spirit of support that you showed so valiantly today…It will take place at ten in the morning at the offices of Seidlin and Schmidt on Main. It would be great if you could——"

Archie held the receiver at arm's lenght and blurted out, "I'll be there," and held the receiver up for Mike and put his head on the bar. Daugherty's disembodied voice only ceased when the phone was back on the cradle.

After draining the glass Archie decided to go home and get some sleep. He left the half full bottle of Black Jack and the fifty on the bar.

Six chairs were assembled in a circle. Damian walked in wearing a gray sweat suit with Georgetown printed across the front.

"I hope I'm not late, I just came from a run," the priest said.

Janine walked in, a demur smile on her face.

Garrett loped in next. "Hey, Doc. How the hell are you?" He had on a new hat. It was red and originally read "Buckeyes," but Garrett had undone some of the stitching to the 'B' and removed the first 'e' so now it read "Fuck yes."

"That's real clever, Garrett," Archie commented.

"Yeah, don't you think? It's glorious. Much better than the "Hard Crew." Got it from a friend who went to Ohio State. Your home state, I figured I'd throw you a bone."

"I'm from Massachusetts."

"Whatever."

"Garrett, why so many chairs?"

"Oh, Doc, I've got a nice surprise for you. While we waited for you to show up I ran into someone you know. Hey Jimmy, c'mon in."

A disheveled kid walked in. Early twenties, gangly and not well groomed. Archie sucked wind. Jimmy Donnelly was the first patient of Wendt's who suicided. The moment Archie had seen him professionally he became worried about what was going to happen to this kid. He came from a single mother and bad circumstances. Father was a drug addict and out of the picture. Mother overwhelmed and mentally ill herself was in no shape to help Jimmy out. And this boy needed boatloads of help. Psychotic and near mute, the only thing anyone could discern was Jimmy's fondness for the afterlife. He spoke about it incessantly and scared the shit out of anyone who cared about him. He had a delusional quality to his beliefs about this world and what waited for him in the next. Coupled with his depression, a truly volatile mix. Sure enough, three months after discharge from the hospital, Wendt received the word. He didn't sleep for a couple of days after that one.

"You know, Garrett, that's a low blow. There's nothing I could have done for this kid. No offense, Jimmy."

Jimmy didn't take offense. He sat down without a word.

"Even with Jimmy that's still only five people." Archie observed.

Garrett turned the chair around and sat a la Vinnie Barbarino, arms crossed over the top. "Who wants to begin?"

"I don't know why I don't wake myself up and get rid of all of you."

"Archie, I'd like to hear you tell us what it was like to lose these people," Damian said. He was leaning forward, elbows on his knees, rubbing his hands together. It was odd for Archie to face this posture. It was a therapist's posture, a pose he struck with regularity.

"Padre - you don't mind if I call you that, do you? I always was a fan of M*A*S*H. Anyway, Padre, I'm not sure if you're here because there's a metaphorical devil in me or a literal one. But I don't need it. I can use my own skills to reflect bullshit platitudes back to myself."

"Can you now?" Garret said as he stood and paced the room. "Booze and sarcasm. That hardly seems an enlightened treatment plan. Father Damian has offered his psychiatric services, free of charge. You might show some appreciation."

"I'll appreciate it when all you ghouls return to where you came from and leave me the fuck alone."

"Tsk, tsk, tsk. Losing our cool, aren't we? You're going to have to keep your head. By the looks of it you're knee deep in another developing shitstorm, huh?"

Wendt rubbed his jaw. "I didn't see that one coming. That's the first time I was associated with a suicide where depression didn't look to play a major part."

"Maybe he did a good job of hiding it," Damian said.

"Good point - I didn't know him that well. But shit, if Morgenstern was playacting, he did an Oscar worthy job."

"You look like hell, Dr. Wendt." Janine always expressed concern for him. Archie tried repeatedly to get her to see that in therapy she was the patient, not him. But she remained a kind soul; death didn't change that. "Why don't you take a vacation and get away from here?"

Archie smiled at her. "You always tried to take care of me." His smile turned down as his furrows creased. "I knew you were on the edge. Foolish me, I believed that somehow I could anchor you to this world. But you had other designs, didn't you?"

Damian said, "Each person is responsible for themselves."

"Father, why don't you take a break and let her speak for herself. She's a big girl. If I have to be here, at the very least I should be allowed candor."

"You come off sounding like a bully, Doc."

"Shut the fuck up Garrett and let Janine speak for herself."

Before Garrett could stand and react, Janine calmed him with a hand on his arm. "Archie is right." She looked at Wendt. "I know you suffered my suicide. I know it, Arch, like I know my own heartache. You should know that I felt your concern deeply and it helped, it really did, but it wasn't enough. Not that *you* weren't enough, I just couldn't hack it. Not your fault."

He grew agitated, stood and paced the room, rubbing his jaw like he expected a genie to pop out of his mouth and start granting wishes.

"Then what the fuck am I in this for? Huh? If my role is simply to be a witness to a patient going down the tubes, then what is the fucking point?"

"There isn't always a discernible point. As a psychiatrist you know that sometimes life just sucks." Damian said. "Sometimes a child is born with cancer that lays dormant until they're seven and then destroys a family. Sometimes a heart gives out in a father of three who spent his weekends volunteering in soup kitchens. It's always been that way. You know that."

Archie stalked around the room, stopped in front of the bookcase. In a flash he grabbed a book and threw it at the desk lamp, sending both crashing to the floor. That satisfied his need to be violent. He spoke: "That knowledge doesn't make it any less devastating. It leaves me feeling helpless - an entirely empty and shitty feeling." He sat hard and sighed deeply a couple of times, the cathartic tantrum receding. "Thank you all for your genuine concern. Even you, Garrett. But I'll be okay." A knock on the door interrupted them. "I think our time is up now." The knocking became louder and more insistent.

"Dr. Wendt, it's a quarter past ten. David Daugherty called and is wondering where you are."

Dr. Wendt. Not a good sign.

He cleared his throat. "Uh, thanks. Tell them I'm on my way."

Lil's voice trailed off as she walked away, "Tell them your own goddamned self."

That was a popular refrain of late, Archie mused; he dressed quickly.

CHAPTER

18

The law offices of Seidlin and Schmidt occupied the upper level of the ubiquitous two story building. Archie arrived at 10:35. He slipped the mini electric shaver into his blazer pocket as he walked through the frosted glass door etched with various ESQs.

"In here, Doctor," a voice called out from a back office.

A balding man in a brown suit sat at a desk, his back to a picture window that looked out onto the street. Chairs in front of the desk. Everyone turned as he walked in. Rose, Luke, Mrs. Morgenstern, and Linda. One more seat available. Archie pulled it next to Rose.

"We can begin," the lawyer said.

"Where's Daugherty?" Archie whispered to Rose.

The man in the brown suit answered. "Mr. Daugherty was Mr. Morgenstern's personal attorney. I handle his estate. My name is Len Seidlin, Dr. Wendt."

"I'm glad that piece of shit isn't here." Rose said.

"Rose, a little decorum if you please."

"Yes, Mother."

"So, I will begin." Seidlin said. "As you know we are gathered to hear the last will and testament of Virgil Morgenstern." He cleared his throat. For effect, for phlegm? Archie couldn't be sure.

"I, Virgil Morgenstern, and so on and so forth…To my son Luke, I leave my stereo, which he always admired, my 1972 Corvette, and a stipend of five hundred dollars per week as of today for the rest of his life." Luke slammed his fist on the chair's arm. Seidlin held up his hand and continued to read. "Unless my son begins to earn his own keep. In that event I will triple whatever his weekly pay is in perpetuity."

Archie thought that extremely generous, but clearly Luke didn't agree. His mother stroked his arm and shooshed his flow of invective.

"To Linda, I leave a retirement stipend of four thousand dollars monthly to begin on the day she ceases her work at the Morgenstern household."

"To my daughter Rose, I leave the contents of my library in the hopes that she does a better job finishing the classics than I did, my stamp collection, and all of my shares in Morgenstern Holdings, Inc." Rose buried her head in her hands, sobbed silently.

"To my wife, Katherine, I leave the house, which she did such a glorious job decorating. I ask only that she allow Linda to keep working until she is ready to retire." Katherine's expression did not change an iota. Everyone shifted in their seats and got ready to leave.

"That's not quite all," Seidlin said. "To Dr. Wendt…" They all turned to Archie, looks of puzzlement and anger on their faces. "To Dr. Wendt I leave the sum of five million dollars in the hopes that he does the right thing with the money."

The atmosphere in the room instantly changed; a torrent of anger blew Wendt's way like the blast overpressure from an exploded IED. Luke broke the silence. "What the fuck! This is bullshit, man, this is fucking bullshit!"

"Control yourself, Luke, for goodness sake. Mr. Seidlin, this is obviously a last minute change to my husband's will, correct?"

"Yes, Mrs. Morgenstern. Completed the morning he —well, the morning of the unfortunate event."

Luke continued his tirade. Katherine took hold of his wrist and stood. "We'll just see about that last minute bequest." Her eyes bore down on Archie like she sought to cut him in half. "I'm not sure what you did to my husband, Doctor, but don't start spending in anticipation of your windfall; you won't be seeing a penny of Lowry money. You can bank on that." She walked to the door followed by Luke, but stopped in the doorway, turned, and said, "By the way, Linda, you're fired," and left.

Linda sobbed. "God bless that Mr. Morgenstern. He always told me he would take care of me. I was never sure. But…great man. Man of his word." She stood.

Rose stood and gave her a hug. "Don't mind Mother. Once she calms down I'm sure she'll rethink letting you go."

"That's okay, Rosie. It's time for me to retire, anyway. Time to travel and live life. If I learned anything from your father it's to grab life when you have the opportunity."

"I can't stand the thought of you leaving. I just lost my father, now I have to lose you, too?"

Linda gave Rose another hug. "You're not losing me, Rose darling. I'll still be around and will always be in your corner." She looked down at Archie and smiled. "Take care, Dr. Wendt." She walked out of the room.

Archie remained glued to his chair. This whole Morgenstern affair had been surreal from the start. Now it entered the realm of ridiculous. Rose sat silently with him.

It was Seidlin who broke the spell with a throat clear and: "I'm going to need my office."

Rose led Wendt out and across the street to a diner.

They sat in a booth drinking coffee.

"I imagine you're still bound by doctor patient privilege."

Wendt looked up from his mug. "He wasn't a patient. Confidentiality with friends depends on the discretion of the confidante. Besides, I am not in possession of any special information that will make any sense of this."

"So, you have no idea why he left you so much money?"

"No." he said.

"Archie I need you to look at me. No idea?"

He locked eyes. "No. I just met the guy. I mean, your father. Sorry." He noticed how piercing her eyes were. Up close he saw they were brighter green than her father's had been. Their angle with her face gave her a slightly feline look and he realized that he found her quite attractive.

"I'm really confused." She brought him from his revery and he refocused.

"You and me both. I got a lot of questions if you're up to it." He said.

"If I know the answer," Rose said.

"Okay. I get your father's attempt to motivate your brother, but why shut your mother out of the money?"

"Out of the money? She is the money."

"What do you mean?"

"My mother's grandfather was the one who started the family business. Her father took over and when *he* died my mother inherited a lot of money and shares in the business. Anything my father has is due to his hard work and investments, shares given to him over the years."

"That explains his leaving his shares to you. Come to think of it, I did know that. Howard Rogoff told me, I just forgot. You know Dr. Rogoff?"

She smiled. "Yes. Lovely man."

Archie sipped his steaming coffee. "So how much are your shares?"

"It amounts to just less than fifty percent. My mother remains the majority holder, but she has little interest in running the day to day affairs."

"How many employees you guys got?"

"All told? About three hundred in the mills, a couple hundred more in the land holdings company. It's a pretty big enterprise, especially for this town."

Archie leaned back. "Seems like your mother is pretty vindictive. What was her beef against Linda?"

"Well, you're the psychiatrist so you may have more insight into that, but I can tell you it's the same beef she has with me and anyone else she thinks is more important to my father. Or was, I guess."

"Linda was more important?" He asked.

"Not in reality. My mother resented anyone who benefitted from my father's attention. She might have appeared cold to you, but I can assure you she loved my father fiercely. More than he loved her, I believe. That led to a lot of resentment towards anyone who my father favored. His kindness to Linda rankled mother." She smiled sadly. "I suppose if I'm being really honest his love for me bothered her, too."

"This is a bit of a delicate question. Do you think he had something on the side with Linda?"

She laughed. "God, no. There was nothing inappropriate with how he behaved towards Linda; he treated her like family. Besides, that wouldn't have been his style. No, he just treated all his employees with a tremendous amount of respect."

"And your mother obviously doesn't."

"Well, you have to remember, my mother grew up with money and privilege. She was accustomed to people treating her with deference. My father, on the other hand, grew up modestly. He drove himself. Mother has a driver. He never got used to the trappings of wealth. My father always tipped the help generously and my mother hated that. She thought

81

the hired help would take advantage of them if they were too nice." Rose paused, then continued. "And I suspect my mother resented everyone liking father more. But that's the way it was. He was the life of the party, you know? The kind of guy who lit up a room when he walked in. Virgil Morgenstern dressed impeccably, always smelled nice, and had a ready joke at hand. And good jokes, you know, topical and witty." She started to cry.

Archie reached across and held her hand. "I'm so caught up in my own shit I forget that you just buried your father."

Rose composed herself. "That was a hell of show we put on at his graveside, wasn't it? But my brother is a complete asshole."

"Were father and son always at odds?"

"Yes. Some things are so cliche. Son never able to live up to his father's expectations. You might be tempted to chalk that up to unrealistic expectations from an unreasonable father, but it wouldn't be accurate. Luke has always been a fuck up. Took after my mother's side of the family. The Lowry's have a host of freeloaders and loafers throughout the family tree. Born into wealth, things handed to them, not being motivated to achieve. Daddy was the opposite. He came up hungry, worked like a dog when he started out in the business. Some people will say that he married Mother just to increase his value to my grandfather. That's short sighted. My father brought an edge to the company, a willingness to take risks. The Lowry's had grown complacent, happy to rest on what they had rather than build more. My father was bold and did a lot for the business - the real estate holdings, for instance. They had so much money they didn't know what to do with it so my father put them in properties and development. You can see how that worked out."

"Your mother takes care of Luke."

"Her husband showed disdain for their son — maybe disdain is a bit harsh, but at least disappointment, so Katherine Lowry came to the rescue and took up the mantel. She saw bits of her brothers and cousins in his weaknesses and took pity on him. But her patience with him is limited. Especially when he hangs around Jed."

"You speak of your mother's family as if they weren't a part of your family, too."

"Maybe I do." Rose reflected. "I guess I've always identified with my father and his spirit more than my mother's."

Archie switched gears. "Who is Jed? I saw him that first dinner when your father effectively kicked him out of the house."

"Who is Jed? Good question. He's many things. It would be accurate to say he's a childhood friend of Luke. Also that he's a low life drug dealer. A hanger on. A shitty influence. An anchor around my brother's neck. He's all of those things and for that reason he is not welcome in our home."

They sat silently taking turns drinking from their mugs.

"My father didn't tell you any of these things?"

Archie shook his head. "He asked me a lot about myself, then he hinted at wanting someone to talk to, you know a confidante who wouldn't be a 'yes' man. That first dinner we shared, last Friday, he asked me to give him an appraisal of his family. You and your brother, specifically."

"A professional opinion based on observations?"

"Well, he didn't specify how in depth it was to be. That was something I thought would be a moving target. Moot now, wouldn't you say?" Archie sat back, stretched his arms over his head. "I have no idea what 'five million to Dr. Wendt in the hopes he does the right thing' means? By the way, why did you call Daugherty a piece of shit?"

"Archie, my mother is dogged. If she is threatening to keep you tied up in litigation, you can bet she will. And it's a long and involved story about David Daugherty."

"I don't care about litigation; I don't want the fucking money. Shit, if it was money I was after I wouldn't be here in Harding, you can bet on that."

"Just what are you doing here in Harding, anyway?"

"Now *that's* a long and involved story. I have neither the energy nor the desire to share that just yet. But I'll tell you when you tell me why you think Daugherty is a piece of shit." He signaled the waitress for the check. "Let me walk you home."

"I'm going to go back to the office. It helps me keep my mind off things. Besides, it's where the fondest memories of my father reside. Thanks for the coffee."

"Thank you. I don't think I could have found my feet without you after that bombshell."

Rose smiled and stood up. She turned to leave, but stopped and faced him, tears again welling up in her eyes. "Things feel like they're out of control, you know." He moved out of the booth, embraced her. She wept silently in his arms.

"I know that feeling. Things will calm down, you'll regain some normalcy." He said it without much conviction, struggling himself, hoping in the inevitability of time to smooth things over.

She spoke into his neck. "I'm not sure how I'm supposed to feel about you, but I would like to see you again." Rose pulled back and looked at him. "I mean, not *see you* see you, if you know what I'm saying. I just need some help right now."

"I understand. I'll be around and try to help as much as I can."

They left the diner and went their separate ways.

CHAPTER
19

Archie worked at his desk catching up on correspondence. Reaching out to patients to reschedule appointments, answering questions. Seidlin, the probate attorney for Morgenstern, called and advised him to get his own attorney to assist in the five million dollar bequest. Archie saw that as low priority; he didn't care for the money. He wasn't being modest or disingenuous. Over his lifetime he came to appreciate the need to earn what you get. Lottery winners and other inheritors of big wealth never seemed happy to him. Those who set goals and achieved them usually had a handle on what happiness could consistently be mined from this fucked up thing called life.

But the situation piqued his curiosity. It harbored a farcical quality. An Agatha Christie novel and he was the protagonist. Only instead of murder, you had a suicide.

He reflected on how arc of this situation resembled meeting a patient for the first time. People always put their best face forward initially. Told you what they thought you wanted to hear. Then, over time, their true colors shined through. Because people are who they are. Not always for the worse. Sometimes the facade hides a more sensitive and likable personality.

This must be how any investigator feels, he thought. At first all you get is the bullshit; sift through that wisely and a lot of good information comes through. As if on cue, someone knocked on his door. He opened it a crack and then all the way to allow Katherine Morgenstern to enter.

"I hope I'm not disturbing you, Doctor."

"Not at all, Mrs. Morgenstern, please have a seat."

She wore a smart pants suit, minimal make up and jewelry, but the effect was well done. As if she went to tremendous lengths to look like she didn't go to tremendous lengths.

"I wanted to be able to speak to you one on one. Hopefully dispel some misconceptions about my family, and see if we can't resolve the issue of the will without further…complication."

Archie stayed quiet.

"You certainly got an inside glimpse of our family. I have to say I wasn't particularly pleased when my husband brought you home. But I allowed myself the hope that your presence meant that Virgil was going to address his alcohol issues. That was dashed when you came bearing a bottle of liquor."

It impressed Wendt that this woman could lace almost every sentence with both an insult and a criticism.

"Your husband wasn't seeing me for therapy. We didn't share a professional relationship. And I wasn't aware that he had an alcohol problem."

"You didn't hear the all the rumors around town? That my husband was a fall down drunk? Literally. Having to be picked up off the ground by strangers. And you not knowing isn't an excuse. For a layman, perhaps, but you're a trained doctor and you should have recognized that he was in distress."

Ouch. This lady has a sixth sense for the jugular.

"Be that as it may I came here to get a sense of what kind of man you are," She continued. "You had time alone with my husband. Time that could have been spent getting a feel for the man and using that understanding to have an influence on him. What kind of influence was it, I wonder? Maybe you took the opportunity to offer him insights that might facilitate his growth." She cocked her head to the side, put on a sneer. "Or maybe you're the Svengali type; someone who would think nothing of taking advantage of the vulnerable. You've only been in town for a few months. Quite a coincidence that you should befriend the wealthiest man in town, no?"

"Just what are you unsubtly insinuating?" Wendt said.

"I'm not insinuating. I'm asking you point blank what your intentions were with my husband."

"There were no intentions. He approached me. And I don't appreciate your accusation that I pulled some sort of mind trick to 'swindle' your husband out of money. This hardly seems like the kind of language one uses to diffuse a situation." Archie could feel his face getting hot. "Mrs.

Morgenstern, I have no idea why your husband left me that money. At no time did I ask for or expect anything. Any intimation that I somehow conspired to make this happen is ludicrous. I can only assure you in so many ways that I have no designs on your family's money."

"So you will renounce the bequest and give it back to the estate?"

Silence. He modeled impassivity; she glared.

"Will you give the money back to the estate or not?" Mrs. Morgenstern looked like a woman who couldn't recall the last time she hadn't gotten her way.

"I don't know exactly what I'm going to do with the money, if anything. Right now, I'm just trying to get my bearings. This has been quite overwhelming for me."

"Then alleviate one issue. Sign over the money to the family trust and let us grieve for our loss unimpeded by this unfortunate obstruction."

"I am not an unfortunate obstruction, ma'am. This whole affair has been unsettling for me, as well. A man who I just met suicided for no apparent reason and wanted me to be a part of the aftermath. I don't have to remind you that I had to cut him down from the chandelier. It galls me that I should have to put it in such stark terms, but you leave me little choice. Until I have a better sense of things, I won't be making any rash decisions about the money or anything else."

"If that's the case, Dr. Wendt, there is little reason for me to continue this conversation. You will be hearing from my attorney, you can bet on that."

"Which one would that be? Brown suit baldy? Comb over stammering D-D-D-Daugherty? Or is there another attorney you have on retainer?"

"You would be wise to watch your tone and language. This is a small town; I can be a real bitch when properly motivated. Good day, Dr. Wendt."

"Good day, Mrs. Morgenstern." He closed the door behind her, grateful nobody witnessed his tremulous hands. He walked over to his desk, sat and yanked on the bottom drawer. An unopened Glenfiddich rolled to the front. Archie twisted the top and drank straight from the bottle, something a scotch man doesn't do on principle, but he couldn't wait for a glass. That spoke volumes.

The single malt calmed him as it went down his throat. He reflected that the widow hadn't shown any of the emotion he felt. Cool as a cucumber that Katherine Morgenstern. Her husband just offed himself and she exhibited no ill effects. What the fuck was wrong with this woman? He tipped the bottle back up with one hand, etiquette be damned.

"She called me a hack. A Svengali, whatever the fuck that is." He already had two more scotches in him, but now from good baccarat crystal.

"Svengali was a character from a French novel." Rogoff said over the phone. "A Jew. He used hypnosis to control a singer. It became a model for the conniving Jew's desire to control the world and added fuel to the fire of anti-Semitism. It's quite an offensive reference."

"I'm not Jewish."

"Then I'm offended for you."

Archie rubbed his jaw. "This situation is spiraling quickly out of control. I feel like I'm in a Hitchcock wrong man piece. And it's insane because a week ago I didn't have anything to do with the guy. He clearly had all this planned when he 'accidentally' bumped into me." Howard stayed silent on the other end while Archie waited for a thought to coalesce. "You know, I didn't sense any vindictiveness in him. I'm not someone who's oblivious to passive aggression; I smell it when it's there and, man, I don't think this represented an attempt to get back at me personally. Virgil didn't do this to me out of malice intent; there has to be something more he wanted."

"What you say makes sense." Howard responded. "I wish I could offer you more insight into Virgil's character, but I didn't know the man that well. His attorney, on the other hand." He trailed off, giving a coy vibe.

"What are you saying, Howard? I don't have the energy for guessing games."

Silence.

"Did you treat Mr. Daugherty and now feel obligated to maintain confidentiality?"

More silence.

"Why the charades, Howard? What the fuck. If you're going to tell me be a man and fucking out with it. If not, piss off. I don't need the games."

"Oh, alright. I treated him. This is the mother of all 'you gotta keep this under your hat.' Daugherty had a thing for Mrs. Morgenstern. And

I'm only telling you to help protect you from a dangerous situation. That and I no longer practice, so what are they going to do, huh? Take away my bathrobe and slippers?"

"Holy shit. That mousey guy was sticking it to the hizzoner's wife? That's more ballsy than I gave him credit for. And I don't wear a hat. Did Virgil know?"

"I didn't say they were shtupping, only that he nursed an unrequited love for her. But Virgil likely knew and the fact that it didn't make him jealous only enraged the wife more." Howard said.

"That explains the snide remarks Rose made about Daugherty. Look Howard, I'm not going to tell this to anyone, you know that. Your robe and slippers are safe. Old and disgusting, but safe."

"Thanks. On behalf of myself and my belongings."

"You sure Morgenstern wasn't unfaithful?"

"Not ironclad, but yeah. It didn't seem to be his style."

"Gambling, maybe? In to loan sharks, banks? Coming up on a very embarrassing stripping of his dignity in some way?" Archie reached.

"I don't think so, but I can't be sure. There has been nothing in the papers; no rumors I'm aware of."

"Rumors. You know, his wife said something curious. That I should have heard the rumors that old Virgil had been such a fall down drunk that strangers had to pick him up off the street. What do you know about that?"

"There might have been grumblings of late. He used to frequent the President's Club, you know, an attempt to remain social, connected to the everyman. Mike said that a couple of times he was in no shape to drive, that someone had to come pick him up."

Archie grew quiet. Rogoff waited patiently, both men accustomed to long silences.

"Who took care of him, internist wise?" Archie finally asked.

"He always went to Ohio State for his care. He gave them a lot of money and talked with pride about his connections there."

"I'd be curious about what issues he had." He swirled his drink. "Think they'd let me see his medical records?"

"I doubt it highly. Though you might be able to curbside someone and appeal to their sense of professional courtesy. It will require you to play the country bumpkin doctor, not the high fallutin' Boston sophisticate. Can you do that?"

Wendt smiled. "I'll certainly give it a try. Thanks for listening to me, Howard. I'll keep you apprised."

"So you're going to go up there?"

"Yes."

"Bring me back a couple pints of Graeter's. Any flavor, but mint chocolate chunk is my favorite."

"You got it." Archie said and hung up the phone.

Archie locked his door, went down the stairs and out into a crisp autumn evening. He loved this time of year, the need for more clothing and such. He felt more secure wearing layers. An extra sweater and hat offered protection. He inhaled deeply.

"I always find the fall air more ripe for memories."

Wendt started. Rose Morgenstern leaned against a lamppost only lacking a cigarette dangling from her mouth at a jaunty angle to complete the picture. She walked towards him. Her mascara had run, but not uniformly. Archie hoped she wasn't there to grieve; he didn't have the energy for that.

"What is it with you Morgensterns and stalking me out here?"

"What does that mean?"

"Nothing." She wore a tweed coat over a short skirt. Looked tired and sad, but good. He contorted his face into what he hoped was a welcoming look. "I know it's not the best of times, but I'm happy to see you."

Rose returned a hint of a smile. "I needed to talk to you, but not having your number I thought this the best way to make contact."

He didn't say anything. Her eyes went to her shoes, then locked on his. "I need to know more of what was going on before my father..." she said softly.

"Let's get a drink. We'll talk."

She nodded and began walking. Without turning towards him she spoke.

"Mother came to see you."

"Yes."

"To tell you to fuck off, I assume."

"She came in as a lamb and left as a lion." He said.

"Wrong analogy. A wolf in sheep's clothing."

"What are you then?"

No answer. Then: "You should take it easy on her. She's not a bad woman, you know. Just jilted. But it's not her I want to talk about. It's him. See, I still can't get my mind around this… this final act of his. It is so out of character. My father could be many things, but a coward was the last thing anyone would call him."

"Why a coward?" Archie asked.

She stopped and turned to face him. "How else would you describe taking your own life? Whatever he was going through we could have tackled it together with me by his side. I thought him the strongest man on earth. How could he abandon me?"

"I don't have an answer for that. I can tell you that he spoke very highly of you. A cliché, but you really were the apple of his eye."

"I know that. He didn't make it a secret that he favored me over Luke, who, by the way, is teetering on the edge of oblivion. He's this close to being cut off by mother."

"Why?"

"You remember we talked about Jed? Well, now that my father is no longer a foil for my brother to play off of mother, she sees Luke for what he is," Rose said sadly.

"Which is?"

"Weak. And vulnerable. Speaking of which, I realize that this represents a bit of a conflict of interests, but I find myself wanting to confide in you and I don't know if that puts you in a bind."

"It's probably the shrink in me that inspires your confidence. And I don't mind. I don't have a professional relationship with any of the Morgensterns." They continued to walk.

"I never understood the reference. Headshrinker, right? Where was I? Oh, yes, my brother and his unhealthy loyalty to Jed Miller. Jed came from a broken home and latched on to my brother. I don't believe it was only because of the money. You wouldn't know it now, but Luke was a generous and kind boy.

"In the beginning, it was harmless. Then as teens, they got into some scrapes, but nothing serious, I mean no major legal issues. But it grew obvious that there was something more sinister to Jed. He was inclined towards not just mischief, but downright vandalism and thuggery. Then the drugs started."

They came to a stop across the street from The President's Club. Rose began to cross; Archie held her back.

"What is it?"

He gripped her hand tightly. A car approached from their right. Rose had a puzzled look on her face. When the car drew closer Archie yelled, "Go!" and pulled her across the street as the driver indicated his displeasure with a long honk.

"What the fuck is the matter with you?" Rose said when they got to the bar's door, out of breath. "Why did you do that?"

"It's a long story, Rose. I'll tell you over a drink."

He held the door for her and they walked in. Mike was in the far corner of the bar shmoozing with a regular. He looked over his shoulder at Archie with a look of pleasant surprise.

"Well, well. The good doctor. And with a guest."

"Evening, Mike, a beer for me, please, and…" he turned to Rose who said, "a glass of red wine, please."

The bartender began pouring the beer from the tap. "'Mike', he says, 'please', he says. Who is this pleasant man masquerading as the psychiatrist I have come to know and love? I wonder."

Archie blushed and led Rose to a table in the back. "I'm a bit of a regular here."

Several at the bar snorted at that remark. Mike walked up and served their drinks. "The good doctor is a regular, Miss Morgenstern, and a purveyor of all kinds of sad tales and sharp insults. Very sharp elbows, indeed, especially when he gets drinking."

"How are you, Mike? Long time."

"Long time, Miss Morgenstern. *I'm* missing your pop. I can't imagine what you're going through. Well, let me know if you need anything." He went back behind the bar.

"My father spent a fair amount of time in bars when I was growing up. My mother would often send me to fetch him. Father would put me on his lap as he held court. He was a great joke teller. I think I told you that already. He could have the whole bar hanging on his every word, waiting on the punchline with so much anticipation…" She stopped talking and leaned back.

"Before we walked in you were telling me about Luke and Jed."

"Yeah, I was. Where was I?"

"Drugs." He said.

"Right." She took a drink of her wine. "For Luke weed was all he ever needed or wanted. A born slacker, he took to marijuana like a fish to water. But Jed was always pushing for the harder stuff."

"How did you know all this?"

"There was a time I was very close to Luke. He confided in me when he felt he couldn't say anything to our parents."

"How much did they know?"

"Well, they knew that Jed was bad for Luke. Several times they turned Jed out, only to have Luke beg them to take him back on the condition he enter treatment programs. Luke felt responsible for Jed because he had no other family. Those periods of sobriety always lasted just long enough for the scrutiny to come off Jed. Then they fell back into the same old patterns." Rose finished off her wine and got up. "Do me a favor, get me another. I'm going to go powder my nose."

As Rose walked by him to the bathroom Archie saw Jed enter the bar. Archie did a sitcom worthy double take. Jed slinked into the bar going to great lengths to avoid being noticed.

"I see you, you dirty bastard. Get the hell out of here!" Mike came down the bar fast, pointing a finger at Jed.

"Alright, alright. Relax. I'm going." Jed held up his hands. "This used to be a free country, you know?"

"Free country? What the fuck are you talking about. Go peddle your shit somewhere else. The only drugs I allow here are the legal ones. Get out now or I'm going to take out your kneecaps." Mike reached under the bar. Jed didn't need to see any more. He hightailed it out of the bar. A couple of the regulars clapped.

Rose came back and sat. "What was the commotion?"

"You'll never believe who walked in here."

She just shook her head not wanting to guess.

"Jed."

Rose shrugged.

"You don't seem that surprised." Archie said. "I found it so coincidental. I mean, one minute we're talking about the guy, and then he walks in."

"Let me clarify." Rose said. "The timing was interesting in just the way you put it. But Jed pops into my life frequently. You see he follows me. Stalks, really. He has a thing for me and that's not just me being conceited. He told me so point blank and despite my protestations he persists. He lacks the ability to take no for an answer."

"I have to say it was kind of freaky. One minute we're talking about him and the next…"

Rose looked around her. "Where did he go?"

"Mike kicked him out."

"That figures. Anyway, I don't want to talk about Jed. I want to talk about my father."

"Okay. I worry that you'll be disappointed with what I have to offer."

"But you were with him towards the end. You're a psychiatrist, for goodness sake. Your thoughts and feelings are more informed than the rest of us, don't you think?"

Archie finished his beer like he was competing in a boat race then held up the glass for a refill. "You want me to speculate and I'm telling you that I don't have any brilliant insights. Sorry to disappoint. If I could dazzle you with acumen, Lord knows I would. I want you to think that I'm smart because I like you."

"I know, I see the way you look at me."

"I didn't think I was that transparent. Or I hoped I wasn't."

"Look, Archie, I find you interesting, too. But this isn't a great time for me, I'm sure you recognize. Anyway, I'm not one to jump in the sack easily and especially not to allay my grief."

"So, no sack tonight? I can live with that if there remains the possibility of future sack."

She laughed.

Mike brought the second beer and Archie cut into it like a man recently come from the Sahara. "Back to your father. Everything happened so fast. I mean I just met him and suddenly I found myself immersed in his life as if we'd known each other a long time. Come to think of it, he must have been trying to pack in as much as he thought was necessary." Archie took another big gulp. "Your father has — sorry had —- a magnetism to him. He drew me in lock, stock and barrel. Now I find myself culling my memories for signs that this was coming, warnings I should have heeded. Though what I could have done I have no idea."

"Any luck with those memories?"

"Not really. And I would have probably let it go were it not for the five million."

Rose bolted upright, an affronted look suddenly painted on her face. "So, the money does entice, huh?"

He smiled. "You got me wrong. Not the promise of the five million, but the reason behind his bequeathing it to me."

Rose's shoulders came down. "So why not renounce it and walk away?"

Archie stopped himself from answering. He wanted to say - 'because you rich folks piss me off. You're used to getting your way whenever and wherever you see fit. Your father, mother, brother, lawyer, even you. All of you think I'm there at your employ and when you see the job as being done, off with you.' But he didn't. Instead he said - "Being the curious sort I need to know. I'm in too deep to just walk away."

"I understand. But refusing the money doesn't necessarily mean that you're walking away, right?"

"What is the hang up with the money? My understanding is probate can take weeks, even months sometimes. It's not like I'm getting that money tomorrow."

"I guess you're right." Rose said.

"If you're interested in getting to the bottom of this, you can help me."

"How?"

"You can tell me if you knew the name of your father's primary doctor."

"Sure. Dr. Len Barber. An internist at Ohio State. My father refused to get his care anywhere else."

They both finished their drinks.

"Listen, Archie, I'm real tired so I'm going to go home. Is that okay?"

"Of course."

"If you come up with something you'll let me know, right?"

"Of course." She got up, reached into her purse. He put a hand on hers. "I'll take care of this."

She didn't argue. "Thanks."

Archie left a twenty on the table and nodded towards Mike as they walked out of the bar. The night air was chillier. Cinching her coat tighter Rose said goodbye and again they headed in opposite directions.

CHAPTER

21

Rose Morgenstern walked up the street, her thoughts returning to her father. The veil of shock slowly receded leaving waves of intense grief. She passed downtown shops and landmarks, each ripe with memories of him.

She always intended on working with her father, but he pushed her to spend some time away from Harding after college. He insisted she get "real world" experience before coming back home to the family business. It was his way of ensuring that she didn't feel manipulated; he didn't want her love and commitment for him to imprison her in Harding. He needn't have worried.

Being a Morgenstern meant something to Rose. She never thought herself better than the people of Harding; she thought herself obligated to them. To work her hardest to keep the business employing so many of its denizens. The singular problem for her was finding a suitable mate among its ranks, a man who couldn't be accused of wooing her for the sole purpose of marrying money. Meeting an outsider like Archie proved refreshing. And seeing how her father had responded to him heightened the sense that their encounter was somehow fated. She longed to stay in his company, to stave off the intense loneliness she felt; to seek solace in someone who understood and together they could explore why her father chose such a jarring capstone to his life. Rose groaned.

You made the right decision, You're not in a good frame of mind to start acting irresponsibly. Besides, you've got enough on your plate taking over all the business operations.

Rose stopped abruptly. Revelation washed over her – her father'd been laying the groundwork for several months. All those meetings about how he liked things done, who to be careful about, who to reward. He'd obviously made his decision and then worked closely with Rose on how she would take over. She'd just assumed that it was in the course of normal succession planning, the importance of which her father had always stressed.

She continued towards her car and stood over it. It wasn't the right time to further complicate her life.

But, there's always tomorrow.

CHAPTER

22

Wendt jogged up the stairs to the B&B and opened the door. He hoped enough time had passed and Lil's anger would be quenched. He started up the stairs towards his room.

"I heard that you've got yourself a new girlfriend."

He stopped midway and turned. Lil sat on a sofa in the living room. Shit, he thought, and slowly descended the stairs. "That's news to me. How come you're sitting in the dark?" Archie turned on a lamp and sat on the sofa beside her.

"Why be coy? Be honest so that we can work it out."

Work it out? Holy hell, he was in deep shit. "Who is it I'm rumored to be dating?"

"Young Miss Morgenstern."

"I'm not sure what you've heard, but I am not romantically involved with anyone."

Lil put her arm on the sofa and turned her body away. "I gave you a home, cooked your meals, provided you with comfort in more ways than one and this is the thanks I get. I should have known better."

"Wow. I'm sorry if I led you on. I was under the impression that this was casual for the both of us."

"Maybe for a New York City slicker like you jumping from bed to bed is natural. But I'm a small town girl and we don't do that."

"I'm from Boston."

She ignored that. "I need to know if you're cheating on me with anyone else?"

"Lil, I'm not cheating on you because we are not a couple and I haven't slept with anybody else, besides." It felt like he was talking to a wall; she paid him no attention.

"Well, Mister, I can tell you that the gravy train is over. My body is a temple and it's now closed to you for worship."

Archie restrained a laugh knowing that he was likely putting his genitalia at risk if this woman felt more humiliated. She had access to all sorts of knives and his sleeping supine body. Lil stood up and left in a huff. He rose slowly and went to his room with the distinct awareness that whatever little world he had succeeded in building for himself in Harding was rapidly coming apart at every seam.

Early in the morning Wendt slouched in his office chair. Several messages. This one lost his Ativan, that one wanted him to know that her husband is still depressed and isn't there something Wendt can do. The final message: "Dr. Wendt, this is Moira Stringer…my husband is a patient of yours. I would like to talk to you…this is awkward. I know that there is doctor patient confidentiality issues, but I need to be able to share some things with you. Please give me a call when you have a chance. My number is…"

Contact with family was always a dicey issue. Where do you draw the line of confidentiality? If you betray the confidence of the patient you're left with nothing to convince them to open up, to share. And the surgeon, Stringer, was already leery of trusting him. On the other hand every clinician fears the headline case - that one in a thousand where something goes horribly wrong and recrimination is in the offing. Thinking about the voicemail gave him a headache. He called the number wanting to get it over as quickly as possible. After four rings he hung up feeling satisfied he'd at least tried.

He rubbed his chin raw. Burn out. He knew the signs. Starting to see each patient as a pain in the ass, as an opportunity to be stressed out. The situation with Morgenstern taking a toll. Wendt looked up his schedule and saw he had only two patients in the early afternoon. He phoned them and rescheduled the appointments for later in the day. That done, he decided to make the trip to Columbus right then. A good excuse to get out of Dodge. Change of scenery, clear his head. He looked up the number for the office of Virgil's doctor, Len Barber. Archie learned the doctor was in, seeing patients all morning.

Approaching Columbus, certainly no metropolis, Archie marveled at how big it felt to him coming from Harding. He drove just west of the city to the medical center. The road wended with the Olentangy River bringing back memories of residency next to the Charles. He pulled into a parking lot and took a ticket. A short while in Harding and he'd forgotten how they screw you to stow your car in almost every other locale.

He found Barber's office in a medical arts type building just off the main hospital. Archie knew the crap shoot of ambushing a doctor without an appointment. Drug reps did it with regularity, but they were better at ingratiating themselves than Archie. He would have to rely on professional courtesy and a kindness owed him by dint of the suicide.

Archie approached the office window and a young woman greeted him with a pleasant smile. "May I help you?"

"Yes, Dr. Wendt to see Dr. Barber."

She consulted her schedule and frowned. "Do you have an appointment, Dr. Wendt?"

"No. Just wanted a few minutes of Dr. Barber's time to discuss a common patient."

"That's highly unusual."

"I'm aware. Do you think that he has a moment to spare for me?"

She shook her head. "Gee, I don't know. This is highly unusual."

This wasn't going anywhere.

"So you said. How about this. You give the message to Dr. Barber that there's a physician in his waiting room who would like a few minutes of his time to discuss Virgil Morgenstern." The mention of the name caused her face to become more somber.

"Can you do that, miss?"

She nodded by way of answering, stood and walked away. She quickly returned.

"He asked that you have a seat. He will try to squeeze a few minutes with you in between patients."

"Be patient for a break in patients?" He said deadpan.

The secretary's brow furrowed. "I'm sorry I don't understand what you mean."

"Nothing. I thank you." Wendt sat down and picked up a year old magazine that promised to shed at least seven strokes from his short game. Some time passed.

"The doctor will see you now."

Archie smiled at that oft repeated phrase. It sounded so old fashioned. She led him down a hallway of exam rooms to an office with a desk facing two chairs.

"Please sit. The doctor will be with you shortly." She closed the door.

Another oldie, but goodie. He sat, looked around the room. Diplomas, pictures of fishing boats, and golf trophies. That explained the magazine selection. He stood to take a closer look at the pictures on the wall when the door opened.

Archie offered his hand. "I'm sorry to barge in like this, I know you're busy."

Barber strode in, all business, white coat flapping behind him like a cape. Looked to be about the same age as Virgil and in the same good shape. "You got my attention mentioning Virgil Morgenstern." He didn't consummate the handshake.

Wendt withdrew his hand. "Yeah, I'm really sorry to use it like that, but I felt certain that I could sufficiently explain why I felt obliged to take some of your precious time."

"You're laying it on a little thick. Why don't you just tell me what this is about."

"Fair enough. My name is Archibald Wendt and I'm a psychiatrist in Harding, recently transplanted from Boston. Virgil and I met days before he took his own life. I didn't see him professionally, but he seemed intent on befriending me. He invited me twice to his house for dinner and hung himself on the second occasion while his family ate dessert."

"You were there that night?"

"Oh, yes. And I couldn't possibly convey how much more difficult it is to witness a suicide than to process it afterwards with a family member." Archie said.

"I'm sorry. I didn't know who you were. You must know what it's like to have someone come unannounced to your office."

Archie smiled. "It's not something I would normally do. But these are extenuating circumstances. Okay if I sit? I'm trying to figure out why a man would do something like this when he didn't, for all intents and purposes, appear depressed."

Barber walked around to his chair, sat, and moved things on his desk. He crossed his arms, looked over at Wendt and grunted. "You are, of course, as familiar with issues of confidentiality as I am. Death doesn't absolve me of my responsibility to protect medical information, especially in the case of someone of his…" he searched for words… "reputation and standing."

"It was my hope that you would afford me some professional courtesy given that I am not a gossip monger or a journalist. And some compassion as I was the one who cut his lifeless body down from the noose. I'm trying to get a sense of Virgil and why he took his own life." Archie offered.

"Look…I understand why you're here, but I don't know if I can give you any answers," Barber said continuing the unending job of rearranging items on his desktop.

"It would help if you could tell me how his general health was."

"You know that death doesn't absolve me from my responsibility for confidential medical information."

"Well, I'm a fellow physician."

"You said he wasn't under your care, so you can't claim to be seeking continuity of care."   Barber said.

"What is going on here? We're going around in circles. I've been up front with you; why are you acting so defensively?"

Barber got up abruptly and walked over to his wall of pictures, stood in front of a sailboat.

He turned and fixed his eyes on Wendt's.

"You a sailor?"

"No."

"I thought, since you said you were from Boston… ever been on a boat?"

"Once. Spent the majority of the time bent over the railing feeding the contents of my stomach to the fish."

Barber laughed. "That's a good one. Anyway, one of the things I love most about being on my boat is the freedom it affords."

"Where is it docked?"

"Florida. You know how they say the happiest days of a boat owner's life are the day he buys and the day he sells the damn thing? Well, that doesn't apply to me. I relish every minute I'm at sea. In fact I spend most of my landlocked days daydreaming about being back on the ocean. Out there I'm The Captain. Me by my lonesome. Very liberating…"

He sat back down. "I admire your directness and I'll honor it with the same. The minute you announced to my secretary that this was about Virgil, my insides knotted up. The defensiveness you pointed out is for several reasons…" Barber trailed off, made to return his desk items to their original positions and thought better of it.

"I knew Virgil Morgenstern for most of my life and I can conjure up countless happy memories with him. But the one that will stay with me forever is the last. Anyway, enough stalling. Here's the scoop.

"Virgil was a relatively healthy man until about a year ago. Hypertension, but easily controlled. Then he came to me with unusual neurological symptoms. General weakness, discoordination. He hid it from people for a while before coming to see me. You know, alpha male, he wasn't going to show any weaknesses. But people started accusing him of being a drunk, falling down as he did. But he wasn't an alcoholic. After an extensive work-up with one of my neurologist colleagues, the best in the business, he diagnosed Virgil with Progressive Supranuclear Palsy. The same illness that took Dudley Moore's life. Curiously, they accused him of being a drunk, as well. Though in that case the accusation was more justified, as I recall.

"Progressive Supranuclear Palsy, huh? I noticed some of those balance issues." Archie said.

"About a week before he took his own life Virgil met with me and the neurologist. In fact, it was right in this office, Virgil sitting where you are now. And we discussed options for treatment and prognosis. He was very intent on getting a sense of how the illness would progress and how long before he could no longer care for himself. Virgil was particularly interested in determining how long before he became a drain on his family." Barber smiled weakly. "That's how he put it, 'a drain', meaning how long before he'd require total support without any hope of improving.

"Now, after the fact, I can see that suicide makes sense from his perspective. But I have not stopped beating myself up for not seeing this inevitability when he sat with me."

"I understand that kind of regret very well."

"I imagine someone in your line of work might. Thank you for saying that," Barber said.

They sat silently then the internist smacked both of his knees and stood. "Well, now you know what was going on. I hope you'll keep this confidential. Obviously this kind of information could have impacted his extensive business dealings, stock prices and such. I don't know what difference its dissemination would make now, but I'd just as soon not be recognized as the source of the leak."

Archie stood, too. "You've been more than kind. I appreciate you opening up especially given the difficulties you laid out. I can assure you I will keep this from causing you any further harm."

Barber escorted Archie to the door of his office and they parted with a handshake.

Wendt drove back to Harding with his thoughts percolating. So Virgil saw the train of mortality bearing down. Not many would blame him for wanting more control over his end. Archie reflected that he hadn't shared with Barber the five million Virgil had left him. He didn't see it as dishonest, more of a need to know issue that complicated matters. It left a residue of guilt that Archie shook. No time for that now.

The illness put the timing in better perspective. Still, questions abound. Why did he choose such a vicious way to end his life as it pertained his family? Why not share his illness with at least his wife or daughter? It also didn't explain the five million. A grinding sound from his car intruded on his thoughts. It grew more insistent when he slowed the car down. He drove straight to a mechanic in town who promised to look into it and call him later.

Archie walked to his office and finished seeing patients.

His day complete, his mind returned to the Virgil puzzle. He ascended the stairs to the B&B with an understanding of the dead man's motives.

"Hey, Arch." Trent stood in the living room.

"When did you get back from the hunt?"

"I got in this morning, tired as hell; I slept until just now. Listen, come close I got something to tell you." Trent sat on the sofa.

Archie pulled a chair close anticipating a good jungle story, not what followed.

"You need to know there's someone sniffing around Harding asking questions about you."

"What? I thought you were going to tell me about Africa."

"I would love to, but someone should alert you about this guy, and Lil won't because apparently you've pissed her off and she won't tell me why. He asked all sorts of questions: How long has Archie been here? Where's his office? Any complaints? That kind of thing. I wanted you to be aware. The guy had a sinister and sleazy feel."

"What did he look like?"

"Thin, dirty blond hair, beak-like nose. Kept blinking his eyes. You know him?"

Indeed. Back from the unpleasantness in Boston that Archie believed he left behind. Curt Cutter, a private investigator. It seemed this particular hound had rediscovered his scent and intended on resuming the hunt.

"Archie, you know him? Cause you look pale."

"I know him. But don't worry about it. Hey, thanks for letting me know." He stood. "And I'd like a raincheck on the safari tales."

"Okay. Take it easy, Archie."

Wendt made his way to his room in a bit of a daze.

A few minutes later there was a knock at his door.

"Arch, you got a phone call."

"Thanks, Trent." Archie went downstairs and picked up the receiver. "Yeah?"

"Dr. Wendt, it's Fred." The mechanic.

"Yeah, Fred, what did you find?"

"Well I put your car up on the rack and gave it a thorough inspection." Silence.

"What did you find, Fred."

"Oh, okay, Dr. Wendt, at first I couldn't locate any problem, so I took her off the rack and drove her a little, you know, to get a feel for what you were describing." Silence.

"And…"

"Oh, yeah, Dr. Wendt, someone monkeyed around with your brakes."

"What does that mean?"

"Someone got under your car and took a knife to your brake line. But it was like they only saw it in the movies, because they didn't succeed in really disabling your brakes, but they did some damage to your car and that's why the grinding sound."

"Can you fix it?"

"Oh, oh sure, Dr. Wendt. Might cost you some, but I can do it."

"Make it happen, Fred. I don't care the cost. Thanks for your help." He hung up.

This was definitely turning into a bad B-movie. Someone doctoring his brakes so that he 'bought the farm.' What the fuck. It didn't take him long to come up with a particular family that might be interested in his downfall. First the investigator, then the brakes. Archie picked up the phone and dialed.

"You have reached the voicemail of Seidlin and Schmidt, please leave a message. If this is after hours and an emergency, please call…"

Archie dialed again.

"Len Seidlin here."

"Mr. Seidlin, Archie Wendt here. Do you remember me?"

"Of course, Dr. Wendt. How can I be of service? Have you decided to hire us to handle your newfound riches?"

Archie didn't appreciate that remark. "No, sir. I wanted to know what would happen to the five million that Mr. Morgenstern left me if I were to suffer some sort of early demise. Is that money mine to disburse as I see fit?"

"No. There's a stipulation in Mr. Morgenstern's will that any money he bequeathed should be returned to the general estate in the case of the untimely demise of any of the principles prior to disbursement. Your money falls into that category."

"Just what I thought. Thank you for taking the time. I apologize if I interrupted anything important."

"Not a problem. And give some thought to whether you want to use our firm. Our percentage would be very reasonable."

"Thanks, I will. Good night."

Archie made absent minded preparations to go to bed. Brushing his teeth for the second time, he felt a weight returning to him. A familiar burden, one that brought flashes of the golden dome of Beacon Hill, the Back Bay, and Cambridge. A flooding of memories. The harbinger embodied figuratively and literally by Cutter. That piece of shit investigator haunted his every move for close to a year after the event. Only now that the burden was back did Archie realize just how fond he had grown of living without it. Curt Cutter, a bad omen, like a coming storm. The incarnation of his rapidly unraveling life in Harding; his past running him down.

He looked long and hard in the mirror. Spoke to his reflection.

"Cutter might be the least of your worries. Those brakes mean someone wants to end your residence here in Harding on a more permanent basis. Having failed they might not be so ham fisted the next time. That's fucking great. What have you got us into, huh?"

He slipped into bed. Pulled the blankets around the top of his head and tucked his arms inside, Egyptian style. In his cocoon he reflected on his visit to Ohio State and the internist Barber. A good man. My kind of guy. Drifting off he thought: almost gives me hope for humanity.

The dreamscapes diffuse, the voices muddled. Scenes floated in and out. As he drifted out of a deep sleep and rolled over to begin another cycle it occurred to him that he hadn't had a drink for a day and he should continue this newfound sobriety. But his teetotalling oath descended with him into another dream, split off and was not to be recalled in the morning.

The top down on the convertible, he saw a winding river. Wind pleasantly whipped his face, easy tones coming from the radio. Then the volume rose and imposed on the harmony of the ride, grated on his nerves. His consciousness returned to the sounds of an argument downstairs. He made out Lil's voice, but not the other. Female and confident. Archie looked out the window. Still dark.

Archie got out of bed, confused, and stumbled out the door to the bannister. He could make out Lil's back and Rose's angry face.

"It doesn't make a difference why I'm here or who I'm here to see. That's none of your goddamned business."

Hands on hips, Lil retorted, "Of course it's my business. This is both my home and my place of business. It is my duty to protect the clients whose privacy and quiet are deeply important. We are not accustomed to 2 AM calls from strangers when they don't have a reservation and especially when they live in town."

"Look, please tell me which room Dr. Wendt occupies and I will be out of your beehive hair."

"You get smart with me and I will call the police."

Archie leaned farther over and the bannister creaked. Both women looked up.

"Dr. Wendt, thank God you're up." Rose started to make for the stairs, Lil threw out an arm bar.

"Lil, please, it's okay. Rose, you were supposed to come earlier; must have gotten caught in that late meeting, huh?"

"Right. The late meeting."

Lil reluctantly let her arm go lax while shooting eye daggers up the stairs after the younger woman.

Rose glared at Archie while pointing her thumb in Lil's direction. She mouthed, "What the fuck?"

He escorted her into his room and shut the door, his back to it. She bodied up to him. He smelled alcohol on her breath. "What's a girl got to go through to pay a man a booty call?"

Archie put his arms around her. "I'm a little taken aback. I thought you weren't the type to jump in the sac to alleviate your grief?"

"I never said that."

"We can review the record. Your honor, can we have the last interaction read back to us?"

"Such as wiseass. Besides, I'm not here to alleviate my grief, as you put it. I'm here to see if consummation is warranted."

"Doesn't a booty call demand consummation, by its very nature?"

Rose kissed him on the lips. "You talk too much."

"No patient has ever accused me of that."

"I'm not a patient. And I'm not patient. Strip."

Afterwards lying in bed, one of Archie's legs dangled outside the blanket, a dazzling white socked foot.

"You're still wearing your socks. That's very sexy, Dr. Wendt."

"Thanks. I often find I need the traction."

"Wow. And are they ever white. How do you get them like that?"

He sighed. "You feel you must know?"

"It seems important. And odd. Important and odd, how I would describe you."

"I buy white socks, I wear them, wash and bleach them once or twice, then throw them away."

"Why on earth do you do that?"

"Now that's a much longer story, and not nearly as interesting as your nipples." He buried his head in her chest. She laughed and they hugged and kissed. When they separated she said, "Hey, what's with dragon landlady downstairs? I thought she was going to kill me. Seemed more personal than just looking after her tenants."

"We had a brief thing together and I fear she misunderstood it as more than it was."

Rose got up on an elbow. "You nailed the landlady? Ha! She's got to have you by twenty years. You must be one hard up fellow."

"That's not nice. And who are you to talk, *you're* with me now."

"Well, she did have a nice figure, I'll give you that."

"Lil's a nice woman. I feel badly that she got hurt. You know, it was really lonely when I first got to Harding. I didn't really know anyone. We spent long evenings talking and one thing led to another."

"I know, I know. Just the other day I was getting my car detailed, I was talking to the mechanic and, you know, one thing led to another…"

"You're rotten."

"I wonder if I've queered your ability to stay here."

"What do you mean?"

"Well, if she's the jealous type, and everything in her behavior earlier suggested as much, she's not going to take this lightly." Rose said.

He shrugged. "I hope you're wrong. I'd hate to think of paying a high price for one indiscretion."

Rose punched him playfully on the shoulder. "And which indiscretion do you mean?"

"I meant sleeping with her. You seem like an endeavor rather than an indiscretion. Though I would appreciate some discretion."

"By that you mean what? That I can't spend the night?"

"It would seem prudent that you not join us for breakfast in your previous evening's attire, so no." Archie said.

"You're a rat, you know that?"

Rose got out of bed and began dressing. Archie felt more intimacy watching her get dressed than seeing her strip. As if letting him in on something she did more regularly.

"What are you smiling about?" She said. "Thinking about another roll, buddy? Fat chance with your 'prudent not to join us for breakfast' bullshit."

Rose looked around the room. "It's interesting to see how you've arranged things. You're a real a place for everything and everything in its place kind of guy."

"This is where I lay my head. Got to be organized."

"And lay your landlady, it seems." She walked around poking at things. Rose peeked inside the roll top desk. "Think you may have a problem here, chief."

"Why, am I low on provisions?"

"Drinking alone is not a good sign. From now on you get the urge to drink along you call me and I'll join you."

"You're a keeper." He said.

Finished with her inspection Rose sat on the bed and sighed.

Archie placed a hand on her back. "You doing okay?"

She shrugged. "I'd rather not discuss sad things. Let's let tonight be about sexual therapy."

"Deal." They shared the silence, both enjoying a rare moment of contentment. He threw on a pair of shorts and a t-shirt and escorted her down the stairs to the front door. Rose looked up the stairs and said, "The B&B has eyes. No kiss."

Archie woke up feeling much better than he should have given recent events and his lack of sleep. He took stock of the situation in the shower; he did his best thinking in there. Unfortunately, the great revelations he consistently made while under the spray vanished with the dissipating steam.

Wendt dressed and poked his head out of his room. Ridiculous. I can't live like this. I'm a grown ass man, I haven't done anything wrong. Archie pulled his tie tight, straightened his back and made his way downstairs. He needn't have worried. Lil was nowhere in sight. Skipping breakfast, he walked out the door and down the stairs. The first unpleasant surprise of the day waited for him at the bottom.

"Hiya, Wendt. Mind if I walk with you to your office?"

Cutter, the investigator from the Mass Medical Board hadn't changed one bit. Wendt felt a chill come over him. Irrational, he told himself, this guy was from another life and had no standing here. That gave him the courage he needed.

"Fuck off you a miserable piece of shit." Wendt stalked away.

"Nah. I think I'll be hanging around here. Check out the sights. Nice little town." He fell into step with Wendt.

For a few paces Wendt pretended he walked alone. Then he whirled and faced the man. "What do you want? You have no jurisdiction with me now. Leave me alone."

"Jurisdiction?" Cutter said. "I ain't no fucking cop. I'm a private investigator with a nice retainer, hourly fee, and expense account. I have you to thank for that. You're going to be my nest egg."

"Somebody here hired you?"

"That's private information, you know that. Client privilege. Like you got, only I don't get to fuck my clients like you."

Wendt walked away.

"I have to say, I am amazed at how many people you've seemed to piss off in the short time since you fled Boston and came here."

"I didn't flee anything, you worthless pile of shit."

Cutter threw an arm across Wendt. "How many freebie insults you think you got with me, huh? Look, prick, I earn an honest living. At least I'm not out there manipulating people when they're at their most vulnerable and putting shit into their heads."

"Don't - put - your - hands - on - me." Wendt tried to put as much menace into his voice that he could muster. That only seemed to amuse Cutter more.

"What the hell are you going to do? Huh? You think you're a hard case? You're a joke." The PI patted Archie. "Look, I'm going to be here shadowing your every move so get used to it."

They approached the office and both noticed the police cruiser parked outside. Cutter chuckled.

"Looks like you're a popular guy. You take care of yourself for now, Doc. And a word of advice - stay away from the booze. You're going to need your composure and we know how you get when you drink."

"I hope you die, you cocksucker."

"Thanks for the good cheer, headshrinker. Bye for now."

Archie jogged up his stairs. The police chief stood leaning against his office door. Unpleasant surprise number two.

"Morning, Doc."

"Good morning, Chief…"

"Lynne. Chief Lynne."

"I have a patient whose arrival is imminent. Is there something I can do to help you?"

"Going to have to cancel that patient. Been getting some complaints. Can we talk inside? I prefer to give you some privacy."

Lynne stepped aside to let Archie unlock the door. He turned the lights on in the waiting room and went into his office, the chief trailing behind.

"What is this about?"

"Well, Doc, you know, we're a small town here. Take care of each other, ya see. When something disturbs that harmony, we have to take it seriously and protect the populace from unscrupulous folks."

"What the hell are you talking about?"

"Not sure what you were doing with old Virgil and why he saw fit to give you all that money. From my vantage point, something smells. Extortion, blackmail…I'm not sure. But I'm going to find out. Until then, I got to ask you to cease and desist your practice."

"You can't do that. I have a proper medical license and have every right to practice here in Ohio." Archie said.

"Well now, I'm not so sure about that. I put in a call to the State Medical Board and they agreed that it was proper to suspend your license and do a proper investigation. They say there's a man in town who can help untangle this web you have created. Cutter, they say his name is. Haven't met him yet, though I will, that's for sure. So, for now, please cooperate 'cause I'd sure hate to have to detain you for practicing medicine without appropriate licensing."

"Listen, chief, my license is paid for and up to date. You have no jurisdiction over my ability to practice medicine."

Lynne took off his hat and put it over his chest. "Well I can you want to play this the hard way. So be it. I'm going to have to see your lease for this office."

Wendt went over to his desk and pulled on some drawers. He stammered. "I don't know precisely where the damn thing is."

"Don't matter much anyway. The owner of the building is a good friend, I'm sure he'll see things my way." He put his hat back on his head and started out the door. "You gonna lose this one, Doc, I'll shut you down no matter what you do. Get used to that idea. You have a good day now." His voice trailed down the stairs.

Archie sat down hard; the weight of the situation sank in. Of the two people who knew what Virgil wanted from him only Archie survived. The others assumed only what they observed on the surface and clearly it appeared more sinister. He struggled to collect his thoughts. Meanwhile, the answering machine mocked him with its blinking red light.

He didn't have the energy to listen to the message. Archie wanted to go to the bar, forget all this mess, but his sense of professional responsibility dictated his next move.

Slippers and robe. "Jesus, Howard, do you sleep in that thing?"

"Such vitriol first thing in the morning I don't need."

"It's nearly noon."

"Thanks for the time, Big Ben. By all means bring your pleasant self in." He stepped aside and let Archie pass.

"You won't believe the shit storm I'm in the middle of."

"I got some idea. Lots of rumors floating around about you."

"If I hear again how this is a small town I'm going to run amok with an AK-47. And where the fuck do you hear gossip?"

"It flies around overhead. I just know how to collect it."

"Can I get a drink?"

Howard pantomimed looking at a watch on a naked wrist. "It's a bit early. Why don't you try telling me what's going on without the Dutch courage." They went into his study where the older man plopped down on his Barcalounger. Wendt sat opposite him.

"I don't even know where to begin. Today I got a visit from two people. Well three, but I'll leave off the early morning visit for now. A private dick met me outside my house. A guy I had to deal with in Boston when I had troubles there. See, the medical board hired this independent investigator. He made my life miserable, hounding my every move. Someone saw fit to bring him here to renew his personal vendetta against me."

Archie stood and paced. "It's like everything is on its head, you know? The more I try to keep things under the control, the less control I have." He ran his hands through his hair, rubbed his mandible to a nice rouged complexion.

Howard sat with the kind of look a father gives his son when the boy comes home to tell him that somehow the girl got pregnant even though they did it just once in the backseat of the car.

"What?" Archie said.

"I'm not judging you. I really do feel badly for what happened. I'm one of the few people who know that you really have been the wrong guy in the wrong place. But, what made you decide to piss off Katherine Morgenstern?"

"Why do you put it like that? I didn't decide to piss her off. She asked me to essentially fuck off and give the money back. I didn't think that was reasonable."

"Well, in a way you chose this path."

"Thanks for that. I also got a visit from Chief Lynne which is what brought me here." Archie relayed that conversation. "I don't know, but this guy has a hard-on for me like I fucked his wife or something."

Howard exhaled through his teeth; it came out a harsh whistle.

"What, for crissakes, Howard, what?"

"Horace Lynne was once married with a son and a daughter. Wife wants a divorce, but old Horace doesn't believe in divorce. 'Til death do you part and all that. So the wife accuses the chief of molesting their kids. Son comes to his father's defense, but the daughter proves to be a vindictive young lass willing to support mother's claim. She goes to a clinic down in Cincinnati for traumatized teens and returns convinced she had, in fact, been sexually abused, but had suppressed the memories because of how horrible they were.

"The courts rakes Horace over the coals and strip him of his parenting rights. I believe the public humiliation was the hardest for him to take.

"Most people who know him understood the situation. Know he wasn't the type to molest anyone sexually. Tax paying citizens and their rights being a different story. But the rumor was out there. Where there's smoke there's fire worked against him. People didn't know what to believe. It may have only been a niggling doubt in some people's mind, but the accusation stuck.

"Our chief suffered and I suppose he sees an opportunity to get a little pay back against someone in the mental health community. Especially when there is the whiff of mind control. Like in this case."

"Mind control. What the fuck are you talking about, Howard? You know the situation; how can you imply —."

Rogoff held up his hands. "Whoa, whoa, whoa. Don't get your balls in an uproar. I speak from his vantage point, not my own. Calm down." He stood. "Maybe I will get us a drink now." He walked over to the bar, mixed a couple and handed a glass to Archie.

"Were you just making a run of the mill crooked cop joke about Lynne harassing honest people or are you insinuating that he is buyable?"

"There is the general belief that if you have money in Harding, you can get out of any minor pinch. It wouldn't surprise me to hear that someone bought his services. Especially Katherine Morgenstern who has more money than she knows what to do with," Howard said.

"How did it come to this? I'm nobody looking to blend into the wall. And now I'm a target for so many people. So much for anonymity and a quiet life here in small town Ohio."

"Why not give the money back?" Howard slumped back down, pulled the lever and propped his feet up.

"I don't know that this is about the money." He took another gulp of the scotch. It's heat burned off his self-pity, rekindled his fight. "And anyway, I want some answers, goddammit. You think I'm going to relinquish the cash and slink off with my tail between my legs? I didn't ask for any of this. But now I'm going to get some fucking answers, I can tell you that."

"There's that Dutch courage," Howard said.

"Look Howard, I need you to fill in for me, see your old patients until I get this straightened out."

"Shit. I guess it's the logical thing, but I really enjoyed my retirement. Not worrying about other people's problems. Getting up whenever I wanted and letting my whims dictate my day." He lifted the edge of his bathrobe and mused. "This thing is addictive. I wonder if I can see people in my bathrobe or will that be perceived as unprofessional."

"You should use the office." He placed the key on the side board. "Thanks for the snort. Time to get my shit together."

"Hey, who was your early morning visit?"

"Rose Morgenstern. I'll have to save that story for another day."

"Jesus, Archie. You're making the rounds on all the Morgensterns aren't you? Just watch out for that weaselly son."

Archie downed the remainder of his drink and left the comfort and safety of Howard's study.

CHAPTER

25

rchie spent the afternoon in the diner putting his predicament on paper; disparate pieces he hoped to put together into something coherent. He plotted his next move. The waitress came over for a fifth time.

"You done sir? Cause you haven't had a refill for a half hour."

Archie looked around the room with vaudevillian exaggeration, arms spread to demonstrate the emptiness of the joint.

She walked off in a huff.

Feeling like he'd pissed off enough of Harding's residents for a lifetime, he gathered his things and walked out to a brilliant sunset. Big orange ball with pink, blue, purple streaks painting the sky. Street lamps came on downtown.

Archie walked the streets back to the B&B, head down, hands in his pockets and brooded. He needed answers about ol' Virgil. There had to be someone with the backstory who might be willing to speak with him. Wife sure as hell isn't in the mood to talk. He needed help unravelling the mystery Virgil left behind.

Thus far he knew only that the neurologically doomed man believed his competent time was short. He couldn't bear the idea that the once proud athlete would be reduced to an invalid relying on others for care in what would certainly be a horrific way to die. Fine, Archie understood that. Must have been something compelling Virgil to enlist the help of a near stranger to carry out his final wish.

His final wish. That's what it came down to, didn't it? Archie could feel his mind coming to something. That feeling you get when you know you are close to the answer, can feel it dodging your grasp like a young boy evading a tag on the schoolyard. Final wish.

He could reach out to David Daugherty. Virgil's personal attorney should be able to answer some of these questions.

His mind otherwise occupied, he let his peripheral vision guide him across the street. Headlights filled his vision; his muscle memory automatically engaged in the familiar practice of waiting for the car to approach preparing to dodge it.

The car bore down on him at an unnatural angle and at a higher speed than anticipated. He jumped to the tree lawn, rolling as the car jumped the curb, barely missed him, and careened down the street.

Breathing heavily, he leapt to his feet and began racing after the car to get a look at the driver. Not used to the pace, his wind quickly left him; he didn't get close enough to get a look inside. He did get the license plate and repeated it in his head as he collapsed on the curb and caught his breath. ARS 348. ARS 348. He couldn't tell make and model, but it looked red.

As his heart pounded he smelled fear mixed in with his sweat. A rank odor he recognized readily from his last days in Boston. He placed a hand on his chest and worked to slow his breathing.

Who could he report this to? Certainly, not Lynne. He'd charge Archie with jaywalking and throw him in jail. Maybe the sheriff - he seemed like a decent fellow. They had developed an easy rapport in Virgil's study and seemed like a man who could be reasonable.

Archie got up and dusted off his pants. The car trying to hit him was the third bad item of the day. It could have been worse.

It dawned on him that Rose knew of his peculiarity of crossing the street in front of cars. He walked to the auto mechanic's shop with that disturbing thought eating away at him.

Fred proved steep with the price, though Archie would have paid much more. He was glad to have his Beemer back. He drove back to the B&B with thoughts of a shower and nightcap dancing in his head.

Approaching the hostelry he saw clothes strewn on the lawn. For a split second his mind registered the similarity to his own apparel and how strange to see clothes so much like his own. Then realization hit like an anvil, for what he saw *was* his wardrobe, scattered about the front steps, the grass, and the sidewalk out front. He parked the car at the curb and jumped out, sprinting up the stairs and through the door, almost running over Trent.

"Oh, Arch. Shit, man, she's pissed with you."

"Thanks for the update Trent. And thanks for saving my shit. You're a pal."

"C'mon, Archie, that's not fair." Wendt raced up the stairs to his room. It was in shambles. And in the middle, Lillie sitting on his bed.

"I want you out of here now."

"Lil, calm down." He began collecting his things and arranging them.

"Don't tell me to calm down you lecherous pig. I trusted you." She lowered her voice and stood. "I let you into my bed. Oh, you are a filthy pig and I want you out."

"Lil, let's just calm down."

"Stop saying my name you quack! I want you to leave this house immediately. That's my right as a landlord and innkeeper."

"Why are you flipping out on me?"

"Like you don't know. Like you didn't sleep with that whore of a Morgenstern, RIGHT HERE UNDER MY ROOF!"

"Jesus, Lil, keep your voice down. I'm right here for crissakes."

"OUT!"

"I can't go anywhere and I'm not going anywhere. I'm sorry if you got the wrong impression of our relationship, if you thought, like a schoolgirl, that we were going steady after sleeping together a couple of times. But I didn't do anything wrong. You have no cause to evict me and the laws will support that." He continued arranging his personal effects.

"I want you out right now or I'm going to call Chief Lynne to forcibly remove you."

He froze. "Why would you call the police? It's the sheriff who's responsible for evictions in this county." Then a thought occurred to him: "Did you already speak to Lynne?"

"As a matter of fact, I did. He was here earlier today and filled me in on all the dirty things you've been doing here in Harding. I suppose I got off lucky that you only slept with me. Maybe you were planning on robbing me like you did poor Virgil Morgenstern before he died."

"It was after he died, you bitch, not before. Get the story right, for crissakes, if you're going to say it."

"So you admit it. Get out now."

"Admit it," he mumbled to himself. "Gladly. I admit that this whole town is full of gullible morons."

Lil stalked out. He could see her in her room across the hall making a real show of calling the police. Picking up the handle, punching numbers, breathing heavily.

"Yes, I'd like to speak with Chief Lynne. (pause) Yes, it's an emergency. Please tell him its Lillie Fagen and that I have a tenant who is unruly and causing damage to the house."

That got Archie's attention. He didn't need to be told twice that his word against anyone's was a losing battle as far as it concerned Lynne. He gathered up as much as he could and threw it all into a suitcase. Ran into the bathroom collected his toiletries and hustled down the stairs. Lil stood in her doorway with a bizarre smirk on her face, her hair disheveled.

Archie stopped in mid-stairs and turned toward her. "The stretch marks *are* noticeable and are *very* unattractive."

He ran down the stairs before she could react and slammed the door shut behind him. Archie picked up some odds and ends from the front yard and put them in his trunk. "Whoever said that shit comes in threes was wrong as fucking hell."

"You fucked up big time, didn't you, Archie?"

Trent sat on the stoop smoking a cigarette.

Wendt slammed the trunk shut. "Looks that way. Think I could borrow your phone?"

Trent dug in his pocket and handed it over. "You still haven't gotten your own? You've been here like a year already."

"Best decision I ever made cutting free from the cellphone. Harder for patients to torture me."

He pulled out his wallet and leafed through the cards to get the number to the estate lawyer. He dialed that and from him got Daugherty's number and the number to the Sheriff's.

"Sheriff Hidalgo. How can I help you?"

"Whoa. I didn't think you'd answer the phone."

"Well, I did. Who's this?"

"Sheriff, this is Dr. Wendt. Archibald Wendt? We met, uh, under unfortunate circumstances at the Morgenstern house."

"Of course, Doctor, how can I help you?"

"I was wondering if you would do me a favor. It's a little embarrassing to be asking, but I need this. Someone tried to run me over tonight and I need a license plate run to see who might be trying to kill me."

"You sure this was an attempted hit and run?"

"No doubt."

"Have you contacted the police?"

Archie rubbed his jaw. "That's where things get dicey. I believe that the chief of police, Lynne, is not terribly fond of me and I didn't think I would get much traction filing a complaint with him."

"You're probably right. He doesn't like you. In fact, he's been asking around looking to build a case against you."

"So he's come to a conclusion and is now looking for facts to support it."

"Pretty much," Hidalgo admitted.

"Jesus. Small town."

"Yes, it is. With regards your alleged hit and run attempt, what's the motive? Money, anger or both?"

"Seems like you already have a handle on the motive."

Hidalgo was quiet on the other end. "Okay, give me the plate number and I'll see what I can do."

Archie repeated it from memory. "How long does something like this take?"

"Where do you plan on being in a couple of hours?"

"The President's Club."

"Alright. I'll see you there."

One down, thought Archie, as he dialed the lawyer's number. Daugherty answered. Two for two. Maybe his luck was turning.

"Mr. Daugherty, it's Archie Wendt, the psychiatrist who you met at the Morgenstern's."

"Of course, Dr. Wendt. How can I be of service?"

"I was wondering if I could buy you a drink."

"Uh, well, it's kind of late. What's this about?"

"The rumor that you were fucking Katherine Morgenstern."

Long pause. "I don't know what you're talking about."

"C'mon, counselor, let me buy you a drink. Maybe I'll be able to make it worth your while."

"Where do you want to meet?"

"The President's Club."

"I'll be there in a half hour."

Archie hung up and handed the phone back to Trent.

"You'd do well if you could see your patients at the bar; then you'd never have to leave." Trent quipped.

"Thanks for letting me use your phone. Guess I'll be seeing you around."

"I'll miss you when I'm here. You're a good listener and a good dude."

"I appreciate that, Trent, I really do. I'll see you when I see you."

Archie walked back to his car. He started the motor, gunned her some to get her back in shape then pulled away from the B&B, tires squealing for good measure.

CHAPTER

26

"The prodigal son returns." Mike clapped his hands.

Wendt took a seat at the bar. "It hasn't been that long; there's no call for theatrics."

"Well, what will it be tonight?"

"Give me a double of the well whiskey for now."

Mike put the glass in front of Archie and poured a generous shot. "Going to be one of those nights, huh?"

"I'm pretty much setting up shop here, Mike. Got some business to attend to."

"From what I've been hearing, you've been plenty busy. Hobnobbing with some high-class trim, word has it."

Archie almost choked. "Holy shit. Word travels bloody fast." He drank the remainder of the glass, wiped his mouth and rubbed his jaw. Pounded the glass on the bar; Mike knew that gesture well. He started the pouring motion nanoseconds before the glass hit the bar and lost not a single drop. Truly a master of his craft.

Daugherty walked in, Archie on his third drink.

"A white wine, Mike."

"You just know everyone, don't you?" Archie addressed the bartender, then turned to the lawyer. "Can we do a shot before we sit."

Daugherty held up a hand. "I'm not a young man like you. I'll stick to my wine."

"C'mon. Just one. Humor a man who's private and public life are being pulled apart by a pack of wild dogs."

The lawyer nodded to Mike who poured all three of them a shot of Goldschlager. "To Virgil Morgenstern" he said. They clinked their glasses and drank somberly. Mike smacked his lips. "Why don't you take a booth for privacy and give me a break from your charm."

Daugherty took his glass of wine to a booth and Archie followed with his drink. They sat, Archie facing the bar's front door.

"What is it you wanted to talk about?" the lawyer asked.

"I want some background on Virgil Morgenstern. As his personal attorney, I hoped you'd be able to share with me some of his childhood development, schooling, things like that."

"And why would I do that? Because you insinuated that I was having an affair with Mrs. Morgenstern?"

"Well, I didn't insinuate so much as stated it as a bold fact."

"Dr. Wendt, your threat is not why I came here tonight, so please dispense with the salacious rumor mongering."

"Salacious? That's a hell of thing for one man to say to another. Well, if you're not feeling threatened then you must be here as an emissary of her ladyship Katherine. See if you can butter me up."

Daugherty stopped his wine glass in mid sip.

"Not bad for a headshrinker, huh?" Archie grinned. "Look, I'm not here on some blackmail mission. Instead of gossiping about who knocked boots with whom, what if I were to cut you in on a percentage of the five million in exchange for the information. Call it an attorney's fee."

Daugherty loosened up immediately. "I'll make you a deal. You want to know about Virgil? I don't mind sharing what I know, but my fee is twenty percent." Before Archie could agree Daugherty continued. "Virgil introduced me as his personal attorney, but I wasn't really that. That was just Virgil's way - you know, a flare for the dramatic. I was in house counsel for Lowry Industries. My father got me the job through his friendship with Katherine's father."

"I heard that he was quite successful."

"Oh yes. Mr. Lowry was probably one of the richest men in the state. A gentleman in all senses of the word. He and my father served in the Army together. After the war, Lowry parlayed some heady investments of his father's into a veritable empire. My father didn't do so well. He struggled with alcohol and combat fatigue, as they called it then, so Lowry came through for his friend and put me through law school. When I finished he set me up with his son-in-law."

"Sounds to me like old man Lowry wanted to spy on his new son-in-law." Archie said.

"Funny you should say that. John Lowry was very fond of his son-in-law. Though a generation separated the two, they were kindred spirits. They saw the world similarly and had uncanny abilities to parlay their talents into reams of money. Virgil was a natural and already a rising star in Lowry Industries when they hired me. John thought this would be a nice opportunity for me and it proved so; I had the honor of learning from two very gifted men."

"It's interesting to hear you talk about Morgenstern as if he were much older than you, but I don't imagine there was much of an age difference."

"You're right." Daugherty signaled to Mike for another glass of wine. "We are, I mean were, the same age."

Archie let the lawyer take a few more sips of wine then asked: "So the rumors about you and Katherine…"

"It's not like you think. Or what anybody else presumes, for that matter. Katherine is a complicated woman. At some point in their marriage either she, or both, grew bored. I don't know the psychology behind it. (He tipped his head to Archie.) What I can tell you is that once the children left the house Katherine wanted to get more involved with the family business. She sought me out and I helped ease her into her birthright. Turned out, Katherine didn't need much help; she had a lot of her father's attributes: methodical, persistent, brilliant." He got a faraway look in his eyes.

"So while working together one thing led to another, is that what you're saying?" Archie snapped his fingers. Daugherty focused.

"No. Katherine isn't a very sexual person. Having an affair with her had more to do with emotional support rather than garters and rent by the hour motels."

"How did Virgil feel about your so called emotional affair?"

"I would classify it as somewhere between willful ignorance and tacit approval. He wasn't threatened when she came to work in the business. He was glad his wife had something to occupy her mind, something he had profound respect for. Her mind, I mean. You understand? And I always wondered if there was another woman…"

Daugherty's focus trailed away again. Jesus this guy was a lightweight; give him a shot and a glass of wine and he can't string sentences together. Archie snapped his fingers impatiently. "Who did you think the other woman was? Linda?"

"Linda? God, no. Where did you get that from? No, he didn't have any sexual feelings for Linda. No one really knows who it was that captured his heart. Virgil was gregarious and charismatic, but the most secret places of his heart he kept to himself. I believe that Katherine sensed that she could never get the whole of him and she harbored a lot of anger towards Virgil for that."

They sipped their drinks. Archie felt buzzed, yeah, but bone tired. Too many things in one day.

"Well, Doctor, if that satisfies you I will call it a night." Daugherty stood. "Here is my card. Give me a call and we'll get the money from the estate."

Archie looked up and took the card. "Oh, yeah. The money. I'll be in touch."

"You will give me a call, won't you?"

"Certainly." Seeing the sheriff walk in he added, "Good night and thank you."

Hidalgo spotted Archie and walked over, giving an imperceptible nod in Mike's direction. The bartender immediately went to work pouring a beer from the tap as the sheriff took the position vacated by the lawyer.

"I got that information you asked about." Hidalgo situated himself in the booth. "Before I give it up, I need to know what's going on. Lots of rumors out there, some very disturbing."

Mike brought over the beer, put it down on the table and put his hand on the sheriff's shoulder.

"Everything okay in the department, John?"

"Holding steady and true, Mike. Thanks for the beer."

"I'll leave you two alone." He went back behind the bar.

John took a sip of his beer, looked over the rim at Archie and said: "Speak."

"I wouldn't even know where to begin. What I can tell you from the jump is I have done nothing illegal or unethical. Virgil befriended me, I never took him on as a patient. He invited me to dinner and after some verbal foreplay asked me to informally evaluate his children. A second invitation followed and, well, you know the rest.

"None of that would matter except that Virgil, for some reason that I'm trying to understand, left me a large sum of money. That's led to my name getting slandered by some powerful people in this one-horse town and they are working overtime to make my life a living hell."

"You're saying all the rumors are false?"

"Rumors? You want to be more specific?"

"There's a fellow who hails from back east telling anyone who'll listen about unethical practices back in your Boston days. Something about sleeping with a patient, her suiciding, and you being investigated. What do you know about that?"

Archie groaned. "That's a long story and has no bearing here. I can just tell you that it's not what you think and I wasn't found culpable of any criminal wrongdoing."

"Then what made you leave Boston?"

"It's complicated, okay? And, again, it's not germane to the things that are happening here. I came to your fine town to start anew using my connections to Howard Rogoff. And things were going okay. Then Morgenstern brings me into his life and, surprise, he offs himself in the most shocking way. I cut him down, something I'm not unsure he didn't plan, and to make matters infinitely worse, he leaves me a huge pile of money for no apparent reason. Everyone here is ready to attribute to me some mythical status as a latter-day Mesmer, putting a strong personality like Virgil under my spell. It would be laughable if I weren't being threatened from multiple sources."

"I want to believe you."

"That's something, I guess. I've started to feel like a small-town Job."

"Some of those misfortunes you brought on yourself." John said.

"Like what?"

"Like bringing a woman to your room and pissing off Lillie Fagen."

Archie smacked the table. "Jesus, is anything that happens in this shithole private?"

"She tossed your belongings onto the street. That gets people's attention. Then there's the matter of Rose Morgenstern."

"What about her?"

John's face reddened. "She's not a plaything or someone you love and leave."

"What business is that of yours?"

"I'm very close to the Morgensterns. Virgil is - was very important to me, goddammit. His daughter was important to him; by transitive property she is equally important to me. I don't want to see her get hurt."

"Whatever is happening between me and Rose is no one's concern but ours." Seeing the reaction this got in Hidalgo's face he quickly added, "But, and I can't speak for her, this is not something casual for me. Okay?"

The sheriff seemed to relax a little. "You should know that Rose has been in trouble herself. Not two years ago she was brought up on charges of assaulting a man she'd been seeing. We never could get a straight story about what happened, but she stabbed him in the genitals according to reports. The guy didn't press charges; Virgil made it go away with a settlement."

"Jesus."

Hidalgo pulled a sheet of paper from his uniform's front pocket. "Here is the report from that plate you asked me to chase down. The car is registered to Rose Morgenstern."

Archie took the sheet and put it away. "Thank you, sheriff."

"You bet. I don't know what advice to give you about the other stuff. You said powerful people and I want to reinforce that. Katherine Morgenstern can be mean as a snake and just as conniving; Horace Lynne is a vengeful man."

"Vengeful. That's a hell of a way to describe the chief of police. Isn't he supposed to uphold the law?"

Hidalgo chuckled. "If we're getting into supposed to's you're in far greater trouble than I thought."

"I see your point."

"Just don't underestimate any of these folks especially when they get a whiff of money. That's how Virgil always described it. He said, 'People hang around the wealthy with the mistaken idea that the rich will shower them with free money.'

"I think that part of wealthn always grated on him."

Archie held out his hand to the sheriff and said, "Well, I appreciate your help. I mean, I wasn't sure where to turn, so I'm grateful you even showed up."

The sheriff took the proffered hand. "You bet. And be careful of Ms. Morgenstern, okay?" Hidalgo looked down furtively at his crotch and smiled. He signaled Mike again and this time the bartender brought his check. Hidalgo reached for his wallet.

"No, Sheriff, please. You've done me a favor, let me. Mike, just add it to my tab, please."

"Look at the big spender. No offense, Doc, but you gonna be able to pay your burgeoning bar tab without a medical practice?"

Archie narrowed his eyes at Mike. "How do you know I can't maintain my practice? Wait, don't fucking say it. It doesn't make a difference if I'm practicing. I have my own money, Mike, so don't worry about my tab. You can stop embarrassing me in front of the sheriff."

Hidalgo stood. "Dr. Wendt, you be careful." And he left.

Archie sat at the table for a few more minutes digesting the new information. He needed a good night's rest to sort it out. He walked out of the bar to his car, unsteady, but able to maintain sufficient balance. The Continental, a hotel that boasted the accommodation of several presidents and Elvis, stood only a couple of blocks away. In his mind he already stretched out in the warm bed. He walked through the sliding doors to the unmanned registration desk and rang the bell. A young man came from the back.

Archie took out his license and a credit card. "You got rooms tonight?"

"Sure do, sir."

"Great, I need a room for the night. Actually, for more than one night."

"Certainly, sir." He took the license; his face fell as he read the name. "I'm terribly sorry, sir. We don't have any rooms to let just now."

"What? You were prepared to give me a room two seconds ago."

"I'm terribly sorry, sir."

"Fuck sorry. You have rooms, that's plain. You have a legal obligation to provide me a room if you have a vacancy."

"Please lower your voice, sir. We reserve the right to refuse anyone who is intoxicated, which you clearly are."

"Bullshit."

"Please do not make me call the police. Just leave, sir."

Archie took back his license and credit card. He turned to leave and his eyes fell on a plaque in the lobby that proclaimed the hotel a proud member of Lowry Properties. Motherfucker. He staggered back to his car with the intention of shacking in there for the night and figuring something out tomorrow. He climbed in and locked the doors. The night had grown chilly. He started the car and put the heat on, eased the seat back as far as it went and fell immediately to sleep.

"It's been a long time, Doc. Where you been?"

"You know how things go, Garrett. Sometimes you get wrapped up in other projects."

Damian took a long drag on his cigarette. "We can start now that Archie has arrived."

Janine took a seat. Garrett flipped the chair and sat with his chest against the back rest. There were some empty chairs, but Archie knew they wouldn't be filled tonight. It was just the four of them.

The room remained a variation of Virgil's study. He wondered if Virgil himself intended on making an appearance.

"You're being awfully quiet." Damian said.

"It took me a lot of training to tolerate sitting quietly with others. To control my nerves enough not to blurt things out. You could always tell the fucking narcissist in a group; they dominated from the opening bell."

Garrett laughed out loud. "You're calling Father Damian a narcissist? That's rich. He's selfless as they come."

"I wasn't calling him a narcissist, you prat. Don't try to stir things up with someone I admire."

"Fair to say your enamor for his character pushed you towards psychiatry, isn't it." Garrett said.

"Really?" Damian asked, sitting back and lacing his hands behind his head.

"I was partial to two psychiatrists of stage and screen and you were one. The other was Sidney Freedman from M*A*S*H."

"I'm flattered."

"You got one of those for me?" He pointed to the priest's cigarette.

"You haven't smoked in years, why start again?"

"What difference can it make?" He took the Camel and lit up. The experience so vivid, he could feel the long-forgotten sensation of smoke filling his lungs, the exhale like the dropping of a heavy bag that's been digging into your shoulder. "I miss these bad boys."

"I didn't know you smoked."

"There's a lot I never told you, Janine. I mean, it wasn't a normal relationship."

Janine shrunk at that comment. He immediately regretted it. "I'm sorry. I didn't mean it to come out that way. You know how much you meant to me."

Damian stood and leaned against the wall. "We're all a little worried about the direction this (he searched for a word with his hand) Morgenstern affair is taking. You're quickly losing control; this could turn out very badly for you."

"Yeah? Thanks for the clarification. You got any more brilliant insights or suggestions?"

"Let it go." Janine and Garrett spoke at once. They smiled at each other.

That annoyed Wendt. Their shared intimacy made him feel left out. The anger took full hold of him. "Can't do that. Too far in." He rocked in his chair, holding the cigarette in a familiar pose he struck when he smoked on a regular basis. "I have to find out why Virgil did what he did. I know he wanted me to pursue this until the end. Say, are you able to bring Virgil here?"

Damian spoke. "No. It doesn't work that way. You don't have a conflict with him."

"That's great. Again, thanks for the fucking help."

Damian ignored that. "While you're farting around with this Virgil thing, you're forgetting what you're forgetting."

"What kind of cryptic fuck all statement is that, Damian?"

"He means that you're letting other shit slide." Garrett said.

"My office was taken away from me."

"Seems like a repeating theme."

"That's a low blow, Padre. That's a fucking cheap ass shot. You have no idea how things turned out in Boston. None of you were around or stayed around (he glared at Janine) when that happened."

"But you were," Damian said, "You know how it went down. Stop wasting time on issues you can't solve and focus on those things you can fix. You can still be a help to your patients who live. Don't forget them."

"Another great piece of advice. You're just full of them tonight, ain'tcha?" He jabbed his cigarette in the man's direction.

Damian stubbed out his own Camel on licked palm. "I think we're done here. Don't forget what we discussed. Good session, guys."

"Where the fuck are you going?" He said. They all exited before he could react, his movements half the pace of theirs. Archie stood and felt the intruding urge to void his bladder.

He awoke with pain in his groin, the sound of rain on his car's roof. The windows were steamed on the inside, blackness pressing down from outside. He pulled the seat to its upright position. His mouth was dry. A knock on the driver's side window scared the living shit out of him. He lowered the window. The rain splattered his left arm; a flashlight blinded Archie.

"I'm going to have to ask you to turn the engine off and step out of the car, sir."

That muted Archie's screaming bladder. He held up a hand to block the light and made out a belt, badge and hat. "What's the problem, officer?"

"Please turn off the engine and step out of the car."

Archie complied and stood in the pouring rain.

"Sir, I need you to blow into this device here so I can get a read on your blood alcohol level."

"Why? I wasn't driving, I was sleeping."

"Sir, please blow into this breathalyzer."

"And if I refuse?"

"Then I have to place you under arrest for suspicion of operating a motor vehicle under the influence and take you into custody."

"This is bullshit. I wasn't driving and I won't blow into your device."

"Please turn around and face the car, sir, put your hands behind your back." Archie turned and felt cuffs being put around his wrists for the first time in his life. He was glad that it was dark and raining, no one around to witness this. The cop led Archie to the squad car. Fear that he hadn't locked the Beemer kept a lid on a deeper unease - the emotional residue from the dream nagging him that he'd forgotten to do something important.

A rchie slept the rest of the night, the only occupant in the police station's small holding cell. In the morning, hungover and irritable, he stood and spoke through the bars.

"This is bullshit, Lynne, and you know it."

"Pipe down, Wendt."

"This is harassment, plain and simple."

"You'll have plenty of time to tell it to the judge."

"I'd like to make a phone call," Archie said.

Lynne ignored him.

"It's my right to make a phone call."

Lynne slowly looked up, his face sans emotion. "It won't be necessary for you to make a phone call."

"What the fuck that does that mean? You have to—-"

Howard Rogoff walked into the station just then.

Archie breathed a sigh of relief. "Thank God you're here."

"Mornin', Horace."

"Good morning to you, Doctor. I don't know why you want to bail this piece of shit out, but you must have your reasons."

"Is that not prejudicial? Can you see how this is just fucking harassment?"

Rogoff held up a hand and offered a reassuring nod of his head, stepped up to the desk and pulled cash out of his pocket. Lynne wrote up a receipt then came over and unlocked the cell door.

"Thank you. You've been tremendous. I know you can't exercise any personal judgment, what with your low IQ and lack of education, but you know I wasn't driving."

"That's enough, Wendt, or I'll re-arrest you for being an asshole."

Before Archie could respond, Rogoff pushed him out of the station.

"What's the matter with you? Arguing with the chief of police in his own station house? How far do you think that will take you? C'mon, you're smarter than that. And why were you sitting in your car with the engine on, anyway? You should have come to my house and slept it off."

"Shit, I didn't want to disturb you. I tried to get a hotel room and they turned me away."

"Which hotel?"

"The Continental."

Howard snorted. "It's owned by Katherine Morgenstern."

"I learned. So I crashed in my car. For crissakes I was drunk; it's not like I was thinking clearly."

"The car was running?"

"Of course the car was running; I didn't want to freeze. But that corrupt bastard knows I wasn't driving. He's just looking for a reason to harass me."

Howard stopped and put a hand on Archie. "Of course he's looking for a reason to harass you and you foolishly obliged him. You better wise up quickly; these are dangerous people you're tangling with."

"Can't you see that they're deliberately setting me up? First the PI is brought in from Boston. Then your beloved chief shuts down my office due to vague complaints to the Ohio Board of Medicine. Now a police officer just happens to be at my car at 2 AM after I was drinking in the Club. This whole thing is a sham meant to intimidate me into returning the five mil."

"They didn't force you to get blitzed, did they? They didn't force you to take the idiotic step of sleeping off a drunk in your car with the engine running. You did those things yourself. By the way, you owe me three grand."

"The money isn't an issue. Come with me to the bank and I'll get you your three grand."

They walked down the street to the bank. It would open in another ten minutes.

"You might think about reaching out to Katherine. She's a reasonable woman," Howard offered.

"What might I be reaching out to say?"

"Truce. Mea Culpa. I give up. Anything that would lead to a compromise and allows the family to save face."

"I'm not going to do that. I'm still in the right." Archie said.

Howard shook his head. "You're stubborn as a mule. Even if you are in the right, which is debatable, are you really going to ride self-righteousness into the ground?"

Archie folded his arms.

"Like I said, stubborn as a mule. I don't want to wait here; I'm going home. Why don't you get your money, collect yourself, and when you're seeing straight again, come to my house. You're welcome to stay with me."

Archie grunted in lieu of answering.

Time seemed to be growing short. Archie might not be able to get the answers he wanted before the hammer fell. The way things were going in Harding he didn't rule out the townsfolk picking up pitchforks and torches and heading his way.

Perhaps it was paranoia or the early stages of the DT's, but he felt eyes on him everywhere he went - in the bank, on the street. Whispers exchanged as he passed by. Having dealt with thousands of paranoid patients he recalled one of his favorite maxims - it's not paranoia if they're really after you. He chuckled to himself, then realized that's the second sign of going insane.

He drove to Rogoff's house, parked and locked his BMW, now mobile home and office. He walked up to the door and knocked.

"Look who's here? The next mayor of Harding himself."

"Can I come in Howard or do I have to tempt fate and have someone take a shot at me from here?"

Howard stepped aside. "Being a little melodramatic, aren't we?"

"You might think so. But no. Someone or some people have already tried twice to take my life. They were half-hearted, but they scared the shit out of me, none-the-less."

They sat in the den as Archie filled the older psychiatrist in on the two attempts on his life. "Both car related, come to think of it. Not terribly creative."

"Who do you suspect is behind it?"

"My first thoughts were of Luke."

"Sure. He's got some knucklehead moves in his past. Avoided prison time by the good graces of daddy's deep pockets. But murder? Why would he do that?"

"He was cut out from the will. Received only a pittance. If I croak, the money gets returned to the trust. Maybe he thinks he can work on Mommy to get him more. She thought it pretty unfair that I got that money, too."

"You hinted at some others. Who else do you think might be after you?"

He wasn't ready to open up about Rose. "I don't know; I'm not sure who I can trust." Archie went over to the side board and mixed himself a little cocktail to take the edge off of the hangover. "This small town shit is getting to me. Everybody's in everybody's grill here."

"Small town living can take some getting used to. Oh, before I forget, Archie, I have a message for you." Howard stood and walked out of the room. He came back looking at a pad of paper. "It's from a Mrs. Stringer; she sounded distressed. Here's her number."

"Shit. I forgot about her message. Goddammit. Can I use your phone?"

"Of course."

Archie took a sip of his drink then dialed. A soft voice answered, "Hello."

"Mrs. Stringer, it's Dr. Wendt. I'm sorry I haven't gotten back to you sooner."

"Yes. Me, too. My husband tried to take his own life."

Archie's body went cold. "Where is he now? Is he stable?"

"He's in the hospital." She sounded businesslike with an unmistakable edge of anger.

"General hospital or psychiatric, Mrs. Stringer?"

"Psychiatric."

Archie exhaled - in the psych hospital meant out of the woods medically.

"I know this is a difficult question, but how did he get to the hospital?"

"I can't really talk now. Thank you for calling." She hung up.

Archie did likewise and put his head in his hands. "Oh shit. That's what's been eating at me. I hadn't returned her call." He got up and paced restively. "Goddammit, I'm losing it."

"What happened, Archie?"

"Surgeon, can no longer operate, thought his life was over. He attempted suicide and is in a psych hospital. Wife didn't give me a lot of information."

"He'll be at St. Anthony's," Howard said.

"I have to go. I have to."

Howard took off his robe and put a coat on over his ragged undershirt. He kicked off his Homers and laced up some boots.

"What are you doing?" Archie asked.

"I'm going with you, what the hell does it look like?"

"I can't ask you to do that."

"You didn't, you blockhead. I'm going because you need me. For emotional support, but more importantly to get you in there. You can't just go in there and barge your way onto the unit. But, they see you with me and the waters will part as if before Moses."

St. Anthony's, a small community hospital, was located just outside of Harding. It serviced several of the neighboring towns. It had the decor of the small Catholic hospital in which Archie had moonlighted during residency - lots of saints and Jesus's peppering the halls in picture and statue form. Archie noted an elaborate dedication plaque bearing the Lowry name.

Lots of people nodded or smiled at Howard. He led Archie through the lobby to the elevators and they rode up a couple of flights accompanied by the Muzak version of a Fleetwood Mac song; it didn't seem possible, but it was worse than the original. The locked psychiatric unit sat on the top floor of the hospital. There was an intercom outside the windowless door.

"Hello, it's Dr. Rogoff—-."

Before he finished his sentence the door buzzed. He looked over at Archie, let loose a thousand watt grin, and held the door open. As they walked onto the unit Archie played out scenarios in his head of how it would go with Stringer. Would the surgeon be pissed off, despondent, catatonic? He felt more raw than after Virgil's hanging. Howard peeled off to the nurses' station with a nod of his head and left Archie to consult the board to find Stringer's room. He needn't have bothered - approaching the unit's common area he heard a loud boisterous voice at one of the tables.

"So then he says, because this is a hardware store." Other patients laughed at Stringer's delivered punchline. Before he launched into another joke he spotted Archie.

"Dr. Wendt. What a pleasant surprise." He stood and walked towards the surprised psychiatrist. Stringer turned to the group in the common area. "This is the guy I see." He turned back to Wendt. "How did you know I was here?"

"Is there somewhere we can talk?" Archie asked.

"My room is over here." They stepped into the small single. Stringer offered Archie the lone chair and he sat on the bed.

"Your wife called me. I hope you don't mind me coming to see you."

"No, on the contrary, I'm grateful for the visit. In fact, I'm glad to see you because I feel like I owe you an apology."

"You owe me an apology?"

"Yeah, because I know that you were trying to keep me from inflicting anguish on my family, but I was so lost in despair and I couldn't hear you. I felt... I felt empty, like nothing mattered and nothing could ever get better. I left your office and continued my preparations for getting my affairs in order. And then I carried it out."

"What happened? How come you weren't successful?" Archie asked.

"Well, I told my wife that I was going to a doctor's appointment, didn't specify where. I left the house and drove about twenty minutes south. See, I didn't want my wife or my kids to find me, you understand? During the drive my mind was amazingly clear with no regrets, only resolution. When I reached a secluded area I put the gun in my mouth angling the barrel as much as I could towards the medulla. Can't be a vegetable, you know? And I didn't hesitate, I pulled the trigger right away, so I couldn't vacillate and change my mind. And then…"

"What?" Archie said, louder than he intended.

"Nothing happened."

Stringer got very animated, stood up. "The gun misfired. It misfired! I checked the damn thing when I bought it, the guy at the sporting goods store demonstrated how it worked. I was meticulous in my preparation. I mean, I broke it down, oiled it, rebuilt it, and loaded it right." He put his hands up in the air. "It just misfired."

Stringer sat back down.

"Well, Dr. Wendt, something about that misfiring broke the spell I was in. Up to that moment I hadn't cried. Not when I was initially diagnosed with the movement disorder, not when it cost me my job, not even when I made the decision to kill myself. But now, with the fucking misfire I started crying. And I'm not talking about silent body shakes, I'm

142

talking about a sob that would put a five-year-old to shame. I couldn't stop the tears from coming. The sheer enormity of my decision to kill myself repeatedly crashed down on me. I threw the gun out of the window as far as I could - as if having it near me was offensive.

"And just like that all my desire to die vanished. All my desire to live, to be a husband, a father, a *man*, (he banged his chest with a fist) came back to me in a flash. I drove my car here and checked myself into the hospital. I called my wife. When she came I told her everything, just like I'm telling you. We cried together; she was grateful I had the good sense to come here. It was as if I needed the attempt to cure me of the need to make an attempt. If that makes any sense."

"I understand what you mean." Wendt said. "What happens now?"

"Now? I go on. I find other ways to occupy my time. I can't operate any more, but there are plenty of things that I can do. In fact, the ideas coming into my head astound me for the variety and richness of options. I can't believe how trapped I felt; it's not possible for me to get into that mind set now. Is that crazy?"

"No, it isn't crazy. I'm happy for you, Paul, go with the positive feeling. Don't lose respect for the depression, though. It's like having a tiger by the tail - you lose respect for it and it can turn around and bite you."

"I appreciate that, Dr. Wendt. What can I say? I'll do what I need to do. If you're amenable to continuing to treat me, that would be great."

It was Archie's turn to laugh. "Right now my practice is in a state of flux. But if you permit, I can introduce you to Dr. Rogoff who's at the nurse's station right now and you can see if he's a good fit. He's covering my patients for the time being."

"You okay?"

"Kind of you to ask. I'm better now that I'm seeing you doing better, that's for sure."

"Just so you know, Dr. Wendt, there's nothing you could have said that would have altered my course. If a man doesn't want treatment, there isn't much you can do to persuade him."

"That's not easy to swallow sometimes."

"I'll bet." He stood. "Thanks for coming to see me, Dr. Wendt."

"Archie."

"Thanks for coming, Archie." They shook hands.

"I feel unbelievably buoyed. Like I had a breakthrough and it wasn't even me that had the breakthrough, but Stringer."

Archie and Howard walked to the parking lot. "So he gave you absolution. How fitting."

"Absolution? Oh, because we were in a Catholic hospital with all the Jesus motifs, that your angle?"

Howard tapped his nose and smiled.

"I don't know about absolution, you old dog, and thank you by the way, for getting me in there. I needed that."

"Archie, please take this in the spirit in which it is offered. You can't take your work that personally. You're too fucking old to be so heavily influenced by your patient's moodish vicissitudes."

"Moodish? I'm pretty sure that's not a word."

Howard shrugged. "I'm an old man. I'm entitled to manipulate the language to suit my purpose. And you got my meaning."

"You're right, I've always been overly invested in the success or failure of my patients; it was my undoing in Boston."

Howard got into the driver's side of his Volvo. He put the key in the ignition, but didn't start the engine; he looked over at Archie who buckled his seatbelt.

"What? You want me to open up about what happened in Boston?"

"I do. I think you need to unburden yourself." Howard solicited.

"No way, Father Rogoff, no matter how close we are to a Catholic institution, I'm not ready to confess that sin." Déjà vu washed over Archie as he made the connection to his dream.

Rogoff started the car. "Okay, my son, when you're ready I'll hear that confession. It will be good for you. In the meantime, are you going to take me up on my offer to put you up for a while?"

"I won't be a burden?"

"You'll most definitely be a burden, but that's beside the point. I weighed the pros and cons in my head and decided that I would prefer knowing you were in a safe place and have to tolerate said burden." He grinned.

"Thanks. I don't know how I can repay you, but I'll come up with something."

"A very expensive bottle of scotch, no doubt. And information, like, what's going on with you and Rose Morgenstern?"

"Don't ask."

"I just did."

"I like her, actually, but I also have reason to suspect that she is trying to kill me." Archie said.

"Again with the paranoia?"

"I met with Sheriff Hidalgo. He ran down the plate of the person who tried to run me over and it's registered to Rose. He also told me that Rose was charged with assault on a boyfriend."

"That's a far cry from trying to kill someone," Howard said.

"She's got five million reasons to kill me; maybe sleeping with me was a way to get inside information on me and throw suspicion off her."

"Keep talking like that and I'll take you back to the psych ward and have you committed."

"So I'm just paranoid, am I? Hidalgo didn't think it so far-fetched." Archie whined.

"Yeah, well it's the worst kept secret in town that the sheriff nurtures an intense love for Rose."

"That I didn't know. But I got bigger problems than Rose. The whole town seems to be turning against me."

"Let's stop in at the President's Club and get a drink. We'll be able to get the town's scuttlebutt from there."

"That's your font of information?" Archie said.

"Among others."

"Like the barber."

"Yes, but I don't like to give up my sources."

Archie shook his head. "I don't know how you can tolerate this small-town crap. It's enough to drive me back to the big, anonymous city."

"That's just it, isn't it? The big, impersonal city where everyone treats you with a cold shoulder."

"At least there's anonymity."

"Did you have anonymity in Boston?" Howard asked.

"I had notoriety, which is worse than anonymity. Maybe I need to go to a big city where they don't speak English, at least then I won't understand the gossip about me."

They got to The Presidents, walked in and sat at the bar. Mike sidled up, towel on his shoulder and smile on his face.

"What will it be, Docs? You know, two psychiatrists walk into a bar should be the start of a joke, but I'll be damned if I can come up with one."

"You're hilarious, Mike, why don't you just give us two Dewar's?" Archie said, then to Howard: "It's probably all Dewar's with this guy, anyway."

"I heard that, you lousy prick. You saying I replace high end scotch with well liquor to save some money and scam my customers?" Mike said, back to them as he poured their drinks.

"That's exactly what I'm saying, you cheap fucker."

"So, this is where you let out all your aggression." Howard said. "I wondered. Cause I knew it had to be somewhere and I hadn't heard of any serial killings around here. But on Mike? C'mon, that's not very sporting."

"Et tu, Dr. Rogoff? Tsk, tsk, tsk."

Howard grinned and put a twenty on the bar. Mike picked it up and gestured as if to say 'all for me'?

"We would like some of your best bartender gossip. Namely, what's the latest scuttlebutt on the town's collective cold shoulder towards young Archie here?"

He pocketed the Jackson. "You mean besides the accepted notion that Archie put a voodoo mind control hex on Virgil that caused him to off himself in the prime of his hoary years and that he snaked several million from the family coffers to boot?"

"Yes, besides that," Archie said in between generous sips of his drink.

"Also, that you're taking advantage of his lovely daughter, Rose, after plundering the proprietress of the local B&B. Though the motives there are not as yet apparent to the hoi polloi. I mean, apart from the trim, that is."

"Well worth the sawbuck." Howard said.

"A twenty is not a sawbuck. A ten is." Archie pointed out.

"No, a ten is a fin."

"No, a fin is a five dollar bill."

"You're wrong. Mike?"

"Sorry, Dr. Rogoff. Arch is right on this one. Fin is five, sawbuck is ten."

"So, what's a twenty?"

"A blowjob, if you're not too picky about the practitioner's oral hygiene." An old regular called out from the other side of the bar; everyone had a good chuckle.

"The whole town thinks I'm that Svengali character. What a cluster."

Mike laid a hand on Archie's arm. "For what it's worth, Doc, I know you didn't do any of those things. I'm sure in the end you'll get it straightened out. Unfortunately the truth isn't always as compelling as a good rumor, but at least you'll know, right?"

"For a lowlife, worthless barkeep, Mike, you're pretty smart, you know that?"

"That's awfully shitty and kind of you, Archie."

"Now that the lovefest is over, pour us another, will ya?" Howard interjected.

They drank another, this time with Mike. Howard swallowed his scotch and elbowed Archie. "What are you going to do next?"

"Get a good night's rest at Casa Rogoff and in the morning reach out to Katherine Morgenstern and beg her to call off the dogs. If not, there's always Mexico." He lifted his empty glass to Mike. "One more for the road, if you will, Señor Mike."

CHAPTER 32

Archie fidgeted, his insides roiling with opposing emotions. Swallowing his pride had never been easy; his ego threatened to blow the whole deal. He knew it to be the prudent move so he cursed internally and rang the doorbell. Better than a phone call, a personal visit demonstrated humility and contrition. He hoped. A few minutes passed with no answer. Archie rang again and peered through the windows. Worthless. He couldn't see beyond his own reflection. He turned to leave when the door opened. Luke stood in the doorway dressed in an OSU warmup suit that looked like he hadn't taken it off in several weeks. The smell of a fraternity hung on him - stale beer and weed. He regarded Archie with a scowl. "The fuck you want?"

"Good morning, Luke, I'm sorry to bother you. Wanted to see if your mother was available."

"Not for a piece of shit like you."

"Listen, I'm sorry if we got off on the wrong foot. I'd like to apologize to you for that. Would it be possible to speak with your mother?"

"She doesn't want to see you for any reason."

Archie decided not to press his luck. "I understand. Please tell her that I came here in good faith to resolve our issue."

"Whatever." Luke slammed the door.

He walked to his car surmising that Katherine made good on her threat to fire Linda. Archie opened the car door and sat, thinking about his next move. A car sped down the street and took the turn onto the Morgenstern driveway like it rode on rails. It pulled right behind him, screeching to a halt inches from his bumper. A red Camaro, license plate ARS 348. Body readied for fight or flight, Archie got out of the car in time to see Rose disembarking with the same velocity she drove.

"Hey, stranger," she said. "Haven't heard from you since our roll in the hay. I have to say, I'm a little hurt."

His heart still racing, blood cold, Archie spat out: "You drive like a fucking teenager who just got her license."

The comment chased Rose's smile from her face like pigeons scattering from a dog. "Whoa. Why the bile?"

"You scared the living shit out of me."

"What are you, a pussy?" Rose challenged.

"Pussy? Because I don't drive like a maniac? You know, there are those who say that driving is a projective test, a setting where one's true character is expressed. How they drive, respond to other drivers, is who they really are, stripped of their defenses."

"Thanks for the lesson, Professor Freud. You going to tell me why you haven't called me or lecture me on my driving habits?"

He took a deep breath, like before plunging into a cold pool. "Rose, I'm sorry, but things are a little crazy in my life right now. I don't know who I can trust."

"What the hell are you talking about?"

"A lot of things are happening to me right now and I'm not sure I'm making the best decisions; I just think it's best if I withdraw and take care of myself."

"Didn't have a problem making decisions the other night, didja?"

"C'mon. That's not fair."

"You know what's not fair? That you come on strong then back away. I'm not a one night stand."

"I'm just asking for some space." And to not get killed, he finished in his head.

She put up her hands in surrender mode. "Okay. Space? You got it, buddy." She turned around and got back in her car, put the window down. "Watch how careful I am." Rose elaborately put on her seatbelt and arranged her hands on the 10 and 2 positions of the wheel. She theatrically checked her mirrors and pulled out slowly, braking every few feet. When her car was clear of his she put it in neutral, gunned the engine then put it in drive. The tires squealed against the pavement of the driveway as she shot up its length towards the separate carriage house in the back.

Archie contemplated the error of his approach while admitting to himself a modicum of success - at least she hadn't run him over.

———— ✦ ✦✦✦✦ ✦ ————

Archibald Wendt hated free time. An idle mind is the devil's playground and all that. Time gave him a practicum on Einstein's theories. Each minute dragged on for eternity as he ached to be busy. He was pulling his hair out, a new wrinkle in his compulsive repertoire.

In one fell swoop Katherine Morgenstern eliminated his practice. He remained incredulous to the insanity of the situation, though a small part of him recognized he could end it all by relinquishing the money, tucking tail, and finding a new place to ply his trade. That would suffice in undoing the damage done. *But didn't I just try that? I went to Katherine in good faith to apologize and that little shit, Luke, kept me from my goal. Well, you took his rebuff lying down. You could be more assertive: give the money back through that expurgated condom, Daugherty.*

Archie crumpled a napkin ferociously.

Be honest with yourself. You didn't want to swallow your pride so you weren't really going to grovel to that bitch.

On an on it went, Archie ruminating over peeled layers of motivation, trying to find a way past his stubbornness. Like the scene from the Princess Bride where Wallace Shawn's Vizzini logics himself into a quick death by poisoning. The irony, of course, that all Vizzini's logic was for naught; he was screwed from the moment he sat down and tried to outsmart the Dread Pirate Westley.

Maybe I'm as screwed as Vizzini. Destined for shit the moment Virgil decided to seek me out. Or maybe the moment I took the advice to move to Harding under the auspices of Howard Rogoff. Or maybe I was screwed when I decided to go into psychiatry.

And on and on and…

"Oh, fuck it!" Archie yelled.

The bar came to a comical halt all eyes fixed on Archie. He looked quite mad, hair standing on end, two day facial growth, hunched over his drink.

"Jesus, Doc, you keep talking to yourself and you're going to make me cut you off," Mike whispered.

"Sorry, Mike." He spoke up and scanned the whole room. "Sorry, everyone. Just a little distraught."

The bar returned to its normal hum. Except for one man who stood with his beer and walked over to the bar stool next to Archie.

"Let me buy a drink for a mindfucker who's morphed into an extortion artist. And a defiler of heiresses to boot."

Wendt didn't look over at Cutter. "Why can't you just fuck off, huh? Go... go fuck a stray dog, do some fucking thing. Just leave me alone."

"Leave you alone? My meal ticket? Never. You're on a roll. Can't say as I didn't see this one coming and even warned you, if you remember." Cutter held up his near empty mug to Mike. "Another, please?" He sat down to Wendt's right. He attempted to put his arm around Archie's shoulder, but was met with a violent effort to shrug it off. "Hey, calm down there, Doc. Just relax. I'm here on a mercy mission. See, I realize that you're all alone here in this little burgh and what you need is an advocate, someone who can help you navigate these waters and get you back to safe harbor, if you'll allow me to stay in the maritime motif."

Archie didn't respond. He pulled away so his back faced the investigator. The man didn't seem to mind; he went on with his proposition.

"Everyone needs good PR. Way I see it, you got to get your message out there. Right now there is just the one theme, which is that you're a piece of shit who bamboozled helpless rich folks out of their hard stolen money." He laughed. "That's where I come in, good Dr. Wendt, where I rescue your reputation and make things right.

"For an appropriate fee."

Archie turned abruptly back to Cutter. "A fee? Are you for real? I pay you to undo the shit you are undoubtedly behind?"

"Your thinking is very narrow on this; I'm not 'behind' anything. Besides, what's done is done. You need to think about what you can do now to improve your position."

"Mike, I need another. This fucking guy's pretzel logic has me tied in knots." He turned to Cutter. "If you'll allow me to stay in the snack food motif."

Mike came over, but held up the pour. "Don't you think you've had enough?"

"No. Clearly dealing with this guy requires being more fucked up just to understand him. Up is down, black is white, we're through the looking glass, blah, blah, blah. Just pour me a goddamned double."

"Doc, you just give it some thought." Cutter patted Wendt's shoulder. "I want a fifteen percent cut of your money. For that all your troubles will go away."

"I can't even be angry. Your bullshit is so far afield I can't even respond. You, sir, have paralyzed me with your deceitfulness and putrescence and that's saying something given the degree of psychopathology I myself have attended to."

"Dr. Wendt, you have a phone call," Mike called.

"Think about it, Doc." Cutter walked away. Wendt stood unsteadily, righted himself and moved down the bar to the phone. He held the receiver and watched the investigator walk out. He cleared his throat, turned to the phone.

"Wendt, here."

"Mr. Wendt, I have a message from Mrs. Katherine Morgenstern." Sounded like someone working to deepen their voice.

"Who is this?"

"Mrs. Morgenstern has said that she will accept you if you call on her this evening. At nine."

Archie looked at his wrist for several seconds before realizing he wasn't wearing a watch.

"Nine o' clock. Okay, I'll be there." The line went dead; he looked at the receiver then hung up.

"Mike!" he yelled.

"What!" Mike yelled back standing not three feet from him.

"Oh shit, didn't see you there. What time is it?"

"It's a quarter to eight."

"That leaves me enough time for at least three drinks before I have to go over there." Archie absently said to himself loud enough for all to hear.

"To go over where?" Mike asked.

"Hizzoner's wife."

"Who?"

"Katherine Morgenstern."

"You're going over there shit-faced? That's a great plan. Should go a long way to undoing the damage you've done." Mike tsked. "You're being a knucklehead. Enough with the booze, Archie, let me get you some coffee."

Wendt groaned, his head falling to the bar. "Coffee'll just make me an agitated drunk. Give me a watered down Bloody Mary; that should do the trick."

Mike shook his head in amazement and got out the mix. He planned on watering it down to its virgin roots. Maybe there was enough time to sober Archie up if he walked there.

In the end, Mike's threat of police involvement did the trick and Archie agreed to walk to the Morgenstern estate. It was an empty threat, though, because Mike, Harding's previous sheriff, held a particular disdain for its police chief. But he knew dropping Lynne's name would get the job done; Wendt would have eaten his own foot to avoid police entanglement.

The walk sobered Archie just enough to convince himself he was completely sober. A dangerous state. Filled with renewed confidence that he could set things right, he walked up to the door and rang the bell.

No one came to the door, but he thought he heard someone invite him in. He tried the door and found it unlocked. The place felt deserted - that hard to explain feeling no one's home.

"Hello?" Archie called out as he took some tentative steps inside. "Mrs. Morgenstern? It's Archibald Wendt. Hello?" He felt like an idiot. In for a penny, he thought, and swayed towards the kitchen. The place looked a lot less put together than when he was here last. His footfalls sounded like hammers to his ears and it dawned on him that in this fucked up town any second the state troopers, coupled with SWAT no doubt, would take him down for breaking and entering. Chuckling out loud he continued his search. He looked up the stairs and decided that was verboten. He turned to his right and looked down a long hall that culminated in the back of the kitchen, if memory served.

He walked with more confidence. "Mrs. Morgenstern? Katherine?"

Turned out she was in the kitchen after all. He noticed her expensive shoes protruding from behind the center island. On the floor.

Oh shit. Peering around the corner slowly, as if cautious movements could possibly alter the landscape, he saw the rest of her body lying on the floor in an unnatural position. Next to her bloodied and matted hair sat a copper frying pan, undoubtedly plucked from the hooks above the island. *Now* he was sober. Instincts took over and he went over to the body, kneeled and felt for a pulse in her carotid artery.

"Shit. Oh, shit. I am fucked." In an instant he got a feel for the whole plan. Call Wendt, get him over there just as you bump off the executor of the vast Morgenstern estate and the crooked eye of the cops will fall conveniently on the already in the crosshair's psychiatrist.

He briefly contemplated the need to wipe down her neck to eliminate prints when the insanity of it all made him stop. He knew he should just get the hell out of there and dissemble later, if necessary.

Archie stood and looked down at the body. Whatever kind of woman she was, she didn't deserve to go this way. Anger welled up inside him as he contemplated someone getting away with this. He made the sign of the cross, something he hadn't done for many years, and walked quickly out.

He passed the stairs, and made for the front door when something in his periphery caught his eye and made him stop - light coming from the far end of the living room. He looked over and saw Virgil's mighty oak door open. The study called out to him, a siren song crooning of Virgil's inner sanctum and the answers contained within. Shit he would love to get in there and look around.

Standing perfectly still he willed his ears to perform superhumanly. No sounds. He made a quick decision. Brisk paces to the open oak door and into the study.

It looked as if someone had done some searching in here. He walked over to the desk and opened drawers. Nothing. Nothing. His mind wouldn't focus and his hands fumbled like he wore invisible mittens. He scanned the shelves. Books, books. There! Notebooks, binders. Archie pulled some out; some looked like journals, but he couldn't be sure. Then he saw a yearbook. Old. Guernsey High School. He opened it to M and found Virgil. His heart raced and his eyes darted from the pages to the study door and back, like the first time snoop he was. He leafed through it. On the back page was the only handwriting in the entire thing. "You'll always be mine. Love, Nina." Nina. Couldn't the bitch put her last name? He started with the seniors. Scanning, scanning. There. Nina Patterson. Cute. He replaced the yearbook. Kept looking.

Back to the binders. Business notes. Then, at the end, correspondence.

From the days of patience, when people relished the process of writing and awaiting responses. Lots of letters from one person, Fred Montrose, Londonderry, Ohio. He went back to the yearbook and leafed through it to the M's again. There, right fucking next to Virgil. He put the yearbook back and made to pull another binder when he heard a noise down the hall.

"Mom? Why is the front door open?" Rose. Someone had planned this to a T.

He tiptoed his way to the door and peered out. She locked the front door and walked down the hall in the direction of the kitchen. "Rose!"

She started. "Holy shit, Archie, you scared the hell out of me. What the are you doing here?"

His heart ached for her at the enormity of the situation. He jogged the length of the living room to block her path to the kitchen. "Rose, I don't know how to tell you this, but someone has murdered your mother."

She went white. "What. No, I just spoke to her a few minutes ago. What? I got to go talk to her about something." In the distance, sirens could be heard.

He grabbed her arms. "Rose, focus, listen to me. Someone called me and told me to come over here, that your mother was willing to listen to me so I could apologize and make things right. When I got here, I found her murdered, hit in the head with a pan. I checked her pulse myself."

"Archie, I don't understand what you're saying." She grimaced, "And your breath stinks of alcohol. I gotta go find my mother."

They went in opposite directions and he called out to her from the front door.

"Please remember what I'm telling you. I didn't do murder your mother." Archie opened the door and listened: sirens approaching, but still afar. He closed the door and ran away from the sound, grateful he was on foot. Somehow it felt more appropriate.

On the run for real now. The smell of rotting wet leaves followed his flight. The odor of decay. *What the fuck am I going to do now?* He didn't even feel safe on the sidewalks. Too exposed. He had to hightail it to Howard's house, collect his belongings and get the fuck out of Harding. He certainly didn't trust anyone to believe in his innocence. This would cement his status as a master con artist and now murderer. Archie could count on Cutter to provide the detailed background onto which they could contextualize all the recent events. No way he'd get a fair hearing here. Running was the right decision.

His mind worked feverishly. Out of the corner of his eye he saw a figure duck behind a tree. He did a double take and ran towards the tree, but whoever it was darted off behind a house.

Archie stopped abruptly. Breathing heavy he put head between his knees. How many movies had he seen where the protagonist makes the exact wrong move, running when he should stay? What real evidence did they have on me? Maybe if I get through the initial questioning they won't have enough evidence to formally arrest me. Then I can work on getting a bead on what the next move should be.

He decided he would do the opposite of his first instincts. He began running again, this time in the direction of the police station, convinced all the while that the figure he had just chased belonged to Garrett.

The lights were on, but nobody was home. He couldn't believe his fucking luck. Door to a goddamned police station locked. Who ever heard? Archie looked around and saw no police cars.

"If I had a busted tail light the whole fucking force would be on my ass." He said aloud, then realized the reason for the deserted station - they were hauling ass for the Morgenstern estate. Idiot.

He stood and rubbed his jaw. The sheriff, that was the ticket. But where was the sheriff department? He spotted a gas station and jogged over there.

The attendant looked him over as Archie, sweaty and red faced, trotted up and asked for directions. "The sheriff's got his station at the edge of town. Just drive straight on High street until you come to a T. If you keep driving you'll plum go right into the waiting area."

Archie thanked him and offered him a fiver. The man looked at Archie funny, shrugged, and took the money.

The walk took him about twenty minutes during which he rehearsed his story. A patrol car was parked out front and the building was lit. His heart raced with his approach. Rubber meets the road time. He put a hand on his chest to steady himself, took a deep breath and went in.

The building had a new construction smell. Didn't have the Hill Street Blues rugged feel. Freshly carpeted, painted, and scrubbed clean. Hidalgo sat in an office behind an unmanned tall desk. He watched Archie walk in with an expectant look.

"Can I speak with you, sheriff?"

Hidalgo motioned Archie in. He crossed a hinged half door and sat down in the office opposite the big man.

"I'm going to tell you a story. Please let me finish the whole thing, then tell me what you think I should do." To his credit Archie relayed fairly precisely the events of the previous twenty-four hours including the request to meet with Katherine Morgenstern, his run-in with Luke, the call to get him to the Morgenstern home, and what he found there. He included his brief encounter with Rose and even the fact that he'd been drinking.

"I didn't drive, though. I walked over to the Morgenstern's and then here. Mike can vouch for me on that."

"I believe you about the walking; you look like you've sweat out three liters of booze, and you smell like a combination of stale beer, sweat, and the outdoors." Hidalgo said.

"I went first to the police station; nobody there. That's why I came here."

"The reason no police at the station house is they were called to check on a possible homicide at the Morgenstern home."

"I figured as much. How come you didn't respond?"

"Now you're asking political questions about the division of law enforcement labor here in Harding. I don't think that's relevant to the story you just told me." Hidalgo said.

"Fair enough. How about this, when did the call come in about a possible homicide?"

"Maybe half hour ago. You'd have to check with the dispatcher for a precise time."

"Is that something you can do?" Archie said.

"It is. What are you thinking?"

"It doesn't take a slide rule and Cray computer. I was set up. I should think by Luke so I'd be implicated in his mother's murder. If I'm discredited the money left to me goes back into the trust; not that it makes much of a difference, I suppose; with Mommy out of the way, he gets half it all, anyway."

The sheriff stood and brought his mug to a coffee pot. "It's an interesting theory. However, Luke is Mommy's favorite. That's well known. So that part doesn't make sense." Hidalgo filled his cup and sat back down, rocked back and forth in his chair. "It's you I'm not sure what to make of. Either you're telling the truth or you're some sort of criminal genius."

"Much of what I told you can be corroborated by the folks at the President's Club."

"Good man, that Mike. You know it was Mike and Virgil who got me elected to this job?" Hidalgo drank. Stopped in mid-sip. "Where are my manners. You want some coffee? It's been sitting a long time, tastes like shit, but you can put in some of the white powder and as much sugar as you can handle."

"Tempting, but I'll pass. I'm already pissing a lot from the alcohol. I would probably burst if I drank coffee. After what I've told you, what do you think I should do?"

By way of answering Hidalgo opened a drawer and pulled out some official looking papers. He slid them and a pen across the table.

"Write out what you told me, word for word. I'll take that statement and present it to Lynne. That may or may not suffice for now. He's obviously going to want to talk to you himself. But at least by coming here right away it shows that you were suggesting you had nothing to hide. In the meantime, you have to do me two favors."

"Anything."

"Stay sober." He pointed a finger at Archie. "No booze, you hear me."

"And the second thing."

"No more trouble. Stay at Howard Rogoff's. Watch the whole Sopranos series or something equally engrossing and stay out of sight while we sort this out. In other words, don't go giving the chief further reason to lock you up."

Archie put up his right hand. "I'll do my best on both. And thanks." He wrote.

The sheriff offered to drive Archie back to Rogoff's house. The porch light was lit and the front door unlocked. John escorted Archie into the house and closed the door behind them.

"That you, Archie?"

"And John Hidalgo, Dr. Rogoff." Both walked into the den where Archie collapsed on the sofa.

"Hey, sheriff. How the hell are you?" They shook hands warmly.

"I'm doing well, Doc. He on the other hand isn't doing so great." He turned to Archie. "Do you mind if I bring the good Dr. Rogoff up to date."

Archie waved it off. "Be my guest," he said. "Let me just get a nightcap before you begin."

"Wendt, for crissakes, you just gave me your word you wouldn't drink."

"Come off it, what are you Mother Teresa? It's a nightcap. Besides, you're here. You can give me a breathalyzer afterwards to make sure I don't drink and sleep."

Howard poured two small cognacs and passed one to John. "Archie, you take a pass like the sheriff says. You're going to need your wits about you."

Virgil Morgenstern possessed an uncanny ability to read situations instantly and maneuver them so he came out ahead. John struggled to explain the phenomenon to others, but he experienced it enough to testify to its veracity.

Just prior to his orchestrated death, Virgil had updated his request vis-a-vis Archibald Wendt. He had taken John aside, and with the ubiquitous arm about the shoulder had given him stern advice.

"A lot of shit is liable to go down in this little town of ours. Many accusations. Your job will be to ignore the major ones and focus on the little details. Keep your eyes on the psychiatrist; he will be under an enormous amount of stress. That kind of pressure can break some men and I need you to keep him from coming apart."

"What kind of shit are we talking about?" John asked.

"Nothing you can avert through the power of your office or your personality."

Sheriff John Hidalgo thought back to that conversation. The psychiatrist showed strain and this meant John needed to honor Virgil's request to be a safety net. That would put him at odds with Lynne. It brought a smile to his face; he'd been fixing for a fight with the police chief for some time.

CHAPTER
36

Archie climbed into bed in Howard's guest room. He sank into the pillow top. Far more comfortable than the Beemer's seat. His mind replayed the events of the night. Howard had listened to the retelling dispassionately, as befitted a man who had spent a career being non-judgmental. Archie had to admit that the sheriff did a near perfect job of relating what had occurred. Now going over the discussion that ensued, Archie's exhausted (and slightly intoxicated) mind turned the information over. John and Howard agreed it was paramount Archie stay out of sight until the sheriff had a better handle on how to manage this. He was grateful the two men had taken his story at face value; he didn't have the energy to defend his innocence and, if pressed, would probably have copped to killing Hoffa.

Time passed in his mind and more of the material broke free from the confines of conscious thought. Archie lost the valiant struggle against the tidal wave of sleep.

Back at the Morgenstern home. In the foyer, standing, scanning the house. Daylight shined through the windows, but corners remained dark, hidden. He looked for something, but couldn't think of what he sought even as the need to find it swelled. A cocktail party materialized filled with people he didn't know. Then Linda happened by carrying a tray of hors de oeuvres.

Katherine's voice could be heard above the din. The urge to find her pressed on him like a weight. He hunted, but after a few steps his leg caught on something. He pulled, but couldn't get it free. He had a court ordered ankle bracelet whose cord was plugged into a socket. Archie pulled hard and freed his leg. Immediately the anklet beeped insistently. He was sure that everyone heard it, but no one made any move towards him. His shirt grew sodden with sweat the pressure to find Katherine building. He waded through the party guests like moving against a strong tide.

"Linda, have you seen Mrs. Morgenstern?"

He couldn't make out her face. "Puff pastry, Dr. Wendt?"

"No, Linda, I need to find Katherine."

"Stuffed mushroom cap? Rumaki?"

He pushed passed Linda further into the house. The next room took him to a bar. Mike stood behind it filling drink orders. Relieved, Archie bellied up to the bar, pressed between others. As he jostled for position Mike moved away. The bartender became engrossed in conversation at the other end of the bar.

"Mike, have you seen Katherine Morgenstern?"

Archie couldn't get his attention. The ankle bracelet's beeping grew louder. "Goddammit, Mike, don't fucking ignore me you piece of shit. Now, in my time of need you're ignoring me? Well, fuck you." He pushed off from the bar and struggled through the crowd. Grabbed napkins from a passing tray to mop his sweating brow. On his toes he espied Rose talking to someone. Archie swam over to her.

"Rose, I'm so glad to see you."

"Archie, I can't talk right now. My mother is not feeling well."

Katherine Morgenstern stood beside her daughter making polite conversation with the other guests.

"Thank God, I found you. You need to call the police. You're in danger." Archie said.

Katherine's eyes were elsewhere. "Linda, you need to circulate more. Circulate."

"Mrs. Morgenstern, I'm worried about you."

Katherine kept craning her head, "Rose, can you see what Linda is doing?" As she turned, she displayed her caved in skull, hair matted with blood. Mortified, he tried to get Rose to do something. She, too, ignored him in favor of the heavy oak door of the study that stood ajar. "Someone left Daddy's office open." She walked towards the open door.

"Don't go in there, Rose!"

He ran after her, his leg dragging, again caught on something. The beeping from the anklet rose in pitch like a pissed off Yorkie. He entered the office; the noose hung from the chandelier, Rose ensnared in its business end.

He screamed. In his dream or in Howard's guest room, he didn't know, but he was awake now, his sodden sheets tangled around his legs. He angrily slammed the top of the clock, its alarm beep set for a hair raising shriek. Archie squinted to see the time. Three AM. Who the fuck sets an alarm for three AM? He freed his leg, sat at the edge of the bed and ran his hands through his hair. Exhausted, he gently lowered himself back onto the pillow. The dream faded, but he remained panicky. He flipped the pillow. Better.

Rose hanging. He knew it wasn't Rose that worried him. She was the place holder for the loss he dreaded most. The one that had unnaturally consumed him and spurred him to attempt an unthinkable intervention. He still couldn't make sense of the twisted logic he justified back then. It ended his esteemed Northeast career. He pounded the bedsheets in frustration. He had done so much to put her out of his mind. Yet she returned again and again.

Archie got out of bed and looked around. The unfamiliar surrounding lent a surrealness to the hour; as if that hour needed more unrealness. He summoned all his energy to focus on what he could control. Get closure from this, from Morgenstern. The dream, the look on Rose's face, the prostrate body of Katherine occupied his mind's eye.

Wendt lay back down, worked on his deep breathing to gain control. The hanging fresh in his mind, he recalled the information gleaned from Virgil's study just before Rose showed up. He rationally understood he had leads to follow. He could work on getting peace from his past later; there were more pressing issues to pursue. It was close to an hour before Archie fell back asleep.

"Archie, get up. Time to get moving." Howard stood at the bedroom door.

Wendt couldn't remember where he was. He rubbed his eyes and sat at the edge of the bed. Overnight his mind turned the material over and regurgitated a path forward. He knew what his next step would be and he found renewed purpose. He dressed and went down to the kitchen. Howard laid out a cup of black coffee and a hard roll.

"John called, said Lynne is already looking for you. Seems only a matter of time before he comes here so you ought to hit the road."

"I know."

Howard put his mug down. "Why do you look happy?"

"I do?"

"Yes, more happy than a person in your position should be. Lynne is going to do everything he can to lock you up for good."

"I know."

"You should be making like Speedy Gonzalez to Mexico."

"Not just yet. I understand now what I have to do." Archie said. "I really feel like Virgil put all this in place for a reason, sought me out for a particular purpose and gave me that money with intent. He's left me crumbs to follow like Hansel and Gretel and I'm getting closer, Howard, I can feel it. If I can piece this thing together before Lynne makes a case against me, I can find a way through."

"There's nothing like denial for someone who is delusional. Very protective."

"Shit." Archie hit his head. "My car. I think I left it at the bar. I can't remember. Can I borrow yours?"

"I don't know how I can say no. Is it unreasonable for me to expect it back without a hail of bullet holes in its sides?"

"You're hilarious."

"Where you going?" Howard asked.

"Check out a Fred Montrose in Londonderry."

"Virgil's hometown."

"I'm counting on him filling in some blanks for me."

Howard raised his mug in salute. "Good luck." He spoke over the lip of the mug. "Please bring my car back in one piece."

It was a cold day, but dry with a blue sky. Archie inhaled deeply and walked to what was once a carriage house and now protected Howard's ancient Mercedes. A diesel, Howard directed him to the glove box to a map that had the stations where the fuel could be reliably obtained. He started up the engine and marveled at its smooth sound after so many years.

Riding with the heat all the way up and the windows down, Archie realized he didn't know where Fred Montrose lived. Or if he did. That trifle didn't bother him flush as he was with the internal certainty that he had caught the scent, was on the right path. He'd figure out all things in the proper time. Or maybe Howard's right, maybe any optimism is delusional. There remained a lingering bit of surrealism to the situation that protected him from deeper despair; as if he were watching someone else go through this nightmare.

The major route out of Harding turned into a country road that became hillier as he drove. The trees were mostly bare, though some still had the flaming remnants of autumn. Lots of farm houses and satellite dishes. He wondered if he could sustain a practice this far out in the sticks. The characters from the Texas Chainsaw Massacre flashed across his mind and he decided it probably wasn't a good idea.

Wendt rode through Londonderry without realizing it. A sign for the next town alerted him that he'd gone too far. He turned around and stopped at a gas station. The attendant, a young kid walked out. Archie rolled down the window.

"Nice car, man. Looks like a '77 240."

"You got an eye for cars. I'm not sure the year, but that sounds about right." Archie said.

The kid walked around. "A diesel. Nice. But we don't have any diesel in this station. I can tell you where the next diesel station is and maybe give you a lift if you're out of gas."

"I'm not, but awfully nice of you to offer. I'm looking for Londonderry."

He pointed in the direction Archie came from. "Next light."

Wendt laughed. "You happen to know people in town?"

"Sure do. Grew up right here. Who are you looking for?"

"Fellow by the name of Fred Montrose."

"Doctor Montrose. Everyone knows him. Only dentist around here."

"You know where he lives?"

"Come to think of it, no, but I know where his office is. Will that do?"

"Absolutely, thank you."

He leaned on the window and pointed. "Take this road here; second light left. First corner on your right look up. Can't miss the sign."

Archie took out his wallet and pulled a ten. "Here, thanks for your help."

"Hey, appreciate that. Good luck."

Back on the road. Second left, right corner. He looked up and saw the sign. Fred Montrose, DMD, like the kid said. Refreshing when things work out. With the sunshine reflecting off the glass he couldn't tell if someone was in the office. He parked and pulled the car's hand brake. The door for the office was around the corner with the same typeset as the sign. Dark stairwell to the second story office door. He walked in to the accompaniment of a chime.

Her world crashed around her in a not to be believed torrent of misfortune. Not a week ago Rose's thoughts centered on inanities. A piece of property for purchase, a disgruntled employee threatening to sue, whether three hundred for a pair of shoes was too damn decadent.

Now her father was a suicide, her mother a murder victim, and the weight of the business fell on her at a time when she only longed to curl up in a ball in a corner. She sat in her office, her eyes unfocused on the paperwork situated on the desk. Normal tasks took twice as long, new chores became unmanageable. She willed her mind to concentrate on work, hoping it would distract her from the intense pain she felt, but all she could manage were vacillations between shock and the enormity of her responsibilities.

Luke proved worthless, as anyone could predict. Always ready to shirk responsibility when their parents were alive, he now neared permanent intoxication with weed and whatever substance du jour he could procure. Their natural roles were reversed. Rose, the younger sibling, carried the burden of safeguarding his interests despite, or because of his laziness.

Her thoughts turned to the psychiatrist. Perhaps it was natural to think of someone who could offer her counseling in this difficult time, but she knew it meant more than that. Archie complicated matters. Crossing the thirty threshold, she'd given up on finding a suitable mate and immersed herself in work. He seemed to fall in her lap and met several of her hard-to-find criteria.

The phone's ring intruded into her brooding.

"Miss Morgenstern, your brother's on his way in," her secretary said.

"Thanks for the heads up."

Luke walked in and plopped down on her sofa, kicked his feet up.

"We need to talk, Rose."

"Make yourself at home."

"I need to know when I'm going to get some funds."

Rose bristled. "What the fuck is the matter with you, huh? Are you completely without common sense? We just lost our parents and you come in here looking for money. I mean, really, just what the fuck is wrong with you?" Her brother shrank at her barrage and that left Rose feeling empty inside. It proved less satisfying to call him out on his shortcomings when their mother wasn't there to pick up the pieces.

He put his feet down, took off baseball cap revealing a mop on his head that looked like it hadn't seen shampoo in many a day. Luke ran his fingers through that hair, then plucked a joint from the cap's lining. He lit up and inhaled deeply.

"Jesus, Luke, what are you doing?" Rose laughed despite herself. She got up and closed her office door. "You do understand this is a place of business, right?"

"C'mon, Rose, leave me alone. You've always known you were stronger than me. Do you have to rub it in?"

She sat hard on her chair, swiveled and switched on an air purifier.

Luke exhaled at it. "You're like a Boy Scout. Always prepared."

Wordlessly Rose opened up a drawer and took out a pack of cigarettes, pulled one out and made a show of lighting it. Luke was overjoyed. "Perfect Rosie and her Pall Malls."

"Camel lights. I haven't smoked in a while, but this seems like an opportune time to catch up with an old friend."

They sat puffing for a few beats. Luke held his draw, sputtered a little. "I know this isn't the best time, but what will happen to me? To the house?" He lowered his voice to an almost inaudible level, fearful of the response. "When can I see at least the stipend that Dad laid out for me?"

"I don't know Luke. Probate is a process that normally takes time and in this case things are much more complicated; I can't give you a timetable."

He put his legs on the ground and leaned forward. "Are you going to make me move out?"

"I don't know, Luke." At that moment Rose saw clearly the extent of her brother's pitifulness. A chill ran through her body.

"Right now nothing's going to change with the house. It's hard for me to think long term, but I won't let anything bad happen to you. I'll float you some money, if need be. Just please give me a chance to get things in order, okay?"

Luke relaxed. Rose walked to a sideboard that held a carafe. "You want coffee? Still warm."

He shook his head. She poured herself a cup, took some sips. The caffeine and nicotine working in tandem brought good sensations, warm memories. Comforted her like a hug. Luke walked to the window next to her. "I can't believe the psychiatrist killed Mom."

She stopped mid sip. "Why would you say that to me?"

"Because I don't want you to let him get away with it. I know you have a thing for him, but you saw him at the scene."

"That doesn't mean he did it. It's circumstantial. He's a doctor, for crying out loud. You think he's capable of that kind of violence? Bashing someone's skull in with a frying pan? It doesn't make sense. I don't believe he could do something like that."

"Don't want to believe, you mean. Rose, I'm your own brother. You trust that shyster more than me? Shit, I thought you were supposed to be smarter than me; how could you fall for this two bit shrink?"

Rose plopped down with her coffee. Used the tip of her last cigarette to light a fresh one. Luke walked over and sat on the edge of her desk. "This guy's hustling you. He's in your head, manipulating you."

"So you said. But I take my own council when it comes to trust."

Luke walked to the door. "There's someone I want you to meet. He can fill you on this Wendt character, cause he's known him a long time."

"I'm not in the mood to meet anyone right now."

"Five minutes, that's all I ask."

Rose didn't have the energy to argue. "Fine."

Luke went to the door and opened it. He motioned to someone leaning over the desk, flirting with Rose's secretary.

Cutter walked into the office flashing a smile a used car salesman would envy.

CHAPTER

39

Three people sat in the Dentist's waiting room - a middle aged man wearing jeans, a flannel shirt and a hat that said "Kenilworth," an attractive woman in her forties in jeans and sweatshirt, and a young kid in his early twenties spitting periodically in a cup. They looked up in unison when Archie walked in.

A voice called out, "I'll be right with you." Archie took a seat and grabbed a magazine.

"Let that set and I'll be right back." The voice came around the corner. Archie looked up.

"How can I help you."

Dr. Montrose had on a short white coat over what looked like suit pants. Expensive shoes. He exuded vibrancy despite his gray hair. Archie stood and extended his hand.

"Dr. Montrose, my name is Archibald Wendt. I came from Harding to see if I can take up a few minutes of your time."

"I'm pretty busy as you can see, but if you don't mind waiting here, I'll get to you soon."

"No problem." Archie retook his seat.

The young guy spoke up. "Doc, I gotta see you. My tooth is killing me."

"Christopher, how many times do I have to tell you to quit the chew and brush your teeth." Montrose turned and walked away.

Christopher continued his spitting ritual. "Shit, I ain't ever going to stop chewing tobacco." He leered lasciviously at the woman.

The trucker spoke to Archie. "Wendt you said was your name, right?"

"Yeah."

"Hate to tell you this, mister, but you got an APB put out in your honor."

"What do you mean?" Archie asked.

"Earlier this morning, came out over the radio. All points bulletin for a doctor up Harding way who's wanted for murder. Said you was dangerous and to call authorities immediately."

"I'm not dangerous, I can assure you. This is part of an elaborate frame; I'm here working on clearing my name. It's why I'm seeing Dr. Montrose."

"Figure to get your teeth straight before you go to the clink?" Christopher said.

"Don't mind that little fella. He still thinks he's smarter than the whole world. But, terms of the frame job, you looking for a one armed man who maybe dunnit?" The trucker couldn't keep the mocking tone from his voice.

Archie smiled. "That's good. I'm a doctor so I get it. Funny as it is, you don't seem terribly afraid."

The woman shifted in her seat.

Kenilworth said, "I'm not afraid because this would be an odd place for a stone cold killer to stop and rest. But maybe we should stop this talk because I think it's making the young lady uncomfortable."

"Don't worry, baby, I'll protect you if it comes to that," Christopher said.

"I'll be fine, thank you. And I'm uncomfortable because of an impacted molar." She said. "And Christopher, your kind speak a big game, but lose your wad before you even get it out of your pants."

Christopher's face blanched.

"Hoo-ah." Kenilworth said. "She got your number, young fella."

A woman came out of the exam room holding her jaw and groaning; Montrose trailed behind.

"Don't eat for the next three hours or you'll undo all my good work. Okay, who's next?"

Nobody volunteered. Kenilworth spoke up. "Best you see this fella here. Seems he's got some business to discuss with you from over there in Harding."

"Is that so? Well, come on in and let's see what you got."

Archie stood and gave a little nod to Kenilworth. "Thanks. Seems I'm in a bigger rush than I realized. You going to call the police?"

The trucker shook his head. "Not in the business of doing police work unless I can be a hero. You take it easy - Doc Montrose has a sadistic streak."

Archie followed the white coat into the exam room. He might have expected a museum of dental horrors, but the opposite proved the case. The room looked like it would be at home in a spa. The carpeting, wallpaper, and accents all looked expensive. There was a flat screen near the ceiling to distract the patient from any painful tools. In the corner stood a tank with some dials and masks.

"Sit in the chair and open up." Montrose donned fresh gloves and a mask. He saw Archie's expression and held up his hands, tugged at the mask. "I hate these things. I can remember a time I'd be up to hairy knuckles in someone's mouth never giving it a second thought. But now with HIV and other communicable diseases, not to mention accursed lawyers, I have to wear all this get-up."

"Doctor Montrose, I'm not here because of a dental problem."

"No one is. Sit and open up."

Archie complied. "I'm here to talk to you about Virgil Morgenstern. You went to high school with him, rig—." His last words cut off by Montrose's contorting Archie's cheeks and lips to examine his mouth.

"Not bad. Looks like you floss every once in a while."

Archie grunted.

"So, you came here to talk to me about Virgil, but nobody escapes without an exam. You inspect the mouth of the folks in my care and compare it to the rest of Ross County and I'm sure you'll agree with my results."

He fiddled around some with a mirror then sat down and pat Archie on the thigh.

"Things look okay. You neglect the gum around your rear molars, but otherwise, you're in good shape."

"Virgil," Archie said softly.

"Yes, I know you have questions. As soon as I read the news I'd hoped you'd come down here." He pulled the mask and gloves off. "I knew Virgil my whole life and been through a lot with him. He was the best kind of friend a man could have. I only wish we could have done better for him. He knew he approached the end of his life and didn't want to end up an invalid and drain family resources for what was a losing battle. As a psychiatrist, perhaps you understand the gut wrenching decision Virgil faced."

Archie said nothing. Montrose continued.

"I believe that Virgil worried about what might happen after his demise. Virgil didn't put it past his wife to seek revenge against Rose in his absence. He went to great lengths to make sure that those he cared about would continue to be looked after upon his demise. Some things he came to his friends for. Others he carried out on his own. And others he entrusted to near strangers."

"Why would Katherine take revenge on Rose?"

"She's a vengeful woman."

A pall came over Archie's face. "There seems to be a gap in the small town gossip machine. I'm sorry to have to tell you this, but Katherine Morgenstern was murdered."

"What? When?"

"Just happened yesterday. Wow, feels like a long time has passed," he added.

Montrose pursed his lips and blew out hard. "That's big news. I mean, I was never a big fan of hers, but that's horrible. Do they have a suspect?"

"You're looking at him. Someone invited me to the Morgenstern's and I found her with her head bashed in by a pan. It was supposed to look like I killed her. A clumsy attempt, but effective in getting me in some temporary trouble; the chief of police is not fond of me."

"Horace Lynne is a simple man." Montrose said. "If an idea is planted in his head he will run with it. Have you reached out to the sheriff?"

"I have and he's been most helpful. But getting back to Virgil, I know he made arrangements for that money; I'm just not sure what they were. And I'm tired. You understand? I'm exhausted from all this shit."

"You know that expression, the one that says God doesn't give you any more than you can handle?" Montrose asked.

"That's just pablum for the masses."

"Well I'm not talking about God. I'm referring to Virgil. He knew that you were going to take some hits and he thought given your past you would persevere."

"I'm not so sure."

"Keep the faith, son. Have you spoken with Nina yet?"

"Nina Patterson?"

"Yes. Go see Nina, you'll like her and understand better what's at stake."

"Who *are* all you people?" Archie asked.

"Childhood friends who stayed close. Me, Virgil, Nina, Lenny, Mike."

"Mike? The bartender up at the President's Club?"

"That's the one."

"You folks are a cool bunch, you know that? You keep your cards close to the vest; I'd hate to play poker with you lot." Archie said.

"You'd lose because we cheat in coordination. Now off you go, so I can try and knock some sense into that adolescent in the waiting room."

Archie got out of the chair. "Okay to use your phone to call someone in Harding?"

"You don't have a cell phone?"

Archie shook his head. "Stopped carrying one."

Montrose smiled. "I gotta imagine that's liberating."

"You're the first person to put it that way. Yes, thank you, it was quite liberating."

"Through that door is my office. Use the phone in there. You can just dial out, no need to press 9 or anything."

"Thank you. And thanks again for seeing me."

Archie walked into Montrose's office and dialed.

"Howard, it's Archie."

"Hey, Archie, how's my car managing in the suburbs of Mexico City?"

"That's hilarious. What's it like in Harding?"

"Predictable. Lynne has been by looking for you. I told him to contact Interpol or the Federales."

"Did he come heavy?"

"Heavy? One day a fugitive and you're already using bad gangland terminology. He didn't come heavy. He came alone and said that if you want to avoid a nasty outcome you're to present yourself to the station immediately. He was calm. In fact, he seemed more reasonable than I expected. Then..." Howard trailed off.

"Then what?"

"Well, then another fellow came by. A crummy looking man who looked like he was caught in the rain and slept in the same clothes. Said he was a friend from Boston."

"Cutter."

"Yes, that was his name. He had the most smarmy smirk I've ever seen. Smarmy smirk. That's good."

"I'm happy for you Howard and your alliterative capabilities. What did you say?"

"He seemed content to just leave the message that he was looking for you. And…"

"And? Howard, you're going to drive me fucking crazy with your pauses."

"Sorry, but I have something on the stove top. Anyway, he said that Lynne is planning on luring you in with a soft sell like I just want to talk, but is committed to pinning this murder on you. Cutter says that the only way forward is with his help and that you'd know what he meant by that."

"Shit. Any more great news?"

"No, that's it."

"Thanks, Howard. I mean it, no sarcasm. Thanks for everything."

"No problem. Just be safe and keep me posted." They hung up.

Christopher was already in the exam chair.

"C'mon, Doc, just a little of the nitrous. Why you gotta be so stingy?"

"You kids and your drugs. You're all hooked on something." He looked up at Archie. "You reach who you wanted?"

"I did. Thank you, you've been most generous."

Fred waved it off. "You just take care of yourself."

Archie saluted and walked out of the office back to his car.

CHAPTER

40

Nina Patterson lived in a modest looking colonial outside of Circleville, Ohio. It was another trek through local roads, then two lane highways, and finally up Route 23. He skirted around Harding not even wanting to be near the place. Bad juju, Archie thought, best steer clear of it. Montrose offered to alert Nina to his arrival ensuring she would be at home. He parked, walked to the door and rang the bell.

A lovely looking woman answered. If Katherine Morgenstern embodied bitterness, this woman was her opposite. She exuded kindness. Shoulder length hair that framed a pretty face with soft features.

"Ms. Patterson?"

"O'Leary. It was Patterson before I got married. Why don't you come in, Dr. Wendt."

He entered and was blown away. The outside suggested a classic up/down colonial, but the inside could only be described as sumptuous. The stairs were central, but everything else was open and airy. The furniture looked modern and expensive. Baby grand piano. He glimpsed a kitchen with top of the line appliances, Wolf, Subzero.

"You have a lovely home."

"Thanks. Years of collecting pieces, one here, one there. A lifetime, really. Come in, we'll sit in the living room. I understand you have some questions."

"I do." He sat on a sectional. Good leather, no cracks. "I appreciate you seeing me like this. Highly irregular, I know, but I've been on a circuitous path that's led me to you."

"How is that?"

"I'm not sure how much you know?" He left it hanging. She crossed her legs and picked up the thread with a soft voice. "I know that you were there when Virgil took his own life. That he left you a fair amount of money. I'm just not sure why."

"You and me both and that's what I'm trying to figure out. What was your relationship with him?" Archie said.

"He was my high school sweetheart, my first love. It didn't work out for us, but he remained a valued friend. A dear man. I don't know if you got the chance to know him, but he was unique in so many ways."

"How so? if you don't mind me asking."

"Not at all. It saddens me that he's gone, but when I reminisce, it feels better somehow. That's sounds weird, doesn't it?" He offered a sympathetic smile. She continued. "Virgil had a style to him that didn't change from when he was a kid all the way until he died. Even as a young boy he exuded charisma. On the playground he organized the sports, the activities. You know, one of those people who could be friends with everyone, no matter who they were and where they came from. But it was always his way, no matter what we did. He would work on you and convince you his way was right by sheer attrition.

"He wasn't a bully, mind you," she quickly added. "Virgil wore you down with logic and his good nature."

"Why do you think things didn't turn out well for you two?"

She uncrossed and re-crossed her legs, thought for a moment. "I've never come to much of a satisfactory answer aside from we were young. How often does it work out for high school sweethearts? I don't know. I don't want to seem like I'm complaining; I had a good marriage, a good life."

Archie saw photos on the piano top, perfectly aligned. He stood and silently requested permission with a head gesture. She responded in kind.

"I'm a sentimentalist. My husband always accused me of sacrificing the moment for a good photo, but I'm grateful I was so dogged in taking pictures."

He recognized Nina in many of the pictures. Her aging laid out story wise fashion in the array of frames. He assumed that the man next to her was her husband. A third collection told the tale of a young boy growing into adulthood. "Your son looks more like you than your husband."

"That would be because he's *my* son, not my husband's." Archie thought he detected an edge in her voice. His eyes traced the boy's development, a familiarity in his visage. When he arrived at the transition to adulthood, Archie looked at the face of John Hidalgo, the sheriff. He turned to Nina and said, "It's the sheriff."

She smiled broadly. "Yes, John is my son. You've obviously met him."

"I've had the pleasure. He's been a source of support for me since this ordeal began."

"I was pregnant with John when I met Dan, my husband. John's father was a GI who went over to Vietnam. We didn't know I was pregnant until he was already over there. When he didn't return, I turned to Dan and we raised John together." She stood and walked over to the piano to look at the photos with him. "The pregnancy was an accident, but I never contemplated terminating. I was grateful to have John, always have been."

She picked up a picture of the three posing together.

"Dan was a good father to John."

"When did Dan pass?" Archie said.

"Some years back." Nina replaced the photo.

"So John's last name…"

"Hidalgo was his father's last name. The one legacy he could leave for his son. Dan was an O'Leary. We wanted children, but it turned out he couldn't, so we doted on John."

"What did your husband do for a living?"

"He was a contractor. Much of his work came through Morgenstern holdings; you know, doing renovations and building."

Something niggled at the back of Archie's mind when he looked at the pictures of John Hidalgo. The same feeling Archie got when he saw an actor in a movie and tried to place his face in other roles.

"His father must have been a big guy." He looked up at her. "I mean, John's a big boy. Do you happen to have a photo of John's father by any chance?"

"No, one of my biggest regrets. Had one of those wallet sized jobs I kept when he went over to Vietnam, but I lost that along the way. John never lets me forget that I misplaced his one connection to his father."

The lie etched lines in her face. This woman didn't look like she misplaced anything. He pushed his luck. "Did he have any contact with his father's family? Surely they would want to be in John's life."

Nina backed up. Put her hand to her mouth and grimaced. "You know,

I'm not comfortable with this line of questioning. I don't think that's any of your business."

"I apologize. Curiosity is a professional hazard; sometimes I forget that in polite company one doesn't ask such forward questions."

Her body language softened a little. He pounced again. "Does his father's family live in the area?'

Nina hugged her arms. "Your apology is not sincere so it is not accepted. I'm going to have to ask you to leave."

"I understand, Mrs. O'Leary. I'll get out of your hair. I'm grateful that you let me in to your beautiful house. And I truly am sorry I made you feel uncomfortable." He showed himself out, Nina still standing in the same self-hugging pose when he closed the door behind him.

A spontaneous and irrepressible smile bloomed on Archie's face as he walked to his car. It was all coming together. He knew where his last stop had to be. Archie started up the Benz, talked to her as the engine came to life.

"Time to go back to Harding and put this thing to rest, old girl."

The radio reception was shitty so he whistled all the way back instead.

41

J ust before hitting town he pulled over into a gas station on Howard's list and tanked up with diesel. He paid inside then stopped by a pay phone, picked up the receiver and dialed. Howard answered on the second ring.

"I was hoping it was you. Are you halfway to Mexico yet?"

"Again with the Mexico jokes? No, I'm just outside of town."

Silence. "You're coming back here, then?"

"I am and I've got it all figured out. But I need to know if Chief Horace Dickhead is lying in ambush waiting for me to cross into Harding."

"Lynne? He's the least of your worries. I received a call from Jed an hour ago."

"Jed?"

"Yeah, you know, Luke's little friend."

"Okay. What did Jed have to say?" Archie asked.

"Just that if you didn't bring the five million with you to the Morgenstern house right away he would hurt Rose."

"What? This guy is unhinged. I don't have the money and if I did, what does he think, I walk around with a suitcase full of cash?" He scrubbed his jaw and breathed heavy into the phone. "You think this Jed is capable of carrying out his threat?"

"I've known Jed since he wore short pants. I thought him troubled then and nothing has changed in his adulthood except he wasn't using drugs as a little kid. So, yes, I'm quite alarmed."

"Have you talked to the sheriff yet?"

"Not yet. I was waiting and drinking, drinking and waiting. Then you called."

"Holy shit. Howard, I'm sorry I've brought this kind of shit to your doorstep."

"Jesus, you're going to feel sorry for yourself?" Howard said.

"Not me, you big dummy. You. But you're right, there's no time for that now. Give me Jed's number so I can call that piece of shit. After I talk with him I'll call you back so we can discuss what I should do next."

"Alright. But I want it on record that I said you should forget this town and drive south until they only speak Spanish."

"And risk Rose? You don't mean that. Just give me the number and I'll call you back."

"Morgenstern household, how can I help you?"

"Jed, I assume."

"Is this Archibald Wendt, noted head fucker? So glad you finally called. Did you get my message?"

"I did. But just in case it suffered from the broken telephone treatment, why don't you relay it to me directly."

Jed sounded jubilant. "Here's the situation. I am in control of the Morgenstern estate; well, the physical home front I should say, and I find myself in a pinch financially. As lord of the manor I need scratch to make my champagne dreams and caviar wishes come true and that's where you come in."

"How so?"

"You took what was mine and you need to make that right."

"I didn't take anything."

"Yes, you did, headshrinker." Jed said. "You are going to give me the five million you swindled from old man Morgenstern."

Archie held the phone away from his body and worked on calming his emotions. He could hear Jed talking into the phone.

"——you used your psychobabble bullshit to somehow——."

"Jed, shut the fuck up for a second. Let's say you're right and I snaked the money from Virgil, how am I going to give you the five million? Huh? I don't have the money, you dumb shit. It's stuck in probate. Do you have any idea what that means?"

"As a matter of fact, jerkoff, I do know what that means. That's why I made sure Rose was able to get her hands on five million of her own money and put it at your disposal. See, Daddy Virgil set aside a fund for kidnappings, and wouldn't you know it, it's raining."

"Are you mixing in a metaphor about a rainy day fund?" Archie asked.

"Fuck you, wiseass. My point is she's able to get her hands on the five mil and you need to go pick it up. I figure, once the money is released from probate, you can pay her back."

Archie put his hand over the phone and let loose a barrage of invective, then got a hold of himself. "And if I don't bring you the money, what then?"

Jed chuckled. "You will. You got a thing for Rose and everyone knows it. You wouldn't want to see me cause her harm. And not just run-of-the-mill stuff, man, I'm talking major harm, you understand?"

"I understand that you're a sick bastard who wants to steal what isn't rightfully his."

Jed laughed. "Ha! Look who's talking? Just get me the fucking money by tonight."

"What makes you think I won't go to the cops?"

"Go ahead, call the chief of police. Tell him I said hi. And if you're thinking about calling that limpdick sheriff just know that it would be my pleasure to kill him, too. I got a score to settle with him."

Archie let the "too" sink in. "Where's the five million I'm supposed to pick up?"

"Now you're using your head. It just so happens that David Daugherty has agreed to act as an intermediary. You can phone him and he'll let you know where to pick it up."

David Daugherty, Virgil's so called personal attorney. What a piece of shit that guy turned out to be, and so innocuous looking. A tiger in meek looking, ill-fitting three piece suits.

"How much you giving Daugherty?" Archie asked.

"Never mind, Buckwheat. Just give him a call and get over here. You be here tonight at 10; no later, no earlier, you understand? If I have to bring violence down on sweet Rose's head I will make sure that she can only be identified by her dental records. And before that, I will take a piece of her ass just like you did. Got it, headshrinker?"

Archie wrote down Daugherty's number. "Ten o'clock. Morgensterns. I'll be there."

CHAPTER

42

The chief of police hated talking on the phone. Lynne didn't appreciate the knowledge that anybody could be listening in and he hated not being able to see the other person. A lot can be gleaned by body language and how a man holds his eyes. In this case he had no choice.

"He's coming to you at ten? Alright, I understand what you want. Now talk to me about how much you intend on giving me."

Lynne listened to the other man on the line. The chief knew this particular fellow well; hell, he had a dossier on him in his files. This would be liking taking candy from a baby.

"Okay," Lynne said, "I'll go along with that. Who's going to get him the money?...That little shit? Okay. I got it. I'll be there."

He hung up. A grin formed on his face and he made quick plans. Lynne picked up the phone, jabbed at the keypad with his finger.

"Hey, baby. I need you to listen and not ask any questions...Didn't I just say no questions? Listen. Gather up a suitcase for yourself and then go over to my place as soon as you can.... Yes, we're leaving town and never coming back. You in or out?... We dreamed about this, but I can make this a reality tonight...That's right, Cancun, on the beach... Didn't I say no questions. You just gotta trust me on this, okay?...That's my girl. Okay, I'll be there as soon as I can...Right back at ya. Bye."

CHAPTER

43

D avid Daugherty was a small man. Both figuratively and literally. At this stage in his life he had come to appreciate that fact. He grew up in the shadow of Virgil Morgenstern and that, too, encompassed literal and figurative aspects. Virgil had always been large and larger than life; David was jealous as hell. In sports Virgil would invariably be picked first, David last. It seemed as though he had been put on this earth to serve as yang to Virgil's yin.

The popular kids liked having David around. Like a mascot. That motif persisted into adulthood with Virgil's father-in-law hiring David fresh out of law school to work with the heir apparent. The pay being more than fair, it was great opportunity. Despite this, or because of it, David nurtured an anger over the years, collecting perceived slights. He watched as Virgil developed a kingdom in Harding pretending he had accomplished more than just marrying well.

Outwardly, of course, Daugherty showed not a stitch of resentment. Inwardly he seethed up to and including the last set of insults. Repeated slaps in the face: the unannounced suicide, bequeathing the empire to his daughter with nary a mention of his many years of loyal service, and the coup de grace, a five million dollar tip to a nobody psychiatrist. When Daugherty saw his opportunity to get a little revenge he jumped at it with gusto.

"David Daugherty here."

"How much are you getting, you shyster piece of scumbag shit?" Archie growled, his body crouched over the gas station phone.

"My good Doctor Wendt. That's quite an earful. We can discuss that at length when you come to my office. It's catty corner to the barber shop,

185

second floor. Be here at nine. That should give you plenty of time to get to the Morgenstern's. Good bye."

"Fuck you, you piece of shit!" Wendt yelled into the dead phone.

He called Howard back. The gas station attendant eyed him crookedly; Archie gave him the finger and turned his back just as shock registered on the kid's face. Small town America not used to big city asshole.

The phone barely rang before Howard answered. "What did he say?"

"You got the gist. Five million. Tonight. The rub is he knows I haven't received it from the probate yet. He blackmailed Rose into getting some of her cash."

"How are you supposed to get it?"

"The ever loyal David Daugherty is acting as intermediary."

"Mealy mouthed Judas. Okay, what's your plan?"

Archie closed his eyes and rubbed them hard. "I don't have much of a choice, do I? I'm not skipping town - that chicken shit I am not. I guess I'll be meeting Daugherty and getting the money. The question is does Hidalgo have the cajones to go at this alone? Maybe not just up against Jed, but Lynne, too."

"The sheriff won't be alone. There are others who can be trusted." He was silent. "You know what, you leave that to me. I'll call in the cavalry. What time you supposed to do the swap?"

"Ten. But you know, there was no discussion of a swap. I get the distinct feeling that whatever happens to Rose Morgenstern tonight, it will be curtains for old Archibald Wendt. Eventually I'm going to need an exit strategy, but for now I'll just have to take it one step at a time and wing it."

"You're not alone, Archie. We'll be there." Howard hung up.

We? Who the fuck is we? Archie walked back to his car not even looking in the direction of the young kid who might have taken the finger personally and had access to a gun. He revved the engine and pulled out of the station, tires squealing. One more fuck you to the world in general.

Daugherty's office was right across the street from Archie's. Small world. Haha. He parked in front of his own building wistfully remembering a time when he used his office for professional work.

I should have bought a gun. I live in rural Ohio and I don't have a gun, what kind of pussy am I. Goddamned Massachusetts and their progressive anti-NRA ways. Too late now. Of course, I don't have any experience with guns; probably blow off my thumb. Archie chuckled. Harry Callahan in his head, "A man's got to know his limitations."

So, first things first. Get the money. That's your first task.

Too quiet on the street; Archie half expected tumbleweed. He crossed over to the lawyer's building, the second story windows all lit. Archie jogged up the stairs to the office and knocked.

"Door's open."

He walked in. There was an empty secretary's desk and an open door to an inner office. "In here," Daugherty called out. He actually appeared happy to see Archie.

"I'm glad you found it alright. Sit down, make yourself comfortable."

Archie remained standing. "Go fuck yourself. How can you act so bubbly while stabbing your lifelong friend in the back?"

Daugherty snorted. "Friend. You don't understand anything."

"Tell me. I want to understand how you can be complicit in blackmail and extortion that affects the man, not to mention his daughter, in whose employ you were for so many years. His personal attorney, for crissakes."

"You know, it's really none of your business. But I'll tell you that after so many years of loyal service I think I deserved better than what I got. And to see you, a total stranger, walk away with five million?" The lawyers face turned beet red. His comb-over came unglued in the heat of the moment. Daugherty sputtered on. "You think it bothers me for a second taking that money from you? You who earned none of it. Promised me some of it, though, you remember? At the bar, you lying filth. You offered me the legal fee of freeing up the bequest in exchange for information. I lived up to my end of the bargain. And you? Hardly." He stood and spat out, "You miserable human, preying on the psychologically weak. I earned this money. I earned it." Daugherty calmed himself, pulled his vest down, and re-laid the strands of hair on his scalp.

"Jesus, you are a miserable piece of shit. Putting it to Virgil's wife wasn't enough, huh? You're pissed because he didn't give you money? Just like every other hanger on to the wealthy, living in a fantasy world hoping that one day you'll be rewarded for your sycophantic dedication with a heap of cash. You're sickening." Archie reveled in the way anger freed him from concern about the impact of his words.

Daugherty seemed surprised, not angry. "I wasn't 'putting it to Katherine' as you put it. Shrinks are all the same: Freud and all things sexual. Think you know something about human behavior. You extrapolate and guess is all you do." He sat back down. "Virgil never loved Katherine, so he didn't deserve her." He gazed out the window. "Naturally she would be attracted to him. Tall, handsome, athletic, what was I compared to him?" Daugherty snapped his head around and shot a look at Archie. In that moment he glimpsed the depths of Daugherty's hatred. "I'll tell you what I was. Loyal. Loyal, Dr. Wendt. Do you have any concept what that means? I was there for her in every situation. She knew I would be around, that she could rely on me at any hour and I would be there. Unlike him. Always off somewhere, *anywhere* else."

"If you harbored a love for Katherine how can you help out her possible murderer? You do realize that it was likely Jed who killed her."

Daugherty turned back to stare out of the picture window behind the desk. He spoke almost inaudibly. "I heard you were the chief suspect."

"C'mon, Daugherty, you're smarter than that. I can even hear in your voice that you know that to be bullshit." Archie thought he might be getting to the man. Then the diminutive lawyer shook his head like a dog just out of the pool. "I've had enough of this scintillating discussion with you." He held out a Gladstone bag. "Here's the money. Take it and get out of my office."

Archie took it and opened it. There were stacks and stacks of wrapped hundreds. "Five million?"

A sly grin on Daugherty's face. "Minus my fee."

"You take a third you greedy bastard?"

Face returning to a crimson shade he gestured dismissal with his hand. "Get out of my office. Take the money. Go help Rose get rid of Jed and we can be done with this sordid business."

Archie leaned in, grabbed a handful of the smaller man's lapel and shirt and mustered all the menace he could. "We aren't done here. I won't forget you and your treachery. This will not stand." He pushed Daugherty into his chair satisfied with the look of fear registered on the red, pinched face.

Archie walked down the stairs, paused outside the door. He bent down and opened the bag. Fuck. He'd never seen this much cash in one place outside a movie. Archie looked up at the sky and blew out a big sigh. I have a tank full of gas and a bag loaded with moolah. What the fuck am I doing still here? He consulted his watch. Ten past nine. He walked over to a phone booth on the corner and put the bag down between his legs. An update from Howard would be prudent. But, alas, no answer.

"Shit."

Archie picked up the bag and walked back to his car. He opened the front door and threw the Gladstone into the passenger seat. From behind him: "I'm going to need you to step away from the car and put your hands on your head."

Archie turned and looked into the police chief's eyes. Nothing but pure menace.

"How long have you been following me?"

"Doc, you got two choices. Put your hands on your head or I'm going to put twelve hundred volts into your body."

Archie did as he was told. Lynne took his right hand and put a handcuff on it. Then he pulled the hand down and brought the left to it. Archie thought he was surprisingly gentle for a man who just threatened to taze him. Once handcuffed he maneuvered Archie to the side and reached into the Benz's passenger seat.

"Are you arresting or robbing me?"

"Archibald Wendt, you are under arrest for murder, aggravated assault, disorderly conduct, resisting arrest. Anything you say can and will be held against you in a court of law."

"You are a miserable fuck, you know that."

Lynne's answered with a fist to Archie's midsection doubling him over. He puked; mostly on the chief's boots he noticed with some satisfaction. He pulled Archie aggressively up by the handcuffs.

"Shit. Easy, easy, you bastard," Archie sputtered.

Another punch to the gut. "I can do this all night wise-ass. You want to keep it up?"

Archie shook his head and struggled to catch his breath. Lynne dragged him to a police cruiser, parked in an alley that made for a nice hidey-hole. Just as he was putting Archie in the backseat, the police radio squawked.

"Dispatch to Chief Lynne. You there, Chief?"

Lynne swore. He used his left hand to hold the cuffs as a means of controlling Archie's movement. With his right he opened the door, leaned in and grabbed the handheld.

"Lynne here."

"Chief, it's Darby."

Lynne cursed, his head turned from the radio. "I know that Darby, you dimwit, what do you need."

"Well, see Chief, there's a situation over at the Crazy Horse."

Silence. "What is the fucking situation, Darby. Spit it out."

"Well, see Chief, we got a call…there are some unruly bikers causing a stir."

"Why don't you go down there and be a cop. Take Laurence and check it out."

"Well, that's going to be a problem. Laurence ain't here yet."

"Alright. I want you to go over there and do what you are trained to do, okay, be a cop, you understand. Do what the job asks of you. Do you copy?"

"Copy, chief."

"No dimwit; repeat back to me the instructions."

"I am to go to the Crazy Horse and be a cop. Got it."

"Over and out." Lynne put the receiver back and shook his head. He turned Wendt around and placed him in the back seat. The chief got in, started the engine and threw it into drive angrily. He was muttering to himself. Archie focused on the dashboard clock - 9:28 with the colon flashing away Rose's fate in second increments.

Hidalgo watched from afar as Archie entered the downtown building that housed the law offices of David Daugherty. The sheriff didn't know the lawyer's connection with Jed, but this didn't surprise him. He never trusted Daugherty.

He waited patiently in his own car, uniform top stripped off to reveal a t-shirt that proclaimed, "There are no such things as ex-Marines." His ability to be on a stake out improved over the years. In the service he had thrived on action. Developing the patience to sit in a parked car took all the discipline he could muster.

Nothing happened for a few minutes then a car appeared in his rear-view mirror. Lynne's cruiser passed him, pulled up next to Howard's classic Mercedes and idled. The police chief scanned the area then reversed his car into an opposite alley. Lynne doused his lights. Sneaky bastard. Hidalgo eased his seat back to be less conspicuous. It had been a good idea to use his own vehicle. He needn't have worried, though; Lynne only had eyes for the door from which both knew Archie would emerge. This didn't bode well for the good doctor.

Archie exited carrying a bad and Lynne sprang into action. The chief made effective use of the element of surprise. Hidalgo lowered his window a touch, but couldn't make out their conversation. Their actions spoke volumes. Hidalgo leaned forward and hissed when Lynne landed the punches to the psychiatrist's gut.

"Fucking unnecessary, Horace, you piece of shit," he muttered. Lynne guided Archie into the alley. When the police cruiser pulled out and made for the station house Hidalgo started his car and followed.

The police chief parked in front of the station. He grabbed the sack of money, got out of the car and slammed his door. Archie expected some savagery, but Lynne was surprisingly tender extracting the psychiatrist from the backseat. Archie wanted to express gratitude, but he didn't think he could tolerate another shot to the gut. Those are harder on the body than they looked on television. They climbed the steps and walked to the front door. Locked.

"Fucking dumbshit." Lynne fumbled for his keys and opened the door. Lights were on. He deposited Archie in a wooden chair. Lynne unlocked one cuff and attached it to a bar affixed to the desk.

"Not sure what to do with you." He sat down next to Archie, a big smile on his face. A large police radio chattered behind him. He picked up the Gladstone. "Well, Shrink, let's see what we have here."

Lynne rifled through the bundles, whistled and looked up at Wendt. The greed illuminated his face.

"I'm rethinking my opinion of your arrival to this town. It's turning out quite nicely for me."

"And you're an officer of the peace," Archie said.

Lynne's visage instantly darkened. "Shut the fuck up before I beat you senseless. I've earned this pension through the years of dealing with the shitheels in this town."

"That's a popular sentiment this evening." Archie muttered

Lynne's attention returned to the money. The radio behind him squawked.

"Darby to Chief Lynne, Darby to Chief Lynne."

Lynne ignored the radio and continued counting the money. His face alternated between sheer delight to irritation each time the radio crackled to life.

Muttering, Lynne turned to his left and picked up the receiver. "What the fuck, Darby. You need me to hold your hand?"

"Chief, I'm outside the Crazy Horse. The situation is this: there is a full on bar fight, some topless ladies, and general rowdiness. Please advise."

"You going to sit here and take this shit from this halfwit?"

Archie turned to his right and saw Garrett in his 'Fuck yes' hat leaning against the wall with a toothpick in his mouth. "I gotta say, I'm disappointed. A big city psychiatrist like you can't outwit a hick cop like this?" He jerked his thumb in Lynne's direction, who was busy berating his hapless deputy over the radio.

"He snuck up on me. I don't see how that qualifies as failing to outwit the hick cop." Archie said.

"Be that as it may, you're in a hell of a jam. Rose in trouble, you in custody. Jed's a sick boy."

"I know, I know." He held up his cuffed hand. "What would you have me do, chew through my wrist like a coyote to free myself?"

Archie's muttering got Lynne's attention at last. "Who the fuck are you talking to, huh? Don't play with me. You want to make an insanity case for murdering Morgenstern's old lady you can do that to your heart's content while you rot in jail. For now shut the hell up."

Lynne turned back to the radio and resumed dressing down his deputy.

"Arch, you got no choice. Time is a'tickin'." Garrett pointed at his empty wrist.

Archie was keenly aware of said time as he scanned the room for anything he might use as a weapon. Garrett smacked his forehead in an exaggerated expression of dismay. "You're sitting on it, man."

Archie stood quietly. The chief had his back to Wendt, all his energy focused on directing his deputy with a mixture of insults and instructions. Darby's quavering voice acted like gasoline on Lynne's barely contained conflagration. He took his anger out verbally on Darby and physically on the handheld. Archie picked up the heavy wooden chair with his free hand and brought it down on Lynne's shoulder and back.

Two things happened: the chair broke in half and Lynne crumpled to the ground. He lay dazed, but conscious. Archie leaned over the prostrate man and pulled the keys free and unlocked the cuff around his wrist. Lynne stirred. Wendt grabbed at the gun on Lynne's belt. He pulled and pulled, but the fucking thing wouldn't come out of the holster. Lynne's body moved against Archie more purposefully and in a panic Archie grabbed the nightstick, which came off the belt easily.

He gave a couple of smacks with the nightstick against the back of Lynne's head. The problem was Archie had no fucking idea how hard to hit. In the movies, they hit once and miraculously the person became unconscious. The first two knocks just elicited a low growl from the chief. Tough bastard. Archie couldn't wait around until he fully came to and he didn't have the stomach to hit him harder so he cuffed Lynne's right wrist to a steel ring on the floor. Lynne didn't offer much resistance.

"Chief? Chief, please advise, over."

Archie picked up the dangling receiver and held it to his mouth. He pressed the button.

"Uhhh, wait for back-up and proceed with caution, numbnuts. Over and out."

"Uh, yes sir. Over and out."

Wendt dropped the handheld and began to panic. For an insane moment he stood paralyzed, struggling to rally his thoughts. The Gladstone on the desk broke the spell. He spoke in a loud and raspy voice. "I need to get over to Rose, get her out of danger then I can flee. Fuck!" He grabbed the bag and bolted out of the station house, down the stairs to the police cruiser and started her up. Now it was 9:44. In his periphery, looming large, was a shotgun. He pulled at that and it came free easily. Archie drove like a bat out of hell to the Morgenstern estate.

He turned off his lights and allowed the car's idle power to crawl up to the station house. Not too close, but the contrast between the brightly lit station house and the dark outside allowed Hidalgo sufficient view of the happenings inside. He wasn't prepared for what he saw. It happened fast and looked like a bad professional wrestling script. Archie came barreling out of the station house bag in hand. He jumped into the police cruiser and took off. For a moment Hidalgo sat torn; a testament to his devotion to Virgil and by extension Wendt. But then his professional instincts overrode emotion and he jumped out of the car and went into the police station.

Lynne lay prone on the ground, breathing deeply, the cuffed arm akimbo. Hidalgo leaned next to him, put a hand on his back. He couldn't see any obvious bleeding. The chief groaned.

"Easy, Horace. Take it easy."

Lynne began vomiting. Hidalgo quickly turned him on his side towards the cuffed hand so that he didn't aspirate. He went over to the sink and wet some paper towels, grabbed a bottle of water from the refrigerator and brought them back for the chief. Bending down he undid the handcuff and helped the man to a sitting position.

"In the cabinet behind my desk is a first aid kit. I got some of those instant ice packs," Lynne croaked.

Hidalgo returned with the stuff and sat down. Lynne opened the kit and took out a bottle of aspirin. He washed four down with the bottled water. Hidalgo took one of the ice packs and kneaded it into activation. He handed it to Lynne.

"I'm going to kill that son-of-a-bitch."

"You going to tell me what happened?"

Lynne looked up. "Shit, you need a compass and a map? He came into the station and assaulted me. Then he stole my bag."

"What was in the bag?"

Lynne scowled. "Police business."

Hidalgo took comfort in Lynne's lies; they eased his conscience.

"Why would a psychiatrist, without a previous history of violence, come into a heavily armed police station and assault its chief?"

"Fuck if I know," Lynne said holding the ice pack to the back of his head. "What makes you so sure he has no priors?"

"I did a background check."

Stubbornness oozed out of the chief. "Well, I don't give a shit what his history is, because his future is going to be brief."

The sheriff stood. "Can I assume you're going to dispense with due process and criminal procedure?"

"Hidalgo, you've been a pain in my ass since you come to be elected. Who's side you on anyways? I just got assaulted - damn near killed and you're talking about 'due process and criminal procedure?' This Wendt is a con artist and a menace. And I mean to put an end to this nonsense."

"I'm not going to step aside and let you do what you want."

Lynne struggled to get to his feet. "You get in the way, Sheriff, and you're going to get stomped." Lynne's threat didn't have the desired impact, perhaps because of the ice pack on his head or the six inches and fifty pounds he gave up to Hidalgo. But the sheriff didn't respond. He just backed away and walked out of the station house intending to find Archie before the chief did.

CHAPTER

48

The stillness of the tree lined street contrasted with the drumbeat of his heart. Archie vacillated on where to park the police cruiser, then realized it mattered little. He pulled up on the curb in front of the house, doused the lights and turned off the engine. 9:50. So quiet. He noticed a worrisome development inside him; he was losing control. Hands trembling, he took hold of the shotgun and found it reassuring.

"I'm coming apart at the seams." His own voice startled him.

"You're doing fine, Doc. Just take some deep breaths."

Archie didn't immediately look over. He could sense the big smile on the face, 'Fuck yes' cap askew. He turned to see Garrett tinkle the air hello.

"Great. I'm a full-blown psychotic. That doesn't bode well for my future prospects."

"Hey, Arch, you got to focus now. Brace yourself so you can get Rose out of this jam."

"How do you propose I do that."

"Courage, my man, courage."

"I'm scared shitless. I think I left my courage back at the station house."

"You will recall the famous words of John Wayne: 'Courage is being scared shitless, but saddling up anyways.'"

"I don't think The Duke said, 'scared shitless,' and he sure as shit didn't add an 's' to anyway. But thanks for the support." He looked over at the empty passenger seat.

"Fuck it all," Archie said aloud. "Time to face the music."

He got out of the car, eased the door back and gave a hip bump to close it quietly. He held the Gladstone in one hand and the gun in the other. Crouching, he made his way to the front door, zigging and zagging. He thought of Alan Arkin in The In-Laws and Peter Falk's advice to "serpentine" his way to safety and had to suppress a giggle. On the front stoop two bushes stood sentinel on either side of the door. Not wanting to be caught with either package Archie wedged the gun into the left bush and placed the bag behind the right one. He rang the bell.

He didn't think there'd be a penalty for being early, but with that psychopath, Jed, who could tell. The frosted glass darkened behind the door and he heard locks opening.

"The good Dr. Wendt. Very glad to see you."

"What the fuck are you doing here?"

"Don't be hostile, Archie, my man, somebody had to quarterback this whole thing and I fit the bill. Right place right time, you know." Cutter spoke with his ever present smirk. "Katherine Morgenstern was paying my expenses. When you croaked her I had to find a new benefactor." He stood aside and let Archie pass. Putting a hand on the psychiatrist's shoulder he added, "In a funny way, I'm glad to see you. You know, a familiar face. I'm not used to these small town folk."

"Where's Rose and is she safe?" Archie shook the hand off his shoulder and stepped into the foyer. It felt strange to be in the Morgenstern home when both host and hostess were no longer Earthbound. He thought back to cleaning out his childhood home after his parents had died. Seemed indecent to be there in their absence. Cutter intruded on his thoughts.

He was smacking and rubbing his hands together like some greedy king of yore. "Where's the money?"

Archie ignored that. "Where's Rose and where is Jed? I didn't come here to fart around with you, you lowlife scumbag piece of shit."

"Always with the sweet talk. I'm a part of this whether you like it or not. I know you so I can vouch for you one way or the other. Best think about that."

Archie turned to him. "Cut the crap; where's Jed?"

In lieu of answering Cutter walked with a beckoning finger through the living room towards the medieval oak door.

Wendt followed him into Virgil's study. Jed sat in the chair behind the desk, hands laced behind his head, feet up like he was the monopoly man.

"Jed."

"That's right, Doc. You and me met a couple of weeks ago before old man Morgenstern cashed in his chips." There was something maniacal about Jed's appearance. A wildness to his eyes, his mannerisms. Archie had only seen that in manics and psychotics. And drug addicts.

Jed put his feet on the floor and sat straight. He brought his fist to his nose and pumped something in there, then inhaled deeply.

Coke. Just fucking great.

"Where's Rose?"

"Where's the money."

Archie didn't respond. "Who I am dealing with here? You or the guttersnipe behind me."

"Now, now, Dr. Wendt," Jed admonished. "That kind of talk isn't necessary. We're all here to make things right again."

"What are you talking about?"

Jed inhaled deeply from his fist, shook his head and pounded the desk. "Whoa nelly, that's some good shit. Where was I?"

"Restitution," Cutter kicked in.

"Right. Doc, you owe my friend Luke a debt that needs to be repaid. That's what brings us all here. Though unless you've got five million shoved up your poopchute we have a problem."

"You have me confused. Who are we making right with this money, Luke or you?" Archie asked.

Jed stood and paced the study. "Luke and I have been best friends all our lives. He's vouched for me and in turn, I look out for him. His parents have never treated him with the kind of respect I feel he deserves. Just as he might be coming into his own, financially speaking, you come around and poison old man Morgenstern into cutting him out of the will. Now it falls to me to salvage something for him." Jed's movements were jerky.

"Where's Rose?"

"We'll get to her just as soon as you show me the money."

Cutter walked up to Archie and put his arm around his shoulders. "C'mon Wendt, don't be such a hard-on. You don't need the money, a rich guy like you. Just do the right thing and hand it over. Nobody gets hurt."

Archie glowered at Jed. "I don't see any wrong that I need to right. Just a shiftless, worthless piece of shit trying to cash in and (turning to Cutter) pond scum opportunism."

Jed stopped mid-pace. "You're awfully ballsy for someone who is powerless. But maybe you don't understand that yet," He called out. "Luke."

They turned to the door and Luke walked in, pulling Rose by the bicep. Luke looked like he aged in the short time since Archie last saw him. Rose appeared unhurt and unworried. She met Archie's solicitous looks with contempt, then she sat on the sofa.

Jed laughed like he was really enjoying the moment. "See, Rose, I told you he wasn't that smart. He came right away when I threatened to harm you."

"You're a genius, Jed. Always have been." Rose looked bored more than anything.

"The threat to Rose was a bluff? Then why would I give you the money now? You don't have anything on me."

"Au contraire, Dr. Wendt. I have everything. I have you." With that Jed pulled out a handgun. "Please tell me you have the money because I'd hate to go through the process of killing you and not get something out of it."

Archie turned to Rose. "You're going along with this? What the hell is the matter with you?"

"What's the matter with me? From the man who manipulated my father and killed my mother. Just looking at you is making me sick."

"How could you believe that I killed your mother?"

"There was a witness who saw you hit her with the frying pan. It makes sense to me. She was threatening to keep that money away from you. And after the things I heard from the detective (she nodded towards Cutter) it all fell into place."

"You were here that day. Why would I hang around and speak with you? And manipulated your father? You were privy to practically every conversation he and I had. Whatever these guys have told you isn't true."

"So you didn't fall in love with a patient in Boston who then killed herself? You weren't married at the time? You weren't suspended from your practice? Are those lies?"

Her words took the starch out of Wendt. "No, those things are all true. But I've never killed anyone in my life."

Jed banged the gun on the desk like a gavel. "I'm sorry to interrupt

Days of Our Lives over here, but I need that money now. So." He cocked the gun and pointed it at Archie. "Where's the fucking money."

What was I thinking in coming in here without the gun? Archie started to panic. "How are you going to explain killing me when the cops come?"

"When Chief Lynne comes I'll explain that you weren't satisfied with just the killing of Mrs. Morgenstern. That you wanted to take out the rest of the family, too. And I shot you in self-defense. I'm sure with enough money I can make that work."

"Did you know that Lynne tried to take all the money tonight? He jacked me outside of Daugherty's office. You sure he'll be satisfied with whatever crumbs you throw him?"

A shred of doubt entered Jed's face. Cutter walked over to him. "Don't listen to him. That's what shrinks do, we talked about this." Jed's face hardened and he re-focused the gun on Wendt.

"Was it your idea to bring poor Katherine into this?" Archie said to Luke. "Huh? You're a mama's boy. How could you let him do that to your mother? That's *got* to be eating away at you."

Luke grew agitated and went over to the sideboard for a drink. "Let's just get this over with. Give us the money and let's be done once and for all."

"She cut you off, didn't she? That's what happened. She said grow up already, be a man; cut loose from Jed once and for all or you're getting nothing. And she meant it. So you killed her." Archie could feel the gun follow him as he took steps towards Luke. "Your mother, for crissakes."

Luke slammed his drink down. "I didn't kill her, you stupid bastard. Now shut the fuck up and give us the money." He looked over at Jed.

"Us?" Archie asked. "Just how many of you knuckleheads are going to divide up the loot? There's Jeddy, Lukey, Curty, Horacey - that's a lot of mouths to feed, nes't-ce pas? How did you plan on making the split? Who decides?"

The men stood silently. Rose walked over to Luke. "You told me that you saw Wendt kill Mother. You pulled the sibling card and swore it was Wendt. Was it?"

"Of course it was," Jed maintained. "He's just trying to pit us against each other."

"Did Wendt kill Mother or not, Luke?"

"Rose, with Luke written out of the will, you stood to inherit everything." Archie raced to get the words out. "Once they kill me you're going to be next. Then the estate falls into probate and Luke is the sole living heir. Don't you see that's——."

Jed pistol whipped Archie; he fell hard to the ground.

"You never said my mom was going to get hurt," Luke said.

Jed walked over to Luke and put a hand on his shoulder. "C'mon, man. You knew the plan, you just lacked the balls to put it in place. Needed me to make things happen. This was the only way you were going to get paid."

"I knew you were fucked up, Jed. But I didn't realize how evil you were." Rose said.

"Be quiet Rose before we reconsider the necessity of you being around."

"Oh, you're going to kill my sister now, too?" Luke threw back another drink. "I should never have listened to you."

"Most of this wasn't my idea. It was his." Jed pointed at Cutter who was doing his best to melt into the wall.

Archie struggled to his feet. "Luke, now's the time to put an end to this. Don't let any more bad things happen. Stop Jed now."

Jed heard. He grabbed Archie by the hair and pulled him out of the room.

"Okay, headshrinker. The time has come for you to get me my money. I know you picked it up because the lawyer called. Give it to me now or I'm going to blow your fucking brains out, so help me."

"It's this way." Archie walked towards the front door. His mind worked feverishly to come up with a way to get the bag of money and gun at the same time.

Jed was really wired now and muttered aloud. "Shoulda fucking killed you right away. Not worth the money."

They reached the front door and Archie still didn't have a plan. He opened the door and Jed pulled him roughly. "If this is some sort of trap my first shot will be at your crotch and we'll go from there."

Wendt shook himself free and reached into the plant on his right. Nothing. he stuck his head in the shrubs and confirmed that the gun was gone.

The sheriff backed his car into a neighbor's driveway across the street and watched the Morgenstern house. He couldn't be sure who was over there and what his next move should be, but the clock ticked. As he pondered, Lynne pulled up to the curb in a cruiser and got out. For a moment, the chief stood in his open door looking in Hidalgo's direction. *He can't see me, can he?* The sheriff squinted his eyes. The chief shook his head slowly, an unmistakable threat directed at Hidalgo.

Lynne slammed his car door shut and walked to the front door. Before going in he paused and looked to his left.

"What are you doing, you mongrel," Hidalgo said.

Lynne reached into the bushes and pulled out a gun. He cocked his head as if he'd heard something and trotted out of sight to the back. Hidalgo got out of his car, checked the 9mm in his shoulder holster and the small Sig in his ankle one. He made a beeline after Lynne.

A rchie cursed silently to himself and pulled the Gladstone out from behind the other bush. He passed the bag backwards without looking. Jed took it and kneeled in the foyer with it. "Hot damn." He pulled out stacks to get a sense of the depth. "Looks close. I'm sure that greedy bastard Daugherty took more than we agreed on, but you done well, doc.

"Now, what to do with you."

Jed absentmindedly used the gun to tick a rhythm against his thigh. "I could shoot you, but disposing of the body could be problematic. And I don't know how much I can count on the greediness of that bastard Lynne. Maybe he just keeps extorting money from me. Then again, I can't have you hounding me. What to do, what to do."

"Maybe the decision will be taken out of your hands, limpdick."

Jed whipped his head around. Both recognized the slow drawl of the chief of police.

"Chief, what are you doing here?" Jed reached behind him to take hold of Wendt's clothing, just out of his reach. Archie eased himself away from the foyer and noted Lynne's reunion with his shotgun.

"Don't look so surprised, Miller. You didn't think I'd sit and wait for you to bring me my cut, did you? It's not in my nature to trust a lowlife like you. Now why don't you drop your gun before I'm forced to put you down."

Jed continued to softly pat his thigh with the gun. "I heard that you tried to take the whole enchilada. Speaking of lowlife, that seems like a dirty move to me."

"Last warning, Miller." Lynne pointed the gun at Jed. "Put the gun down. Now."

Archie drifted further into the living room, pointed in a direction perpendicular to the two men and yelled, "Look out!"

Both men froze long enough for Archie to scamper towards the study. He turned to see if he had pursuers when a big blast echoed throughout the house sending Jed backwards. Archie darted into the study, slammed the heavy oak door and locked it.

He stood against the door, safe in the knowledge that a cannon couldn't breach the tough oak. Rose and Luke stood, shocked looks on their faces. Cutter crouched under the desk.

"What the hell just happened?" Rose asked.

"It's been some time since I was in medical school, but I think Chief Lynne just blew a hole in Jed."

Luke took the news with placidity. "Serves him right far as I'm concerned." Rose's face registered a deeper meaning.

"Think Luke. If he's taken Jed out, what do you think he has planned for us?"

"I can't speak for the Morgenstern clan," Archie said, "but I can tell you what it means for me. And where the fuck did that piece of shit Cutter go?"

Both sister and brother pointed under the desk.

Archie began a search of the study pulling on books, testing walls, and looking behind paintings. "Your father ever talk about a panic room? Or some cache of weapons just in case of home invasion?"

Again with the shrugs.

"Thanks, you guys are a big fucking help."

"Look, our father didn't invite us in here often. It was his room. He never spoke about it with me. How about you, Luke?"

He shot her a disbelieving look. She turned back to Archie. "I didn't think so. Sorry. What are we going to do?"

Before they could answer there was a hard knock on the oak door.

"Lenore?" Archie called out. He stood behind the desk, pulling on drawers looking for anything that could be weaponized. Nothing in them and the top middle draw was locked.

"Open up, Wendt." Lynne yelled.

"Go fuck yourself. We've got provisions and lots of booze. We can be happy in here for many years."

Luke started for the door. Archie leaped across the desk and blocked his path to the door.

"What the hell are you thinking?"

"Getthefuckoff me, shrink. I'm not staying in here with you. I got nothing to hide from Lynne."

Luke attempted to pull free from his grip. Archie looked over at Rose for help. "Don't you fucking get it, Luke? He has no reason to keep you alive. You'll make a justified claim for the five million that he thinks he deserves. You need a fucking diagram?"

Lynne continued banging on the door. "Open up you piece of shit!"

"Why should we trust you?" Rose asked Archie. "You still stand to get the five million."

"Your working thesis is I'm focused on the money right now? I had you pegged for smarter." Archie continued to pull against Luke who's steady diet of weed and laziness rendered him weaker. "And besides, of the two of us, I'm the only one that hasn't tried to kill someone."

"What?" Rose looked genuinely perplexed, a look not easily feigned. Luke, on the other hand, had the more recognizable sheepish visage associated with guilt. It grew quiet outside the study. Rose began to talk again and Archie held up a hand and shushed her.

"Don't shush me—-."

"Listen."

Archie's slackened his grip; Luke took advantage to rip his arm free and bolt for the door. Both Archie and Rose sprang into action. Luke pushed a high back chair in their way and made it to the handle. They tried to pull him back as he opened the heavy door revealing nothing behind it. Just the dark living room. Luke listened at the door, then cautiously stepped out into the living room and stopped. Archie and Rose peered around him willing to use him as a human shield, if need be. Cutter stood from under the desk, thought better of it and crouched again. The living room was dark and silent. The only thing visible from the foyer's light was a pair of legs jutting out from the front entranceway some fifty feet from them.

CHAPTER

51

The back door stood open. Hidalgo listened for noises inside the house, anything that would give away positions. In his mind he walked the rooms like so many times before doing a threat assessment. Lynne was just one of his concerns. Jed Miller had long nurtured a rabid hatred for John Hidalgo, both of them in love with the same woman. Male voices carried from the front hall.

He peeked in the window and surveyed the empty kitchen. Crouching, he pulled out his 9mm and duck walked his way in. John moved in the direction of voices, through the kitchen then double-timing it to the edge of the dining room; he flattened himself on the floor, gun extended. He peered around the doorjamb and saw Jed, playing with his gun and talking to Archie.

The sheriff jumped when he heard Lynne's threatening voice boom out. John pulled back and sat up, his back to the wall, breathing heavy. Another peak around the corner just in time to see Archie point in his direction and yell. Hidalgo tucked his head and crawled, keeping Lynne's voice as a reference, looking to flank the police chief. A blast tore through the air and shook the pans hanging overhead. The echoes reverberated throughout the kitchen. John covered his ears and squeezed hard to quiet the noise in his head.

After a moment, he crawled back to see what became of Jed. Just then Lynne passed by. John pulled back and held his breath. The police chief was so focused on his quarry he didn't notice the man crouching seven feet to his left. The chief looked briefly remorseful as he examined his handiwork. Then he bent down and picked up a bag, opened it and smiled.

Lynne's footsteps receded down the living room. John inched a little further forward and used the wall's edge to cup the pinna of his ear for better sound pick-up. He heard the chief bang on the door and a muffled response from behind the door. Then silence. Hidalgo strained to pick up any further sounds. He dared a peak into the living room. Empty. The quiet pressed on him. Then:

"You gonna sit there and wait for me to shoot you in the back or do you want to turn and face me like a man."

John raised both arms and used the wall to stand up. "You don't want to do this, Horace."

"I got a bagful of money that says you're wrong and a gun that says you're going to walk with me." He took the sheriff's 9mm and used his own pistol to point towards the study. "I think I saw another way to get to that medieval looking door."

"You've got the money, why in the hell don't you just get the hell out of here? I'll give you three days before any pursuit."

"I appreciate the advice, jerkoff, but seeing as you've always been a puppet for old Morgenstern you'll forgive me if I don't trust you; just keep your opinions to yourself. Now move."

Hidalgo walked, shaking his head. "You can leave right now with the money and nobody else gets hurt."

Lynne let out a bark of a laugh. "I ain't only about the money. I have some scores to settle including with your shrink friend. Plus, and I don't mind saying, I imagine old Virg' kept some treasures in that office of his just in case. That should sweeten the pot."

"No use other people getting hurt."

"That's enough. Over here to the left." They walked through a short hallway; Lynne pulled Hidalgo to a stop a few feet from the study door just as it slowly opened.

Archie advanced slowly through the door and into the living room, past Luke. Cartoonishly slow with an exaggerated lifting of his shoes from the carpet.

"You look like a Scooby-Doo cartoon. Dufus." Luke pushed by Wendt. When he drew near the foyer Luke slowed and peaked around the corner. "Fuck." He said and put his hand to his forehead. "He's fucking dead. Holy shit, there's a lot of blood."

"What did you expect, Luke? Shotguns blow holes in people. We need to get back to the safety of the study. Lynne didn't just disappear; he's here somewhere. Now that his shotgun has the taste of human flesh it's not going to stop."

"He's right." Rose said. "Let's get back to Dad's study and we can figure this out."

"Figure what out? Jed is dead. Oh, fuck. What the hell am I going to do now." He crouched down with his hands laced over his head, elbows flapping at his ears.

"You're going to do just what your sister said, dickhead. Get back in the study."

They all turned back to the study door and saw Lynne nudge Hidalgo into the room. The light wasn't great, but the gun illuminated the situation nicely. "C'mon back here." The chief seemed to sing as he motioned the three into the study. "This is a good place as any to keep you all in my sights while I figure things out." They slowly walked into the study, heads hanging down. The chief closed the door after them. "All of you on the sofa. Not you Wendt, you stand by the bookshelf."

Luke, Rose, and Hidalgo crammed onto the leather couch while Archie walked over to the shelves behind Virgil's desk. Lynne came to stand next to him and smiled. Then he raised his left hand and fired a bullet from Hidalgo's 9mm into the oak door.

The room amplified the sound a thousand fold scaring the shit out of all of them except for the police chief. He walked over to the door and examined the hole, probing it with a switchblade he pulled from his pocket.

He turned to Hidalgo. "This is one tough fucking door, I'll tell you that. Should make for recovering the slug nice and easy." Looking over at Archie, he said. "Shame you thought fit to fire at the chief of police. And with the sheriff's own gun."

"Don't do what you're thinking, Horace, it isn't worth it." Hidalgo looked positively alarmed. He stood ready for action.

Archie wasn't grasping it yet; he looked perplexed and dazed.

Lynne's face contorted into anger and he raised his right hand to fire a shot from his own pistol. Hidalgo jumped forward and hit Lynne's arm as the gun fired. Archie's body spun counter clockwise as the bullet struck his left shoulder.

"What the fuck, Horace, have you lost your mind?" Hidalgo shouted.

Lynne turned his gun on the sheriff. "Goddamn you, man. I warned you not to get in the way. Now sit down or I'll put you down, too."

"You're not going to shoot me. I'm going to check on him, so you just relax." The police chief kept the weapon up, but didn't protest.

Hidalgo trotted over to where Archie lay crumpled on the ground, his shirt darker around his left shoulder. More familiar with gunshot wounds than he ever hoped to be, he pulled off Archie's flannel shirt to examine the wound, front and back. There was a neat hole in the undershirt and crimson all around. Archie was breathing rapidly, looking at Hidalgo with wide eyes.

"The fucker shot me. He actually shot me. I am actually wounded by a gunshot."

"Yes, Archie, this is actually happening." Hidalgo tore up Archie's shirt into a couple of strips and two wads. "He got you in the deltoid. The bleeding is local; I don't think he hit any major artery. I'm going to bind it, so just sit tight."

"You know," Archie said, his eyes becoming more focused, "it doesn't even hurt that much."

"That's because adrenaline and endorphins are rushing through your system. You know that better than me, doctor." Hidalgo smiled in an effort to be reassuring. Time and again he did that on the battlefield in the waning moments of a fallen comrade's life. He placed the balled up shirt pieces on the entrance and exit wounds, the latter more ragged and responsible for bleeding. The strips he looped around the armpit and tied to each other.

"That should hold for a bit." John helped Archie off the floor and onto the sofa next to Rose. He stayed standing.

"Don't look at me that way, Hidalgo. You shouldn't have intervened when I was serving justice. Wendt knows what he deserves." The chief eyeballed Archie, finger on the trigger of his gun. Lynne suddenly changed course and looked at the brother and sister seated on the sofa. "Well, young Morgensterns. It goes without saying my career as police chief of Harding has run its course. I've got money, but I could always use more. Where did your father keep cash?"

Neither sibling answered. Lynne pointed the gun at Rose.

"Where did ol' Virgil keep walking around money?"

"I don't know. My father didn't share those things with us," she answered.

"Come now. You were daddy's little girl, everyone knows that. Give me a guess."

"She doesn't know, asshole, stop badgering her," Archie said.

"Archie for crissakes, keep your mouth shut," Hidalgo snapped.

"Shrink, your time on this earth is quickly coming to an end. If you want me to speed you into the next life, by all means, keep pissing me off." Lynne walked around to the desk.

"Well lookee here. In all the excitement, I failed to take a full rendering of the room. Why don't you stand and go over there with the rest of them."

Cutter got out from under the desk and sheepishly walked over.

"You truly are a weasel," Archie said.

"I never claimed to be a hero," Cutter whined.

"I'm going to need you guys to stay over there and keep quiet. If I hear things I'm going to assume you're thinking of giving me the bum's rush and I will start firing. And I'm a great fucking shot at this range." Lynne turned his attention to exploring the shelves, pulling at books, pushing at molding looking for a trapdoor.

Hidalgo leaned back and exhaled.

"You gonna take this shit?"

Archie turned to him. "What choice do we have?" he whispered.

Hidalgo shot him a puzzled look. "What?"

"You said, 'you gonna take this shit.'"

"I didn't say anything."

Lynne didn't pay attention to their conversation, too busy now was he with the desk. Pulling drawers, poking around papers. The chief inspected the locked middle drawer more closely, then disappeared under the desk.

"You've been pushed around long enough, haven't you? Why don't you stand up for yourself?"

Garrett stood in the corner rolling a quarter through his fingers like it rode a wave.

"My psychosis has returned," Archie said and stood.

Lynne's head snapped up from under the desk. "You better sit back down or I'm going to paint the rear wall with your intestines." He ducked back down.

Archie turned to the couch sitters. "Do you see a man standing over there?" He pointed at Garrett.

Rose and Hidalgo sported dual worried looks on their faces, though Luke didn't give a shit. "Archie, sit back down. You're scaring us."

"Sit the fuck down, Doc. Don't be playing your crazy head games with me or I will shoot you down like the dog you are," came a voice from under the big desk.

"This guy is not a good guy, Arch, I'm telling you. He extorts, shakes down drug dealers; he gives even crooked law officers a bad name."

"Thanks for the tip, Garrett, but best you let me handle this my own way." Archie ran his right hand through his hair. "Chief, just what are you prepared to do, huh? Kill all of us in cold blood. C'mon, that's not going to happen."

Lynne stood up again feeling all around the underside of the desk, a frustrated look etched on his face. He appeared ready to react to Wendt with another threat when he ducked his head under the desk again. "Shit, there's a goddamned keypad under here. Any chance either of you brats know the code to Daddy's desk?"

"If I may be of assistance, uh, Chief. I saw that myself."

Lynne stood. "Just who the fuck might you be, peckerwood?"

"The name's Cutter and I might be someone who can help you get into that desk. Dollars to doughnuts there's something valuable in there."

"I suppose you'll want something for the trouble."

"A little something, but not exorbitant," Cutter said.

"You never miss an opportunity to be a snake, do you Cutter?"

"Nobody asked for a shrink's opinion, so just shut the fuck up." Lynne spat. "If you've got help to offer, Cutter, best do it fast."

"Gotcha." He turned his attention to Rose, pushed his dirty blond hair out of his eyes in a practiced move of seduction. "Miss Rose, I'm hearing you were the apple of your daddy's eye. I'm guessing you're the key to that desk. What's your birthdate?"

Rose sat silently with a stone look on her face.

"I don't have time for your bullshit." Lynne said and fired off another shot from the 9mm into the oak door. Rose shrieked and put her hands over her ears.

When the reverberations died down Lynne spoke slowly: "What - is - your - date - of - birth?"

"October twentieth,1984."

"That's 10-20-84," Cutter said.

Lynne just glared at him for a moment, then ducked down again. They heard six beeps and a clicking sound. He stood, grinning ear to ear. "This is the payoff for persistence, boys and girls, let that be a lesson." Lynne opened the middle drawer and pulled out a metallic box, like you would find in a safe deposit box. He placed the 9mm on the desk and his own Baretta in the holster.

Lynne's attention was focused entirely on the box and didn't notice Cutter reach down into his own ankle holster and pull out a snub nose revolver.

"Chief, I hate to be that guy, but I'm going to ask you to drop your gun and step away from that box."

Lynne looked up, but didn't comply. He slowly replaced the box in the drawer and closed it with a click. "Mister, I don't know who you think you are, but ain't no way I'm doing either of those things. Why don't you put that thing down before you get yourself killed."

"I'm not going to be able to do that," Cutter said.

"Put the gun down right now." Lynne repeated and exposed a badge clipped to his belt. "You see this, dickhead, it means I can shoot you without skipping a beat."

"Horace, calm down. Nobody needs to get hurt." John stood, pulled at his ankle holster and brandished his compact Sig. "Everyone, just keep calm."

The three armed men stood triangulated in the study, the two Morgenstern progeny wedged on the couch in the middle of the isosceles. Wendt paced just outside the line connecting Hidalgo and Cutter.

Lynne laughed. "Looks like we got ourselves a good old fashioned Mexican standoff." he said. He alternated the business end of his gun between Cutter and Hidalgo. "You ever been in one of these John?"

"Can't say I have. You?"

"No. But I'm familiar with them. It ain't the first guy who shoots that's got the advantage. It's the second. Unless an advantage can be garnered in the meantime."

"I'm not looking for an advantage; I want all of us to live to tell this tale. So why don't we all just calm down."

"Fuck that, John. I know you. You think because you were a Marine sniper you're a better shot than me, but what will you do about Limpdick over there." He tilted his head in Cutter's direction.

"Just what is your interest here, Cutter?" John asked.

"You could say payment for services rendered. Perhaps we can work something out."

"Here's what we can work out. Put your gun down, you're under arrest," Lynne said.

"Ha! On what authority?" Archie taunted. "You're an outlaw now just like Cutter. In this triumvirate, the only one who still represents law and order is the sheriff and you know it."

The chief spared his attention from the gunmen a moment to shoot a practiced wilting look at Archie. He'd used it for years to good effect. Archie held the gaze, a wild look in his own eyes. The chief spoke menacingly. "Whatever happens here I can promise I will get you. I will not forget you blindsiding me back at the station house."

Garrett moved from the corner, walked along the bookcase examining books. "You know he has to kill you all now; no way he can let any of you live."

"I know, I know." Archie said.

"Listen, Horace. We all lose if someone starts blasting so let's just relax for the moment and talk this out. What if we all agree to lower our weapons and sit," John suggested.

"I'm not giving up my gun, Sheriff John Brown." Cutter said gripping the pistol tightly. "So you can save the negotiating tactic."

The sheriff smiled and turned to Cutter. "My name's John Hidalgo, but I like Marley, so I'll let that go. I don't want to die and assume you feel the same way. So, lower your weapon."

"I thought Clapton's version was better. And I'll agree to a detente if Chief Asshole over there does the same."

John turned back to Lynne. "What do you say, Horace? Willing to at least set our guns down for a moment and talk this through? It's not like you can't re-draw that gun at any time."

"You're goddamned right I can draw it anytime. I am the Chief of Police for Harding, the ranking officer of the law in this town, so sure as shit in this fucking room. You, sir, are obstructing justice. Put your gun down now."

"Do you see this?" Archie gestured wildly with his left arm. "This guy is fucking delusional. How can anything good come out of this with this psychopath holding a badge and a gun?"

John kept his eyes on Lynne, but spoke to Archie. "Stop inflaming the situation. Sit down and be quiet. Let me work this out so that no one gets hurt."

Garrett leaned against the wall. "You're not looking good, Doc, I can tell you that. You've lost some blood and you're probably in shock."

"Look who's talking, you ghoul," Archie said.

"Who are you talking to?" Rose said.

Damian, who'd joined Garrett holding up a wall, lit a cigarette. "Archie, it's time you came clean about what happened in Boston."

Archie paced like a caged panther in a three foot enclosure. "How is talking about what happened going to change anything here?"

"This might be your last chance," Damian said. "The gunshot wound might not kill you, but Lynne isn't going to let you live now. He's too far gone; his only way through is to complete the task."

"I agree with you there."

Lynne grew more restless. He used his gun to point to the sheriff. "You better get this nutjob under control. His bullshit is pissing me off." He raised his voice to Archie. "Don't think just cause you're acting batshit crazy I won't shoot you. I'll shoot crazy as much as I'll shoot normal."

Archie stopped his pacing and looked at Lynne. It had such a piercing quality that Lynne actually took a step back.

"You're willing to trade in whatever little good you've done in your life for a little bit of money. That's got to be the sorriest thing I've ever heard."

"It's not a little bit. It's five million dollars and I earned it after all the shit I've taken from the assholes in this town. Years of service to ungrateful bastards. Having to kowtow to the all powerful Virgil Morgenstern; it's enough to make a man puke." He lifted the Gladstone bag. "This is my severance and muster pay."

"Unburden yourself. Open up about your past sins." Damian said.

Archie flashed anger and yelled, "Fuck off, Father. With all the suffering I've imbibed from patients over the years one confession won't negate the intense antipathy I have for God and all religion."

"Don't punish yourself. Confess and be absolved, Archie." Damain soothed.

Everyone froze, spell bound by Archie's one man show.

Luke broke the silence.

"If we're going to be cooped up in here, I'm sparking up." He pulled a joint from his back pocket and lighted it. He looked at the sheriff and police chief in turn. "If I make it out of here alive, you can arrest me."

"Horace, if it's true that you're intent on going on the run, leave now. Take your money and go in peace. We'll stay in here and give you a head start," John said.

Lynne shook his head. "You must think me a goddamned idiot. I can't trust any of you."

Cutter cleared his throat theatrically. "You're damn right not to trust us, Chief. I ain't letting you leave. Mayberry over there doesn't speak for me," he said.

While the gunned gentleman bantered, Rose turned to Archie. "What's happening to you? Your little tics and peccadillos were cute before, but this level of crazy is concerning."

"She's cute. This the one you shtupped?" Garrett asked lecherously.

Archie turned away from Rose and said, "Shtupped? Where did you pick up a word like that?"

"Who are you talking to?" she asked again.

Hidalgo spoke up. "Stress has gotten to him. I saw it happen when I was in the Marines; combat makes some men crazy."

"Battling the fine folks of Harding, as it were." Archie offered a wry smile.

"C'mon, Archie. Stop torturing yourself; the Lord will forgive you if you will just make a confession." Damian pleaded. "Do it before it's too late."

"Nobody wants to hear my tale of woe."

"That's not true, Archie." Rose stood and walked over to him. "Come sit down on the couch and tell us what happened to you before you came to Harding. It will do everyone good to take a break from the threats."

"Shut your mouth, missy. I ain't interested in what he has to say," Lynne said.

"Give it a rest, Horace. Nothing will happen if we take a moment. The guns will still work." John kept his gun up, but moved to sit on the sofa's broad arm.

Archie got Lynne's attention and held it with his eyes. His face was etched with pain and concern, and once again, the force of it moved Lynne despite his best efforts. He spoke in calm, measured tones.

"Chief Lynne, I am truly sorry that your ex-wife took advantage of the power of accusation to poison your kids and the court. That kind of shit destroys credibility for the rest of humanity who really experience brutality and caused you immense pain, no doubt."

Lynne's facial expression relaxed, the gun lowered; he tacitly offered the floor.

Archie prepared to speak when all heard a loud crash followed by cursing.

Everyone tensed. Guns were immediately re-raised. Shouts were exchanged.

"Put it down!"

"You put it down!"

"Easy, Horace. Everyone be easy." John modeled deep breathing and restored order. "I'm going to walk slowly, open the door, and see who's out there."

"The hell you are, asshole. You move and I'm going to blast away," Lynne said.

"Think, Horace. If that person sounds the alarm you'll have more company, not less."

"Good point. I'll get the door."

"You forget about me, *Horace?*" Cutter chided, tensing his grip on the pistol.

"Why don't you move as one." Archie said. "Like the group hug in the finale of The Mary Tyler Moore Show." Nobody responded. "I guess you all don't watch classic television. Your loss."

Cutter moved slowly backward for the door, his eyes fixed on the two law officers. He opened it and stood facing the room. "Okay? I'm just going to peek out." He poked his head out. "Why don't you join us in here?" He flashed the gun to whoever was standing on the other side.

Howard Rogoff walked in the room slowly and took in the triad of guns. "Clearly I can see I'm interrupting; I'll just see myself out."

"Is this your idea of a rescue? Nice work, Howard." Archie said.

"Rescue? I don't know I had such delusions of grandeur. Thought I'd check in on you, though, make sure you're not in imminent danger. I appear to be too late. You've been shot."

Archie threw him a sarcastic thumbs up. "Your medical skills are sharp, Quincy, MD."

"Have a seat, Dr. Rogoff. You're not going anywhere." Lynne gestured with his gun to an empty chair and Howard sat.

"Good to see you, Howard." John said. "Apart from stepping into an obviously volatile situation, we could use your professional skills. Archie here is having some sort of nervous breakdown, talking to imaginary folks in the room."

Howard nodded solemnly and walked over to Archie. He looked at the triad of pointed guns while he kneeled in front of the younger psychiatrist, checked vital signs. "The Mexican standoff. Used to be a staple of the old westerns, but became cliché. Nice to see it being resurrected.

"And you, boychick, have you finally crossed over to frank psychosis?"

"I would be the last to know, wouldn't I?" Archie said.

"Reasonable question. Another might be when is the last time you had a drink?"

Archie furrowed his brow. "You know I can't remember. I think it was yesterday evening, but it feels like an eternity."

"Hold up your hands."

Archie complied, the trembling visible to all.

"I would say you might be in the early stages of the DTs."

"DTs?" Rose asked.

"Yes, alcohol withdrawal can turn nasty with visual hallucinations and agitation. Has he been agitated?"

"Yes," three people said at once.

"Doc, you got some sort of sedative you can give him?" John asked. He'd been an EMT and seen all sorts of drunks.

"No, I don't have sedatives on me. The only person who carries such things around are ne'er do wells looking to slip a Mickey to some unsuspecting lass. However, alcohol will do. Luke, make yourself useful and pour a generous drink for Archie."

Luke rose and busied himself at the bar.

Damian lit up another cigarette. "Archie, the floor is technically still yours. Let me hear your confession and give you some absolution."

Archie labored to focus on the priest in his gray Georgetown sweatsuit, lazily enjoying his Chesterfield King. He took the proffered glass from

Luke and drank it greedily. It's effects on his nerves were rapid. "I agree it would be a good idea not to die with this on my mind and I would like to share if you'll let me." He took the silence as collective acquiescence. This would be the first time in his life that Archie would avail himself to the group experience. He cleared his throat and spoke.

CHAPTER

55

"She wasn't terribly attractive. Seems cruel to start with that, but I want to set the tone that I was a seasoned psychiatrist, not given over to crude animal longings. But there was something about her that hit me the right way. The more I saw her the more I couldn't get her out of my mind. Each appointment I sat and daydreamed about her as she poured her heart out to me. I looked forward to those days she had a session."

"My marriage was on the rocks at that time and I found myself seeking emotional connection elsewhere. For some reason I can't quite fathom, I focused all that love starved attention on Janine." He shook his head. "Poor Janine, with her low self-esteem and constant thoughts of suicide. Normally I'm able to handle a patient's flirtations with suicide. I mean, if you hospitalized everyone who had a suicidal thought the hospitals would overflow. But, I found it harder and harder to hear her contemplate taking her own life. Finally, one session she told me that she had a plan to overdose and had even taken a few pills to see if she could keep them down and not vomit. I panicked. Not like a doctor does over his patient but more like an addict does when his stash runs low. I was that obsessed with her. To combat her suicidal intentions, I convinced her to come in for extra sessions, multiple times per week and of course she readily agreed."

"That's a recipe for disaster," Howard interjected.

Archie nodded. "So it was. Because as Howard will attest, when you reward suicidal behavior with more attention, you only increase that very behavior. Which is what happened. So, continuing in that desperate theme I suggested we check in by telephone in between sessions. One thing led to another and I was seeing her outside of the office in a personal capacity. I convinced myself that a connection to me would keep her alive. She went along with every suggestion."

Archie spoke to a point in the wall where it met the ceiling. "Janine was so innocent. It was completely inappropriate of me to breach treatment in that way."

Rose directed a question to Howard. "Isn't it unethical to date patients?"

"You can lose your medical license," he responded.

Archie got irritated. "Of course the ethics bothered me, but I felt justified. Self-righteous, even. I was on my own, no one looking over my shoulder and I believed I was saving a life.

"Look, I'm not asking you to see things my way, just trying to explain it from my vantage point. If you want to judge, then fine."

"Oh shut up, you sanctimonious prick, and go on with the story," Cutter spat.

Archie sulked for a moment, then continued. "The relationship was doomed from the start. What exists in the office is artificial, not real - a fantasy because all the realities that exist on the outside are muted in the safe confines of the four walls of a therapist's office. As a real couple, we were mismatched. I knew what I wanted to do for her, but it didn't dawn on me to ask myself, 'What can she do for me?' It was all about my wanting to save her."

Rogoff spoke up. "The white knight syndrome. Particularly caring clinicians become enmeshed in saving patients. Usually those patients are aware that they can have that effect on others and they use it to manipulate. They can be very seductive."

The room turned its attention back to Wendt. He sensed an unasked question.

"We didn't have sex. Came close to it, but something kept me from doing that. Knowing that it would seal the deal, so to speak. And I quickly knew I didn't want that. I tried to return us to the office relationship." He laughed. "Do you hear what I just said? What an idiot, right? I offer her infinitely more than just a doctor patient relationship and then I try to put the genie back in the lamp. The toothpaste back in the tube. Anyway, you can imagine how that went over.

"She made threats that she was going to suicide unless we got back together. I told her that I wouldn't be able to live with myself if she did, but I couldn't give her what she wanted; to tell her we would be together again. No matter how much I wanted to, I couldn't force my mouth to form the words. She then lapsed into a silence in our sessions that was a combination of anger and resignation. I tried to get her to talk about once again feeling rejected. Can you believe that? I was still trying to be a therapist, working to therapize her from my own actions against her. How fucked up is that?"

"I began living in fear. Fear that my actions would be exposed, that I would be revealed for making the cardinal sin in therapy; that I might be the very reason that pushed her over the edge to seal the deal. All of it. In a desperate bid to keep her from hurting herself I doubled down. I told her that I was in love with her, but conflicted because of my marriage. I made her promise not to kill herself; she refused. Then I told her that if she killed herself I would end my own life. She didn't buy it so I upped the ante; I entered into a suicide pact with her. I didn't want to die. But I believed I could keep her tethered to Earth by her conscience.

"We joked about Glen and Val. That was how we referred to the suicide pact because we were going to take a bunch of Valium with a nice bottle of Glenlivet. I never intended on honoring my end of the bargain - for me it was a complete bluff. But to Janine suicide was all too real. Her previous attempts took the mystique out of the process and they weren't cries for attention."

"As her hurt and anguish intensified she kept pushing for a hard date. I hemmed and hawed, kept postponing, putting her off, so she set a date. The night that she scheduled for our collective check-out, I went to a bar, got blackout drunk, and woke up in the gutter. Literally. The next morning, I convinced myself that there was no way she went through with it. When she didn't show for the appointment I didn't panic so protected was I in my cocoon of denial. I got the call from a family member the next day. She overdosed and cut her wrists in a bathtub just to make sure."

Everyone was silent, then Hidalgo said, "What was the fallout?"

"Of course, her family sued me. When a person dies prematurely everyone is filled with unimaginable grief. Anger feels better so it's natural that when there is an outlet for the anger, like the doctor, people use it. My hospital put the full weight of their legal department behind me and for a little while it looked like it might be dropped. Then one day their lawyer subpoenaed my private files."

"Private files?" Howard asked.

"What does that mean? Why are you asking him that way?"

"Because, Rose, psychiatrists have one set of records. They're not supposed to have private files."

Archie shifted on the sofa. "I kept process notes."

"What are process notes?" John and Rose both said.

Howard answered. "While conducting psychotherapy it helps to get supervision from someone who has been doing it for a while. The trainee, or novice therapist, writes down as much from a session as he can recall and brings it to the supervisor. They go over the notes together."

"I produced those notes for the court; plaintiff's council made an additional request. They wanted any material I produced while Janine was in my care; they wanted my private thoughts.

"While we were becoming more intimate I shared with her that I kept a journal. Janine pestered me to see it, but I didn't share it with her. She must have confided in one of her sisters that I kept a diary."

"Well you didn't give it to them, right?" Howard asked. "I mean, those kinds of personal musings are not the purview of the courts."

"That's what my lawyer argued. We had a hearing to discuss those journals. We lost. Judge ordered I produce them."

"What was in them?" Rose asked.

He looked at her. "In them?"

"Stop stalling. What had you written about Janine?"

Archie silently held her intense gaze. "That I loved her. That I would have done anything to stop her from killing herself."

"You gave over the journals?" Rose asked.

Archie nodded.

"Holy crap, Archie. Why didn't you burn them, bury them, tell the judge to go to hell. What were you thinking?" Howard said.

Archie shrugged his shoulders. "The only thing I can come up with is maybe I saw it as a penance for letting Janine exit this world alone."

"This is all so fucking touching, isn't it?" Lynne weighed in. "This goddamned shyster dupes and kills that poor girl and you feel sorry for him? What a bunch of bullshit."

Everyone ignored him.

"Is that what brought you here?" Rose said.

"Yes. After I produced the journals the case took an obvious turn for the worse for me. Now my lawyer was on her heels. The family wanted blood, but the judge pressured for a settlement. In his chambers he said he felt sorry for me; he could see I was overwrought and that my actions, though clear breaches of standard of care, were not malicious and criminal, but the desperate attempts of a fool in love. He made sure that the settlement included a sanction with the Massachusetts Medical Board that didn't preclude me practicing elsewhere. He was kind in those chambers, but the public humiliation proved unbearable." Archie absentmindedly stroked his chin. "With the revelation of the journals my wife, of course, left me. It was only the straw that broke the camel's back. We had been a poor match from the beginning."

"Those journals. When Virgil read about those he became fascinated with you." All eyes turned to John. He seemed surprised that he had the floor. "He couldn't believe that someone could have that kind of integrity. He kept saying, just like Howard, 'Why didn't he just burn those books? Why on earth did he hand them over when he knew they would condemn him? That's the kind of man you can trust, John, that's the kind of man you can depend on. Like Socrates, he kept saying. Like Socrates.'"

"You guys are a gullible bunch, aren't you?" Cutter sneered. "He screwed his patients and you think he has integrity."

Archie shrugged. "Maybe Cutter's right. I certainly have contempt for myself."

"Alright, enough of the pity crap," Howard said. "What the sheriff says jibes with me because Virgil asked me a fair amount, too. He asked about the laws of privacy and such. I wasn't sure what his angle was back then, but I guess he wanted to see if you could be trusted."

"Trusted for what?" Rose asked.

Archie turned to her. "He wanted me to believe that he was looking for a fresh opinion about his kids. That was the payoff he gave me after buttering me up with a great meal. And I bought it at the time because it made sense for succession and such. Luke was such an obvious fuck-up (from the couch Luke took a lazy pull from his roach at the sound of his name) I accepted that Virgil sought some help with him. Funny, though, I worked hard to train myself not to accept the first impression a patient laid out because it was usually bullshit, a screen for some deeper need or wish."

Howard nodded his agreement. "What do you think he meant?"

"Oh, I know what it was." Archie stood and resumed his pacing.

He walked by the bar, ran his fingers over the bottles. He picked up a distinguished looking bottle. It had a small model horse and rider on the cap. Like a hood ornament. Archie held onto its neck with his right hand and continued his walk and talk around the study, the bottle swinging with his gait.

"See, Virgil had a lot of secrets of his own. Things he didn't want to get out even after he was gone." Archie's pacing took him by Lynne whose hand tensed on the gun in his lap. "He saw me as an entrustee of his secret. Not only as a psychiatrist, who like a priest guards secrets, but one who had an integrity he prized. Who would have thought that my idiotic behavior back east would come off like a strong scent to a bloodhound? And for what secrets might he need the secure vault of my masochistic integrity?"

Archie stopped, aware that he had the room hanging on his every word.

"Secrets. Some are guarded to spare a person humiliation like sexual preference or a predilection that isn't societally acceptable. Others anxiously guard a secret they fear will humiliate those they most respect and admire." He walked by Cutter, not giving him a look.

"What was the secret, Archie? What did he entrust to you?" Rose asked, literally on the edge of her seat. He stopped and looked at her, the hint of a smile forming on his lips. Then in one fell swoop he gripped the bottle's neck tightly, swiveled his hips, and swung the bottle as hard he could upside Cutter's head.

everal things happened in quick succession. Cutter went down like someone dropped the floor out from under him. John and Lynne together made the intuitive leap of what three minus two meant and drew on each other. Their shouted threats caused a din. In that noise Archie dropped down on top of Cutter. The private investigator was unconscious and bleeding profusely from his temple. Archie grabbed Cutter's gun and pointed it at Lynne. The chief, now target of two weapons, kept his gun pointed at Hidalgo while looking at Archie on the ground.

"Put that fucking gun down right now, Wendt!"

"Horace, stop this now. Let's put the guns down and figure this out. No loss of life."

"Shut up, Hidalgo. You're not going to shoot me. And you, put the gun down right the fuck now, Wendt, or I *will* shoot you. Now!" Lynne turned his gun towards Archie on the floor. The yelling sounded far off, not related to him. Time slowed and Archie had an out of body sensation. Standing, as a matter of fact, next to Garrett who looked completely relaxed. Bored even. He spoke in even tones to Archie.

"You gotta shoot him first. He won't be satisfied with just killing you. He'll kill everyone to keep that money. You'll be saving lives starting with your own."

Archie nodded. "I got you."

The yelling grew louder. Archie, back on the floor, loosened his hold on the gun and made as if to put his hands up in surrender.

"That's more like it. Put the gun on the floor." Lynne barked.

Wendt feinted as if to let go, then gripped the pistol again with the intention of turning it on Lynne. The chief, long trained to never take the bait on any deception, felt a wave of calm rush over him as he pulled focus on the psychiatrist and squeezed the trigger.

The bullet sailed six inches to the left of Wendt and for a frozen moment Lynne was supremely confused: in that close setting, with his skills, that bullet should have torn the aortic root from the psychiatrist's heart. But with the blast that accompanied his own shot, he didn't appreciate other sounds, specifically the blast of John's Sig that struck the chief in his left chest and spun him around. Archie pulled the trigger on Cutter's gun until the barrel emptied. Lynne's torso absorbed several of those bullets, the others tore up the leather-bound books behind him.

CHAPTER

57

"Okay, Archie. Be easy." John pried the gun gently from Wendt's hand.

"Let's sit down. Howard, you want to help me?"

Rogoff lie on the ground, hands over his head. He got up slowly and helped the sheriff put Archie on the sofa. When they had him seated Howard said loudly, ears still ringing from the gunshots, "How about a drink? Everyone up for that?" He didn't wait for a response, but walked through the smoky air to the bar and poured five generous glasses. Luke held up his hand to demur on the alcohol and used a shaky hand to relight his joint. Rose sat on the sofa and hugged herself. Howard handed out the drinks.

John put his glass down and walked over to Cutter's supine body. He ripped a strip from Cutter's shirt and tied it tightly around the fallen man's head. It staunched the bleeding. The wound required stitches, but that could wait. He walked over to Lynne, crouched down and checked for a pulse knowing full well he wasn't going to find one. John looked over at Archie who met his gaze and asked, "Well?"

"Congratulations. In less than thirty seconds you single-handedly took out both your tormentors."

"I didn't plan this. Shit, I didn't plan any of this." Archie downed more bourbon.

There was a tentative knock at the door. Everyone tensed.

"Who's there?"

"John, it's me, Mike. Is it safe to enter?"

"Yeah, c'mon in."

Mike came in holding a rifle, followed by Paul Stringer, the surgeon recently released from the hospital after his own suicide attempt, likewise armed.

"Everyone okay?"

"We're fine, Mike, but we're going to need a new chief of police."

Mike looked down at Cutter. "What about this fucking guy?"

Howard answered, "Archie cut him up with a bottle kind of like you do when someone doesn't pay their tab. I'm glad you came; just in the nick of time," he added sarcastically.

"They were with you?" Archie asked.

Howard held up his open cellphone, its face recording the running time of the call. He pressed end. Mike held up his own and closed it.

"We heard everything. We just weren't sure when there might be a good time to intervene, I mean, holy shit, this is a nightmare scenario. Closed room, several guns, loose cannon like Lynne. What did you expect?"

"That's why you were so clumsy coming through the window, huh Howard?"

Rogoff looked sheepish. "Yes. All part of the plan, my good sheriff."

Archie laughed weakly. He looked at Stringer. "What are you doing here?"

"When I heard my favorite psychiatrist was in trouble I offered to help. And when Howard and Mike filled me in that Virgil was involved, well that clinched it."

"That reminds me." Archie said and rose out of the sofa. He walked behind the desk and found the Gladstone on the rug and picked it up. Walking across the room he offered the bag to Hidalgo.

"Thank you, Dr. Wendt. I was going to grab that for evidence."

"No, not evidence. It's yours."

"What do you mean, it's yours."

Archie exhaled. "Look, this money was never intended to be mine."

"It isn't, you remember?" Rose interjected. "It's mine."

He waved that off. "Semantics. When the five million in probate gets released it goes straight to you Rose. This money belongs to John Hidalgo."

John looked puzzled. "Archie, you're in shock. I don't want your money."

Archie shook his head. "I'm thinking quite clearly, I'm surprised to say. Believe me when I say, it was always intended for you."

John sat down. He reached into his back pocket and pulled out the folded envelope he'd been carrying. On the front was written, 'Archibald Wendt'. He handed it to Archie.

"Who's this from?" Wendt asked.

"Virgil Morgenstern." John whispered.

"What's in it?"

John shook his head. "No clue. Didn't open it."

Archie took the envelope and stared at it for a moment. He scanned all the faces in the room and then slowly opened it, began to read to himself.

"Read it aloud for fuck's sake," Howard implored for everyone's benefit.

CHAPTER

58

Dr. Wendt,

*If you are reading this it is because after a long and (likely)
torturous journey you have arrived at the doorstep of the fair
sheriff of Harding. By now you know that John Hidalgo is
my son. It might seem silly to you that I went to such lengths
to keep this a secret and then provided such a circuitous route
to his inheritance, but if you're reading this you've already
offered him money, so my risk is rewarded! It's the kind of
letter one writes basking in the glow of hoped for success.
I'm not a huge believer in the afterlife so this letter serves to
confirm my calculation that you'd be the right man to do
what I couldn't do. Let me explain.*

*My childhood was bereft of love. The Great Depression
overwhelmed my father and he ran away leaving us destitute.
My mother did her best, working several jobs and so was
largely away from home. My older sister tended to the rest of
us kids. I worked hard in school, but wasn't a natural scholar.
When I met Ben Lowry, an industrialist with great wealth,
my life changed. Working for him opened up opportunities I
had only dreamed of. More importantly, I became infatuated
with the man. He was everything I thought a father could
be. Can you, a psychiatrist, imagine what impact it had on
me to not only find a man of such strength of character, such
resolve of will; but to find such a man who saw those same
qualities in me? It was a revelation! I came to understand
that Ben harbored great disappointment in his own son and
saw me as an alternative. He poured in me all his wisdom*

and love. It's no wonder I became successful. Come to think of it, I didn't do any better with my own son. I was profoundly disappointed in Luke; I didn't learn from Ben's mistakes. I poured my energy into Rose and, surreptitiously, John.

While rising in the ranks of Lowry Industries it was only natural that Ben would have me over his house and that I would become acquainted with his daughter Katherine. At the time I was in love with Nina Patterson; she was my high school sweetheart. But I couldn't disappoint Ben. He so wanted me to marry his daughter that I might formally join his family. It broke my heart, but I married Katherine even after finding out that Nina was pregnant. It was the decision that laid the foundation for my successful career. It both made me and killed me.

Katherine is a brilliant woman. I grew to admire her and, in my own way, love her. But it was nothing like the intense love I felt for Nina. Nothing like young passion. And Katherine knew it. Maybe she didn't know the name of the person, but she was perceptive and always resented the part of me that I withheld. As the years passed her anger grew until it consumed our relationship. Her bitterness led her to inflict little tortures on me. Death by a thousand cuts.

It never occurred to me to divorce her. At first it was out of my eternal respect for her father. Then for our children. In the end, though, I think I did it for penance; to make up for my original sin of choosing a father over a wife. It was never the money that drew me to Katherine. It was the praise I got from her father when I did well; it felt to me like a son should feel when he pleases the man he admires most. That was the energy that fueled me.

I lived a good life, Archie. This letter is not intended to be a gripe against choices I made or to express regret. It's meant to give you information so that perhaps a man of your education and perspective can figure out my life choices.

I didn't share this with you, but in the last year I was diagnosed with a disease that was going to rob me of everything I was. Facing that, I chose the less courageous path of suicide. I'm disappointed in myself for making such a decision. But as death draws nearer and with it the specter of the misery, not that I would endure, but that my family would have to bear, both financially and emotionally, I came to see suicide as an option offering me more control. I could cheat Illness of his prize and go out on my terms.

But what to do about John? It was always my intention to take care of Nina and John, but how to do it without drawing the tremendous ire and will of Katherine Lowry. Over the years I had come to respect and fear the spirit of vengeance that my wife harbored. Not just fear for my secret family, but for Rose. It occurred me that Katherine would see no problem in destroying Rose knowing just how important our daughter was to me. To preserve all my children (though I knew that Luke was favored by his mother and would be taken care of, no matter what) I came up with what seemed like my only option. I couldn't trust those I knew; Katherine knew them, too, and they would be additional firewood for the pyre that my wife would light to burn my plans to the ground. It had to be a stranger, one who had both curiosity and integrity.

When you came to town it was almost as if you were sent specifically for me. I discovered that you were suspended from your practice after a patient suicided. That you had meticulously documented the feelings you developed for that patient. And that you handed over those handwritten notes to the authority for inspection. Handed them over! I said to myself, there's a man who's got convictions and integrity even if it meant bringing himself down. Surely you could have burned those papers, said they were lost, claimed your dog had eaten them. Anything, but hand them over and be hung by their admission of inappropriate love. I knew then that you were my man.

So let my next words be a profound apology. If my suspicions of my fellow citizens of Harding are correct, they will have given you a hard time. It will have looked to their feeble eyes that you manipulated me and were able to con me out of my money. You will know the truth. John will know it. But the rest have to believe the lie if you are to prove kind enough to see this plan through to its conclusion. That's where I think proper reward is necessary. So I propose you take a ten percent finder's fee as compensation for all that I have put you through.

Dr. Wendt, I know you are my kind of man. The type with an internal compass guiding them to what is right and just. Someone who can be relied on to complete a task that is hard, but worthwhile.

You have given me the ability to do right by those I loved, but for whom other commitments prevented me from living up to my obligations. It took me a lifetime to learn what was really important. I don't regret my career achievements, yet I would probably give it them all back to spend a lifetime with Nina. Hindsight and all that. Regardless, Archibald Wendt, thank you and I wish you peace of mind knowing you have done a worthy and just thing. Farewell and best wishes,

Virgil Morgenstern.

Rose looked at John. "You're my brother."

He blushed. "That's confusing to say the least."

"You know, my father used to tell me that you were a tomcat who couldn't be trusted. He didn't want me getting involved with you romantically."

"He told me that you stabbed another man in the balls and he had to pay off big time to get you out of trouble. Is that true?"

Rose started laughing as she shook her head. Both of their faces registered the look of someone who finally sees the picture emerge from a computer generated 3-d art poster.

"Thank God for Virgil's head games, huh?" Howard said. "He obviously didn't want you getting involved and having two headed children."

"How long you been toting that letter around?" Archie asked John.

He thought it over. "A few days before he died."

Mike cleared his throat. "This is all fascinating and I'm mean that seriously, no sarcasm. But we have two dead bodies here that will require an explanation."

Hidalgo didn't respond. He seemed to still be in a daze, his gaze fixed on Rose and Luke.

Mike snapped his fingers. "John! You are now the ranking peace officer in Harding. What do we do about this?" He gestured to the dead chief of police.

"I'm not sure."

Rose spoke up. "It's pretty obvious to me what happened here. Archie came to rescue me. Jed and Chief Lynne got into an argument over the money and in the fracas that ensued they shot each other allowing the rest of us to escape relatively unscathed."

"And what do we do about the bleeding PI on the floor?" Hidalgo asked.

"He can be bought off. He's as crooked as Lombard Street." Archie said.

"We'll have to move the bodies around." Mike said. "John, will you come with us and we'll arrange them two to make it look half believable. Then we can call in the state troopers and let them take over the scene."

"Sounds good."

They broke like a football huddle. Mike, Stringer, and Howard began pulling the bodies out of the study. "Hey, Cheech," Howard called to Luke, "Get over here and help."

Archie walked over to John who was still stunned.

"You know, a part of me always wondered about Virgil," he said. "I mean, we had a lot in common. But I didn't have the nerve to ask anyone for more specifics, not wanting to upset the apple cart. I was just grateful to know him."

"He looked out for you. Looks like he funneled money to your mother by hiring your father, or stepfather, or whatever you want to call him, to do renovation jobs on his properties. Kept you well supported. In turn your mother rewarded him with loyalty, by not betraying the secret."

Rose took the letter from John. She poured herself another drink and sat reading the last missive from her father. She gently shook her head side to side, weeping silently. "I knew there was something wrong. The falling down, the weakness. I knew he wasn't a drunk."

Archie sat next to her, put a hand gently on her back. "You must know how much he loved you."

She looked away and her body silently shook with each tearful paroxysm.

"You know, for a little while I thought you were trying to kill me to get the money back."

Rose furrowed her brow.

"Someone tried to run me over with a car registered in your name." Archie said.

"It was Luke and Jed." Rose wiped her eyes. "They plotted how to take you out. I didn't take it more seriously because I didn't think they could stay sober long enough to carry it off. The cars are all registered in my name because Luke is such a fuck up."

Archie tried to stand up, but the blood loss coupled with the bourbon sent him heavily back to the couch.

"We need to get you to a hospital, young man." Howard said. "You look like shit."

Archie shook his head. "No, no hospital. They are mandated to report a gunshot wound to the police."

"He's right," John said, "but we can take him to the ED and have Trent work on him, I'll do the paperwork and that will be the end of that."

"That work for you, Archie?"

"Fine, Howard. I don't have the energy to argue. But make sure Trent knows not to admit me no matter what. I'll convalesce at your place and then I'm getting the fuck out of here."

"What do you mean?" Rose said with a note of panic.

"What do I mean? I'm blowing this popsicle stand; making like Catholics and pulling out. I mean getting the fucking out of this town before they put me on trial for kidnapping Lindbergh's baby."

"Why? We're not going to let you take the heat for what happened to Lynne," John said.

"You'll excuse me, Mr. Sheriff, if I don't rely on the good intentions of the denizens of Harding. I'd rather take my chances south of the border."

"You're fleeing the country? Isn't that a little melodramatic?" Rose asked.

"I don't think so. Because of my interactions with the Morgenstern clan I am persona non-grata in Harding. I'm pissed off at your father. He could have put some money in a blind trust and given it to Hidalgo that way; left me out of this godforsaken family."

Rose shook her head. "My father knew his wife. Knew that she'd account for every last penny because she always suspected something. And he knew, as well, that she'd have no issue taking out her anger on me. Father intended for you to be the anvil on which my mother unleashed all her anger. I have to say for an impromptu plan with his life ending, it was a pretty good one."

"Have to say, do you?" Archie smiled despite himself out of fondness for Rose. "Regardless of your admiration for the plan I now need to reset my fortunes. So with that I will take my leave, hopefully with some of that money you got, John."

"I'm okay giving you the whole bag, Archie, I don't want it." He handed over the Gladstone.

Archie took it. He stood slowly and shuffled over to a garbage can and pulled out the empty bag. "I appreciate the offer, but I'm not interested in the whole thing. Though I am going to take more than the ten percent finder's fee. How does twenty percent sound?"

John just nodded as Archie counted out stacks of money into the garbage bag. He stopped midway. "You mind if I take the Gladstone? I'm going to need it for my trip."

He dumped all the money on the desk, counted out a million and put it back in the Gladstone. Then he remembered something, stopped and bent down over the middle drawer, back in its locked position.

"What did you say your birthdate was, Rose?"

"October twentieth,1984."

Archie punched in the numbers and grinned when he heard an audible click. He opened the middle drawer and his smile broadened further. From the box he took out more bundles of cash and a black felt bag the size of his fist and laid them on the desk. He prized open the bag and a rainbow of gems glittered back at him. Archie pulled the string of the bag tight and looked up at the Sheriff. "You keep the extra cash, I'm taking this."

Archibald Wendt made for the door.

"Stop."

He turned to face Rose. She said, "I didn't sleep with you for kicks. I really do like you."

A glint showed in Archie's eye. "I like you, too. Feel like a vacation?"

The Mercedes diesel chugged down the highway, a southwest course. In it were a fatigued driver and a Gladstone bag. In the bag a million dollars, a smaller felt bag, and a change of underwear. Well, minus ten thousand he paid to Howard for the car.

Archie was filled with a light airiness. He turned on the radio and Paul Simon sang out about feeling groovy.

"I've got no deeds to do no promises to keep, I'm dappled and drowsy and ready for sleep, let the morning time drop all its petals on me, life, I love you, all is groooooovvvvvyyy." Archie sang along and only part of his euphoria was due to the Percocet.

He felt like Red at the end of Rita Hayworth and the Shawshank Redemption. And the feeling was as good as it seemed in the novella. Heading for Mexico. It wasn't true that he had no promises to keep, though. There was one debt he still owed to Rose that he intended on honoring.

The road hypnotic, his mind wandered.

"You did good, Doc. We hope you got the closure you needed. We always knew you cared and that meant a lot to us."

"I know it, Garrett, but thanks for saying it all the same."

"She's at peace. We've all found peace, a reprieve from the torment. That's something that we want you to understand."

"That helps to hear. It doesn't take away the pain, though," Archie said.

"We're here for you."

And he *could* feel their presence. Garrett with his baseball cap and sardonic grin, Janine and her warm, soft smile; even Virgil, basking in the glow of a successful plan to provide for those he loved most.

Archie had only a vague notion of his destination or what he might do once he got there. The pacific coast. Maybe the far east, who knows. The not knowing heightened the excitement, the anticipation. He was warmed by the companionship he felt in his car, the travelers with him in spirit.

He promised Rose he'd come back once his head cleared sufficiently. Archie could hear Virgil's voice extolling him of Harding's virtues. Or maybe it was the wind. Either way, a vacation first and then possibly a moustache.

Harding wasn't such a bad place, after all, but he'd need a new place to live. Maybe there were rooms to let above The President Club. He would christen life anew with Glenlivet and a fresh perspective. Or maybe it was time to switch to gin.

99372295R00152

Made in the USA
Columbia, SC
09 July 2018